VICTIM OF LOVE

VICTIM OF LOVE

Dyan Sheldon

THE VIKING PRESS   NEW YORK

Copyright © 1982 by Dyan Sheldon
All rights reserved
Published in 1983 by The Viking Press
40 West 23rd Street, New York, N.Y. 10010

LIBRARY OF CONGRESS CATALOGING IN PUBLICATION DATA
Sheldon, Dyan.
Victim of love.
I. Title.
PS3569.H39265V5   1983   813'.54   82-20001
ISBN 0-670-74586-3

Printed in the United States of America
Set in Bembo

VICTIM OF LOVE

1

At the very top of the tree – which is full, and thick, and green, and artificial – an old and fragile angel perches. She is dressed in yellowed white satin, dusted with silver stars; her halo tilts, her smile is half chipped away, her angel sleeves touch at her center, as though she has hands that are clasped in quiet prayer.

"I didn't believe it myself at first," says Lillian, her golden bracelets jangling as she speaks, "but it's really terrific. All you need is a half pound of chopped meat, any vegetables you want and a packet of this mix. It's fantastic. You can feed four on it easily." She sips her drink and raises her chin. "Jimmy loves it. Don't you Jimmy?"

Jimmy picks off the tinsel which some child has draped across his arm when he wasn't looking. "It's great."

Linda smiles an enthusiastic smile. "I'll have to try it."

"Of course," says Lillian, lips wet and almost glistening, her tiny teeth as white as Chiclets, "it probably doesn't mean that much to you, but for us a penny saved is a penny saved," and laughs without humor.

Linda shifts in her chair from the burden of being better-off. "Oh, no, I'm always looking for ways of saving money," and smiles at her brother-in-law. "Everything costs so much."

Jimmy laughs. "You can hardly afford to be poor any more."

"And of course," his wife continues, "I buy most of

1

Angela's clothes secondhand. Or make them myself," sighing, twisting her mouth into a sad little grimace, she who barely knew how to thread a needle until she was twenty-four, she who used to buy her clothes at Bloomingdale's and celebrate birthdays at expensive clubs.

Linda sighs and fiddles with her new necklace, her present from the adorable Angela, which is made of clam shells and a wadge of something silver-colored that looks very much like a penis. "And how are things at school?" she turns to Jimmy.

He shrugs and chews at the edge of his tar-black moustache. "Oh, you know, it's okay. Some of the kids are pretty wild, but it's okay. Some of them are pretty wild."

"No discipline," says Lillian. "No discipline and drugs. They're all into drugs. Aren't they Jimmy?"

"Some of them come from pretty rough homes," he laughs, apparently for no reason. "But some of them are. Some of them are pretty wild kids."

Paul doesn't hear them. He watches the little angel, the hem of her robe dappled with red and blue and green and yellow light, as he has watched for every Christmas for as long as he can remember. She once had a name, but it is gone now – along with the wrappings and the crinkly tinsel and the angel hair like spun sugar; along with the dolls and tin soldiers, the bikes and catcher's mitts – and at that thought he sighs. It is 6:30 on Christmas day and Paul is pretty drunk, though not so drunk that he would have to admit to it. He is feeling at this moment mellow, nearly content. Around him his family gathers – mother, sister, wife, children, niece and brother-in-law – faces shining, lips smiling, and for a few warm minutes Paul allows feelings of peace and devotion to wash over him like a fine, tepid shower.

It is not a mood that ever lasts for long.

Paul has spent the month or so leading up to this day of days in a state of gloomy agitation: predicting disaster, cursing Christ, raging on about the materialism and commercialism that has turned a holy day into a three-ring circus. He says that if there were a God He would throw them all into hell just for this, for making a mockery of an event that symbolizes

2

some of the more noble and enduring of man's feelings and desires (meaning peace and love as opposed to lust and power). On two separate occasions he was forced to banish his children from the dinner table, appalled by their unending whine of IwantIwantIwant, angered by their grasping self-interest and greed. Paul said that there was no use in anyone buying him anything because no one ever gave him anything he liked anyway. Not ever; not since he was thirteen and his father bought him a stolen bike, which was identified only three days later as he was riding it to the store for his mother. Linda said she would have thought, under those circumstances, that he'd have been relieved no one ever bought him what he liked.

Paul had said that they either bought a small, unpretentious tree this year, or they did without. Their tree at home is barely three feet high, thin and pale, its bumpy brown branches defeating not only the flimsy, unconvincing leaves, but the armloads of plastic balls (they have never bought glass balls since the advent of children and cats), paper chains and strings of popcorn and cranberries (Paul suggesting that these would seem more homey, more earthy, closer to Christ) with which they tried to disguise it. Patricia made a star with seven and a half points for the top. Paul, watching his wife and children decorate it from the vantage of his easy chair, immediately declared it a success. "It has character," he decidèd, ignoring the puckered foreheads on Linda and Patsy. "It's a nice, friendly family tree."

"Katie Wilson has a family tree," said Patsy, bending her head at a right angle to her body, as though that might make all the difference, "but it was so tall that Mr Wilson had to cut the top off to get it into the apartment." She bent her head at a right angle to her body, but in the opposite direction. "The piece they took off is bigger than this tree."

"Maybe," said Linda, that strained note of politeness in her voice which meant that she was trying to be tactful, "maybe we should take a few of the decorations off. It looks a little crowded."

Patsy put her hands on her hips, considering. She was wearing dungarees and a plaid flannel shirt, an outfit which made her look like a sixteen-year-old midget. "Then it would look like bones." It is her father's considered opinion that though only eight, Patricia has all the makings of a first class nag, if not of a sarcastic bitch, class A.

David, of course, didn't mind. He giggled, he sighed, he clapped his hands in childish glee, screaming for presents, waiting for magic. Some might say that his being so easy to please is directly related to the fact that he is only four, but Paul knows that it is really his son's easy-going disposition and simple nature (so much like his own) that are responsible. And so he said, sitting behind the standing bodies of the females, his girls, "Isn't it beautiful, David?"

And David had hurled himself past mother and sister to land on father's lap, shrieking, "Yessss!"

Paul also said, during those hectic weeks of frenzy and panic – through which he passed almost untouched, stopping only long enough to sample a cookie, lend a finger for ribbon tying, suggest or veto a gift, the pressures of his world being too great to allow him much participation – that Linda became too carried away with the pomp and circumstance and forgot the substance. And that she was spoiling the children with too many presents, he had certainly never gotten as much as they did. And that the children's teeth would rot out of their heads, falling onto their laps like so much crushed peppermint cane, if she and his mother didn't stop buying them so much junk. And that he was tired, sick and tired, weary, of the meaninglessness of modern life; what had happened to the real, old-fashioned virtues? He implied that it was people like Linda, who put up artificial wreaths and bought candles that looked like Christmas trees and Santas, who cheapened the holiday and perpetuated its crass profitability. He intimated that it was people like Linda, who bought $1.99 Christmas Hits albums, who insisted on staying up until one in the morning to watch *White Christmas* and who bought pre-made egg nog in tarted-up milk cartons, who cluttered life with squalid trivia, making it that much more difficult for others to find any real meaning.

For weeks he had raged and grumbled, complained and

4

looked bored, his only concession his annual trip with his children to Rockefeller Center to see the tree, an excursion he assures them they will learn to appreciate when they get older. He named their own tree Chiquita, saying that if there were ever a Third World tree that was it, but he appreciated the joke and its subtleties alone. He even threw David's jolly little Santa Claus out of the window onto Riverside Drive because he had woken up with it sitting on his chest saying over and over, "Ho, ho, ho, Merry Christmas" in a voice that was almost a squeal.

But all that is behind him now. He has survived the morning, he has safely chauffeured them to the perilous shores of Long Island (a place he sees as a sort of purgatory on earth, its only contribution to the culture being drive-in stores, if you wanted to consider that a contribution) and he has navigated himself through the first sober minutes of the afternoon with his sister (the cow), his brother-in-law (the Frito Bandito) and his niece (the little witch). He has withstood the tedious hours of his mother's conversation, even managing to seem surprised and restrainedly delighted (just as he had last year and the years before that) when he opened his present to find neon red and orange socks and a baby-blue T-shirt, one size too small, and has triumphantly ignored the syrupy singsong of his mother's chatter with the children, her continual insistence that her remembrances of the past are exact and correct when clearly they are not. He even had a seven-and-a-half-minute conversation with Jimmy while the women were gathered in the kitchen, wriggling the turkey leg up and down to see if it was done, Rita peering into the gravy pan searching for lumps, saying, "I always used Gravy Master myself", Lillian whipping the spoon from her hand with a significant grimace, though he has forgotten what it was about.

Now he sits, sipping his scotch, gazing at the glistening branches of what he usually refers to as the Tinkertoy tree, imbued with a feeling of indiscriminate kindness – affection, even. Jimmy has fallen asleep again, lightly – near him the women swap their stories of chest coughs and friends deserted

5

or betrayed by feckless husbands or lovers, and to one side is Rita, enthroned, the two smallest children precariously balanced on one knee each, Patricia standing near a shoulder, trying to see over David's head. It is easy to imagine haloes; effortless to envision the shadowy shapes of ancestors, little Davids, Angelas and Patricias, fatter and thinner Ritas, reaching behind them into the beginnings of families; simple to see the continuity.

Paul Sutcliffe is thirty-eight years old. He has one wife, two children, a mother, a sister, a brother-in-law, a niece, and two lovers. He is a college professor (which he admits to with a shrugging of shoulders and a jaded disdain; it's not such a big deal), a relatively successful one, and a writer (which he admits to with a forceful show of humility; there is, after all, an intellectual elite) on the brink, he would like to think, of considerable success and reputation. He has known struggle, Paul Sutcliffe; he has known also the rewards of persistent effort. Intelligent and highly educated, he lives by a simple and flexible liberal, humanitarian code. Ambitious (but kind) he does not submit easily to either deflection or defeat. Now he observes the scene which he so often ridicules and mocks, and he is moved. Paul Sutcliffe is thirty-eight years old and he is concerned about the meaning and potential of life.

Is this it?

He closes his eyes, jiggling the ice that remains in his glass, listening to the chug-chug-chug of the female conversation, the comfortable sound of Jimmy's gentle snoring, the hum, the babble and the giggle of Rita and the kids, Angela's left foot thumping against the chair. He is five, he is two, he is fifteen, he is twenty, he is eleven; he is every Christmas he has ever known; smelling the trees, touching the tinsel, shaking the boxes. He wishes he could stay here for ever, just like this, rainbow colors flashing across his face, his hands, his gray corduroy suit.

Jimmy wakes up, tipping the ice water that was in his glass onto his shirt. He curses softly and blinks. "You want another drink?" he calls to Paul, disturbing the reverie, and then he titters, a nervous habit.

6

Paul nods, but he will not look, he will not speak. Already his demi-euphoria is melting away like an early morning fog. There are at least two hours more before it will be acceptable for them to prepare to leave. Paul watches Jimmy shuffle from the tiny living room, and then re-looks at the others: at the children, grubby and already glassy-eyed, the blood of countless chocolate elves and angels dried around the corners of their mouths; at Linda and Lillian, bobbing and nodding their heads at one another like old crones reading the leaves, mouths mobile, oh, yes, yes, I know just what you mean, oh, yes, I understand; at Rita, round and beaming, graceless and gay, lavishing on her grandchildren all the things she would never let him have.

The spell which had enchanted him has been broken; the magic and mystery which had enveloped them has spun on down the road. Paul sighs. They will probably make him eat a cold turkey sandwich as well before they let him leave.

They are standing on what Lillian calls the porch (although it is not really a porch, it is a stoop with a roof over it), hugging and kissing and laughing good-bye. Jimmy pumps Paul's hand several times, and giggles. Lillian rubs face powder on everyone's cheeks as she lands small, sticky red kisses near their ears. Rita is crying, but no one pays any attention to her since she always cries when she's drunk, and that is what they all assume she is. "It's okay, Ma," they take turns saying, patting the black wool shoulder of her good winter coat (bought three years before for her own mother's funeral – though the old lady has yet to die), "it's okay." The children, sleepy and grumpy, do not participate. "It was a beautiful day," whispers Rita. "It was the best Christmas I ever had. Wasn't it the best Christmas?" Lillian smiles at her, Jimmy smiles at her, Linda and Paul murmur their agreement. Except to get her through it without a major scene, no one really cares what Rita thinks. Linda repeats how much she enjoyed the meal, especially the stuffing, she really must get the recipe for that, as Paul eases the misting mass of his mother down

7

the garden path. "We really should get together more often," someone says, and other voices say, "Oh, yes," "I know," "Time." Merry Christmas, Merry ChristmasMerryChristmas. Jimmy and Lillian shut the door on the cold and raining night. "Well," says Lillian, "thank God that's over."

It is now 9:28 on the Long Island Expressway and traffic is moving steadily, though not always perceptibly. In the back seat, Rita has fallen asleep, her jaw hanging slightly open, her black patent leather purse clutched to her stomach and part of her breast, the fake-fur leopard skin pillbox hat she is wearing tilting at an angle that makes her look deformed.

Paul has the classical music station on. It helps to calm and soothe him. His belt feels too tight, his body feels sleepy and sluggish, he is still tense from the effort of being happy, jovial, polite and well-behaved for so many hours on end. He knows that if he closes his eyes, his ears and his nose he will still see mouths chewing, fingers shoving stray bits of meat and cranberry sauce back into the sides of mouths; still hear the family's repetitive, inane conversations, underlined by the women's sighing disguised as breathing; still smell Jimmy's cheap cigars, the residual odor of Lysol in the bathroom and the totally unintoxicating aroma of Lillian's homemade peach brandy. He is sober now, back in reality.

The music – to him so restful, so isolating – promises that soon he'll be back in his study, door shut, radio on, worlds away from the lack of adventures of the day; safe. The news comes on; behind him his mother snores like an old bear. The weatherman, sounding resigned, prophesies that the rain will change to heavy snow. Next to him, and for most of the day not actively speaking to him, Linda mumbles an unemotional, "Oh, shit, snow."

Where has the magic gone? Paul wonders. Where the surprises and delight? Next to Rita, leaning against her like human dominoes, one on top of the other, the children sleep. His children. His daughter and his son. His babies. In real life they are very often headaches, heartaches and general pains in the ass – but in theory they are one of the only redeeming features of his life. He turns to look at them, his hope and his future, over his shoulder, but they only appear as dappled rocks in the shadowy light. The music returns, somewhere up ahead a horn sounds, Linda squeaks a finger across the side window. Christmas is done.

Paul has been so busy lately – though, when isn't he busy, when does he have a chance? – that he hasn't paid much attention to Linda's inattention to him; hasn't noticed that she treats him more with a polite coolness and benign disinterest than with devotion or well-worn friendliness. He has noticed her sometimes peculiar behavior of late (like the time he asked her for a cup of tea, a simple, one bag cup of tea, and she poured it into the bowl of ice cream he'd been eating – though they hadn't been arguing, had, in fact, been having a normal conversation), her growing forgetfulness, increasing tardiness in the simplest tasks, late-blooming signs of irresponsibility. And he has wondered, casually and occasionally – as today, when she greeted his well-chosen jokes and anecdotes (which would once have delighted her) with frosty smiles from across the room, the Snow Queen of Manhattan – just what the hell is going on, but (knowing women as well as he does) he knows it would be madness to ask. On the one or two instances when her behavior has disturbed the smooth running of his life he has inquired as to whether or not there was something wrong, and has been told, "No", and even "No, of course not". And he is more than content to leave it at that. Her leaving him alone, so long as she doesn't forget to feed him, or collect his shirts from the laundry, or make love to him, is better than having her nag or argue, or pursue him with phone calls through his days, whereareyoucouldyouwhynot?

And yet. And yet it is Christmas day and she has said almost nothing to him except "Don't forget the box in the hallway", "There's coffee in the pot on the stove" and "Have you remembered the booze?". Has she even wished him Merry Christmas? What happened to the mistletoe he had hung so provocatively in the shower?

9

Linda shifts her weight, responding to some sleepy noise from one of the children. At some point during dinner – while he was taking his second helping of white meat he thinks – she looked at him because of something he had said and he clearly saw her turn him off. He had been correcting some misguided memory of Rita's at the time and, feeling Linda watching him, had caught her eye just as she threw the switch, click. Since then she has been neither cold nor uncivil; she has simply left her body behind and been off somewhere else, probably having a good time.

With a sudden jerk on the wheel, he moves the car into the next lane, which immediately stops moving. Paul sighs.

"All I want," says Linda as he begins to make aggressive sucking noises on the pipe which has been dead for the past twenty minutes, "is a hot cup of coffee."

He taps a tune on the steering wheel with his short, clean nails. "I want a scotch."

"More?"

"More than what?"

But she doesn't want to play that game tonight. She doesn't even look at him as she says, "More than enough."

They edge towards the exit for the bridge. Maybe, he thinks, maybe it's just the holiday blues. Or maybe she's getting her period. He hums along with the radio, assuring himself that all is well.

In a few weeks, or a few months, or perhaps not for a few years, he may regret his own human gullibility in thinking that a situation which hadn't even begun to define itself had actually been resolved. Or, to rephrase that, he may damn his own stupidity in diagnosing as gas what will turn out to be a massive myocardial infarction.

David is leaning, almost lying, on top of Patricia, who, in turn, is leaning, almost lying, on top of her grandmother. In the position of the bottom domino, Rita's head rests on the chilly metal of the door and Patsy's elbow digs into her stomach. Awake now, Rita listens to the children's steady breathing and David's rhythmic sniffling, worrying about his little lungs. She hears Paul tap out a tune with his fingers and

10

immediately switches from worrying about the baby getting pneumonia to worrying about her son developing ulcers, high blood, pressure, or an unhappy homelife. Instead of speaking, or sighing, or clearing her throat, she makes her breathing even more shallow than it was, as though making her presence as faint as possible will avert all possible trouble. As a rule to live by, this is one which Rita has adopted only lately, this tactful, almost apologetic passivity. She used to be – according to her son – the screaming bitch on wheels of all five boroughs, a human bomb set to detonate at the smallest provocation, too highly explosive to be introduced to friends or the parents of friends, too unstable to travel with in public – a mother who could not be told the dates of PTA meetings, open nights at school, or important Little League games. For most of her motherhood and wifehood, the cry which trailed after Rita as she stood in doorways and hallways and stairways, arms akimbo, was "Oh, shut up will you", or, "For God's sake shut up", or, "Shut up. Shut up. Shut up". And now, for all practical purposes, she has.

Rita's good blue pants suit, which she bought in the January sales two years ago – and which she still thinks of as being rather daring – has four different stains on it, all acquired during the day's festivities. The first is cranberry, gotten in an attempt to be helpful; the second is red wine, gotten in an attempt to keep Angela from eating all the chocolates; the third is gravy, received when David threw his fork at her; the fourth is, or was before she wiped it off with soap and warm water, vomit, received as she threw up her Christmas dinner.

For most of the day (for most of all her days it sometimes seems) Rita has been treated either with a short-tempered "oh, mom"; with a patronizing "oh, mom, isn't that nice"; with a dismissive "mom, do you mind"; with a vaguely threatening "mother". She was expected to play with and entertain the children when no one else wanted them, but not to interfere with them in any other way. Despite the bitterly cold day, she went down to the lake twice to feed the ducks, and then was yelled at by Lillian because she took the wrong bread. Despite the expense, she bought David the Official

United States Air Force Tank and Helicopter he had pointed out in Woolworth's, and then was lectured by Paul on his views on war toys. She was snapped at and sniped at by everyone, except Jimmy, who almost never argues with anyone. Even Angela, who is only two-and-a-half, called her a "stupid bitch". Every time she went to touch something in the kitchen Lillian would raise her pencilled eyebrows, make a sound similar to that of escaping steam and say, "Ma, why don't you go and sit down?". On more than four occasions, Paul interrupted what she was saying, and once he told her to be quiet (what he actually said was, "you're full of shit"). Lillian denied that the stuffing recipe was the one that her mother had given her, and even Linda responded curtly when asked if she needed any help with the potatoes. No wonder Rita cried.

A tiny hand flops on top of Rita's larger one. Once more tears are loosened. Rita is tired, nervous, lonely and frightened. It is true that Rita hasn't always been the easiest person to get along with, but now she is an old lady, and, as many old ladies do, has come to see herself, viewed through her children, as either a pain in the ass (when she is around) or a not-so-great memory (when she isn't).

Linda says something to Paul, but Rita doesn't catch what it is. She stares down at the mittened hand on top of her own. The mitten looks like a raccoon. This has been Rita's last Christmas. Inside of its cocoon, she knows, Patsy's hand, so perfect and so small, is a miracle of ancient science; its smooth, unblemished skin, its miniature knuckles, joints and cuticles all make it look just like the hands she used to hold at a time when she knew she would live for ever and would always be called mom and trusted and loved.

Rita has been dying for a very long time, but she has been able for most of that time to ignore it, to shove it behind her as something else; something she'd eaten, something she hadn't eaten, gallstones. Now she can no longer deny the pain, the nausea, or the bleeding – so she tries instead to get along with them. She hasn't yet been to a doctor, because she knows what a doctor will do. A doctor will whisper words of reality and concern – words like "riddled" and "keep as comfortable as possible"; a doctor will put her into a hospital and then she will begin, instantaneously, to die in earnest. They will put tubes up her and down her, debowel and degut her, stick her in a bed against the far wall, a chart at her feet, a plastic, waterproof and nearly indestructible bracelet on her wrist with her name on it so they can identify the body if they mix up the beds.

Rita had promised herself that all she was waiting for was Christmas, to have one last Christmas like a perfect snowflake with her kids. But now she's wondering if she couldn't hold out just a little while more.

Linda, dying only in a general sense, is also exhausted. Her feet hurt, her mouth aches and her brain feels like mashed bananas. Without having to actually take out a pocket flashlight and a compact mirror to make sure, she knows that tiny lines, like bits of thread, are criss-crossing the skin around her eyes. Punishment lines – but for what?

Linda is still in her thirties, but she could easily pass for forty-five. On most days she feels far closer to sixty. Her normal level of functioning is just below collapse, though she has been in this state for so long that it is doubtful that she herself even notices any more. Neither particularly ambitious nor particularly maternal, she has a career and a family because she thought she should have them – and at least partly because Paul thought she should have them. She is not so much his wife and helpmate as she is the horse harnessed next to him; where he has gone, she has gone; what pace he has set she has followed, if often breathlessly. Guessing that if she didn't keep up with Paul she would be left behind, she has tried to match him through the years; to live up to his standards and expectations; to be a wife he could be proud of.

If there has been a slight imbalance between them, she is only just becoming aware of it. She put him through graduate school, shielding him from the tedium of household tasks and crises; she made curtains, sewed her own clothes, taught herself how to strip furniture and how to cook. He orchestrated her career, telling her when to move on, when to move up, when to press forward. At the first significant signs of trouble in their marriage they had had Patricia – that is, Linda had had Patricia. David was the remedy to the third, or perhaps it was the fourth, sign of trouble.

With each year that has passed – with each social, economic and professional advancement made by Paul – Linda has had to run just a little faster, puffing just a little more audibly, putting just that little bit more effort into getting ahead, staying ahead and fulfilling Paul's ever-changing specifications. Linda's own desires and ambitions were satisfied years ago (a nice child, a nice apartment, a good job), but not so Paul's. The more he gets, the more he seems to crave; the more he has, the more he seems to need; the more he possesses, the greater his sense of loss. And so, on an ever-increasing, inflationary scale, Paul's ambitions, lust and need for love have all risen proportionately to his achievements. While Linda – who has little ambition of her own, who has only fleetingly experienced lust and who is now too exhausted to be able to recognize it, and who has always assumed Paul's love (which, he has constantly assured her, has never failed for even the wing-beat of a hyper-active butterfly) as the basic foundation of her own happiness – has spent the last seven or eight years panting beside him, bearing baskets of babies, suckling pigs on silver trays, neatly typed manuscripts and tastefully chosen clothes, wallpapers, bedspreads and dinnerware. She has been supportive, patient, understanding and tolerant; bright and entertaining when she would rather have stayed home and made popcorn; aggressive and go-getting when she would have preferred to do nothing; a perpetual tiptoer along the mined and highly sensitized corridors of her husband's ego – shhhhh.

In return, she has received a lovely home in the city, a beautiful home in the country, a large income, two perfectly passable children, status, position and, within a small but not totally discountable circle, prestige. As well as the direction, focus and drive she knows she would never have had without him. Certainly, she is grateful to him for helping her escape the fate of being Linda Teresa Miller for her entire life; living

14

in the suburbs of Minneapolis, married to a man like her father, steady but boring, reliable but reserved, respectable but taciturn, dutiful but dull, she herself spending most of her life in a neutral-colored station wagon with a St Christopher medal hanging over the dash and an American Legion sticker on the bumper. Close call.

But, then, what is wrong? Why has Linda been behaving so strangely lately? Why, if you look behind the drawn and puffy mask of tiredness, do you see only unhappiness and worry? Paul, certainly, has no answers to these questions – assuming that he has ever had the questions. Does Linda?

Linda gazes dreamily out of the window, bubbly with rain, as they bump along under the El, a princess in her tower gazing across the rolling blue-green hills towards happiness.

Could it be that she simply doesn't like Paul any more?

Lately she has begun to view him from a different angle, one where his obvious charms are less apparent. This afternoon when Paul – after having spent the early part of the day sniffing and sniping, metaphorically running his white-gloved finger along everyone else's door-frames – jumped on some twenty-nine-year-old Christmas memory of Rita's, telling her, "Don't be ridiculous, you're full of shit", chuckling good-naturedly, Linda thought that she could hear one of the very last straws thumping on top of the pile. The old lady – who used to have more fight, more spirit – visibly withered. And Linda had watched Rita's face, the eyes dissolving away from the center of that moment into some memory as she concentrated on helping Angela to more potatoes. Suddenly she had seen, like a building passed for months and never noted, Rita sitting at countless tables, in endless rooms, on infinite occasions, trying to talk, attempting to converse, sneaking her way onto the edges of conversations, and always, always, being shunted aside, testily told that she was wrong, patronizingly appeased, genially ignored, lovingly convinced that she didn't know what was being discussed. Over this image of Rita – turning to dish out more food, or take away a plate, or carry a child into another room – came an image of herself, Linda the loved and the lovely, listening intelligently to deadly discussions on the forgotten genius of Leopoldo Alas, or the difficulties of translating modern South American writers into English, then slipping away to baste the roast, or tuck in the children, or call about the babysitter for the next night. Paul tells everyone, especially his lovers, what a brilliant children's editor Linda is, what a fantastic gourmet cook, what a gifted mother. He also tells everyone, though not especially his lovers, that his mother makes the best meatloaf and the best sauerbraten in New York. When Paul introduces Rita to people he says, "This is my mother"; when he introduces Linda he says, "This is my wife". Today, during the second lap of Christmas dinner, it occurred to Linda that the difference between the two introductions was, somehow, negligible. She had turned to look at Paul, who was stowing lumps of turkey, dripping with bloody cranberries, into his mouth, and thought to herself, paying special attention to the twitch in his left eye, who is this man? No answer came.

The children breathe through their early winter colds, Paul taps his pipe against the door as they stop for a light, Rita says, "Wasn't it a lovely day?"

Paul says, "Um."

Linda says, "We all had a really nice time". She could leave him – or, more to the point, she could ask him to leave. She would be free, liberated: no longer would she have to help edit his journal, do his laundry, cook food she doesn't even like, answer the phone to his students who thirst after enlightenment and knowledge during all hours of the day and night, conform to his sexual, intellectual and domestic fantasies. She could be whoever she wanted, do whatever she wanted, explore the limitless, phantasmagoric possibilities of the universe.

"Didn't Lillian look well? She's lost a lot of weight."

"He's put on some," says Paul.

"She looks very well," says Linda, imagining herself going to dinners alone, to parties alone, on vacations alone, backpacking across America all by herself.

Linda has yet to discover that every time you forget you're a woman, some man reminds you.

From his nest in the back seat, David whimpers, "Mommy, Mommy, are we home yet?"

Or some man's child.

Linda doesn't feel like turning, and she doesn't feel like having a small body climbing onto hers, squashing her breasts and bruising her hip bone with a pointy knee. But Rita says, "Now, now, sweetheart, don't bother your poor mother, she's tired," and Paul says, as a darling, tousled head bobs up directly in line with the rearview mirror, "Come on, David, don't bother Daddy when he's driving. We'll be home soon and then I'll give you a ride into the house," and so Linda says, "Do you want to come up front and sit with me?"

Patricia also sits up, whining, "Are we almost home?", prodding Rita's wracked and weary body with an elbow and then a heel.

"Don't hurt Grandma," she says, rather futilely, then gives the little girl a hug and a kiss, smooths a strand of damp hair from her round and flawless face. "Would anyone like a mint?" as though it could be a question, dumping a handful of green-foil-covered discs onto her lap, looking like some legendary pirate currency in the non-glare public lighting.

Patricia immediately resumes her place; David, just coming in for a head-first landing on his mother's lap, quickly slams his feet down, skimming his father's shoulder, and makes a quick U-turn.

"David! You have to sit still while Daddy's driving."

"There, there," croons Rita, helping the little boy back to the dark safety of the rear. "You just come and sit with Grandma."

Paul grinds his teeth into the stem of the pipe. What Rita means, Paul knows, is not "don't bother your father", but "pay no attention to your father"; his mother humiliating, castrating, dismissing him. He, a man who commands respect, admiration, envy and even small amounts of power and adoration in the real, intelligent world, has always been infantalized and deballed at home by a woman who only has a High School Equivalency Diploma. "I don't want them having too many sweets," he states.

It is the same thing she did to his father: preying on his kindness, his weakness; bullying him into a life he didn't want; sucking his creativity from him with her crazy straw of petty, materialistic demands and dearth of imagination. Not a bad woman, of course, but simple, narrow, prosaic. What had his father ever seen in her? "Fuck."

In a few minutes, depending on traffic, he will finally drop her off, see her safely upstairs and inside (thank God she has her own apartment, isn't too sick or too senile to live alone), and then he can return to his own home, pour himself a stiff scotch while Linda gets the kids to bed, go in to tuck them in and read them a short story, making the faces and voices he knows they love, receiving in payment the hot little kisses which always just miss his devil-may-care Pancho Villa moustache, and lock himself into the sanctuary of his study.

He is writing a novella – his longest work so far. As with all of his poems and stories, it will be published (either whole or in part) in the small but prestigious literary journal which he founded and runs. As with all of his previous work, it will be published under a pseudonym. There is no deceit or dishonesty intended in this; if the work had no merit he wouldn't publish it – he is simply providing public space for an unknown, but acknowledgedly talented writer who otherwise would have no forum. He periodically publishes the work of close friends and mistresses on the same grounds.

That is all he wants from life: a little peace, a little quiet, a little time to himself. A space in which to create his universe and dream his dreams. The traffic, the understated threat of the city, the silently antagonistic presence of his wife breathing next to him, the grating voices of his children as they stuff their faces with forbidden sweets (will his mother never listen to him? who does she think pays the dental bills?), all of them fade into the hum of the engine as he contemplates the real world of his boiling brain.

The light changes. Behind, a car horn honks impatiently.

"The light," says Linda.

"The light," Rita says.

"For Chrissake, I see the damn light."

18

They plunge along the streets and avenues of the Bronx, the war zone. The sturdy white Volvo and its five weary occupants roll towards Rita Sutcliffe's street. Magically affixed by armies of elves, glittering hoops of balls and tinsel and plastic molds of Santa, candles and joyous carollers swing easily across the major roads.

"Oh, look," commands Rita.

"Ooh, look," echo the childish voices.

The car rides over something solid as he pulls up to the curb. "What was that?" It would be just his luck to ride over a drunk. Or a piece of wood with a nail sticking out of it, planted by the local gang. So that, as he bends to see what is wrong with the tires, they will emerge from the shadows, wearing their berets and their bandanas, club him over the head, grab his wallet, rape the women, and then vanish, laughing and whistling, down the deserted road.

No one else noticed that they rode over anything. In front of Rita's building, the statue of the Virgin Mary glows in a halo of Christmas lights – as she does every night of the year.

"I hope the tire's all right."

"You don't have to see me up," and she heaves herself from the back seat, narrowly missing banging her head on the door. A pain like twenty torches lights up the bottom half of her body, red, orange, gold, glowing like the plaster Virgin. She prays that she won't be sick again before she can get upstairs.

Paul silently sighs. "Don't be silly. I'll make sure you get in okay," taking the plastic shopping bags from the back, leading the old lady up the path, hoping to make her hurry. At the front door he realizes that she is still back at the car, kissing them all good-bye, bye-bye, call me when you get home.

"Mom!" The landlady's fox terrier begins to yap. Rita travels slowly over the concrete, hunched inside of her coat as though it is an outgrown shell. Paul sighs, audibly this time. Once she has finally reached him he has to wait while she rummages through her purse for the keys.

"Why don't you keep them in the zip compartment," he advises, for perhaps the twenty-eighth time.

19

"I usually do," she lies, locating candies, pencils, a tin packet of aspirins, three old address books, two key rings, a rubber dog eraser pencil top, a small plastic doll, a miniature flashlight that doesn't work and an old brooch with a broken clasp.

He leans the bags against the door; they let off soft moans. "Let me look." He has just found an opened safety pin when she locates the keys in her coat pocket. He takes them from her and opens the door. This part is always exactly the same.

He never enters his mother's house without being assailed by two opposing desires: the first, to leave; the second, to stay. But they are impulses of which he is no longer aware; just as he is not aware of the clean, cheap linoleum, or the yellow plastic dish drainer, or the over-sized wooden spoon and fork that hang on the wall.

He kisses his mother on her powdery cheek. "Have a good day?"

"Is everything all right?" holding on to him. "What's wrong?"

She does not ask this, he knows, from any genuine concern, but from her delight in doom. Rita likes to read the trashiest newspapers and magazines, looking up from some grisly tale of drunkenness and cruelty, murder, pillage and mayhem, to fix her beady lizard eyes on whoever was luckless enough to be in the room, wheezing exclamations of horror, shock and outrage. "Terrible, terrible," Rita would say; "Do you believe this? Only eleven . . ."; "And then he stabbed her twenty more times . . ."; "They even found fingers and toes in the playground, miles away . . ."; "Seven children and her almost paralyzed with arthritis and he ran off with a sixteen-year-old nymphomaniac . . ."

He holds her at bay. "Everything couldn't be better."

"You look overtired. You're doing too much." She squints at him, searching out the first traces of destruction and decay. "You can't burn the candle at both ends."

She wants to be able to say "I told you so", she wants him to need her, she wants him to be unlucky. "I've never felt

20

better in my life," he says, stepping back from her, and this is true.

"Linda doesn't look very well," coming around from the other side. She takes off her coat. Rita doesn't look so well herself.

"Linda's fine. She's just exhausted herself. You know Linda, she always does too much for the holidays, and she just won't listen to me." He re-kisses the wrinkly cheek.

Defeated, she kisses the rim of his ear. "Drive carefully. And call me when you get home. I want to make sure you get home safely."

"Are you sure you have everything?"

She doesn't look at the bags. "Uhhuh. Make sure you call."

"You haven't left anything in the car?"

"That's everything."

In the morning he will find on the floor of the car a plastic container filled with creamed onions, and an old shower curtain that Lillian was going to throw out but gave to Rita instead. Even as he now descends the stairs, Rita watching from the landing, he knows that he will find something in the morning. He almost always does. At the bottom of the stairs he stops and turns to wave again; her whisper whistles through the hall, goodbyegoodbyeMerry Christmas.

The children are asleep once more.

"Is she all right?" as though he would have left her if she weren't.

"Of course she is."

"She seems very tired."

"It's been a long day."

Linda cranes her neck to make sure he isn't going to pull into the path of a runaway cab. "I didn't mean just today. She's calmed down a lot lately."

He looks over his shoulder, checking where she has checked. She once directed him right into the path of a cream colored Cadillac as they were entering the Expressway. "She's getting senile, not mellow, if that's what you mean."

Linda yawns.

"It's been a long day for all of us," he says, leaning over to pat her knee – a gesture which either means that he wants to make love to her tonight, or that he doesn't.

"It went pretty well," all-in-all, given all the things that might have gone wrong. She yawns again as he makes an illegal U-turn and speeds down the street, fearing, perhaps, that if he lingers masked gunmen will leap from behind trash cans and out of alleyways to dance on the roof and hood of his car, your money or your life. Ever since being mugged in September Paul has had a more than cautious fear of what he calls "bad neighborhoods". Even though he lives in one.

"Lillian never could make gravy."

"It wasn't bad," says Linda. "The sweet potatoes were terrific." She shuts her eyes; will he believe that she has fallen asleep in .1 second?

But no. "I just don't know how she puts up with that imbecile," and, remembering the radio, clicks it on.

Linda watches the speedometer. "He's not so bad."

"He's a fool. And that incessant giggling of his. He just sits there with that inane grin on his face. If one of us dropped dead at the table, he'd laugh." They lunge onto the parkway. "Lillian is anything but perfect, but I can't see what it is in him that she fell in love with."

They swish along, Linda watching the silhouetted families in other cars, wondering how happy they are. They have had this conversation before. She once suggested that Lillian might have married Jimmy because she was thirty-one and desperate. This was greeted with much hurt hostility, an angry attack on her own cynicism and emotional frigidity and a short but eloquent speech on Love. Paul believes in love; being a democrat he believes in it for everyone.

So now Linda answers him with a shrug that he can't see because his eyes are on the road.

"And that kid," he continues, "what a pain in the ass. I can't decide which is worse, the way it tears around destroying everything, or the way Lillian tears around after it making sure it doesn't get any dirt on the tips of its shoes."

22

For perhaps the first time all day, Linda laughs. "Did you see the look on Lillian's face when Angela dumped the spoonful of cranberries down the front of her dress? I thought she was going to try to kill her in front of everybody." Their laughter froths all over the front of the car, loose and familiar, comfortable and warm. "That's nothing, did you see the way she tried to dislocate its wrist when it called her a stupid bitch?" he can barely squeeze the words from between his gasped giggles.

The tension has been snapped; conspirators, their similarity sizzles. She tells him what Lillian said about Rita always getting in the way and spoiling Angela; he tells her Jimmy's story of setting fire to himself with the bunsen burner during a class demonstration (Jimmy teaches science and coaches the basketball team at a local high school). She tells him about Lillian going Christmas shopping with Rita and, having had too much wine at lunch, getting into an argument with the Santa Claus at Macy's; he tells her how Jimmy was supposed to pick Lillian up at some Tupperware party or other and instead he got drunk and drove the car into a highway divider. She leans against his shoulder, and their laughter trails off to friendly sighs.

Everything is all right. Merry Christmas, twinkle the lights of Jersey.

They bump off at the 125th Street exit, under a sky that houses neither star nor moon, just drizzle. Ghosts flutter forlornly down avenue, street and alley, flickering with fragility on the perimeters of light, beckoning with stunted arms, calling to long-vanished lovers, friends, family and foes in voices that sound like thawing ice falling through branches. As he rides the car up on the curb, trying to jam it into a too-small space in front of his building, he tries to imprint on his mind the image of timelessness, of separate, parallel realities which has suddenly overtaken him. Sometimes it's hard to live poetically on 110th Street.

Babies, blankets, washed bowls, foil-wrapped slabs of pie

23

and flaking white meat, a stringy stuffed bear with an Adlai Stevenson button for a nose, extra sweaters and David's emergency changes of underwear must all be brought back into the house. The elaborate lock and alarm system must be set in place – so they will know when the car is being stolen. This is the part they all hate most. The children begin to whine, at the same time feigning sleep. Linda buries herself beneath bundles, her bag hanging down from her elbow, banging against her leg as she leads the limp Patricia down the block, fumbling for the keys in the pocket of her coat. Paul will carry his son.

He holds the boy in his arms, protecting him with his own breath, his heartbeat. Paul Sutcliffe is not a happy man – in a world as flawed as ours, on a planet populated by fools and lunatics, bozos and bozettes, part of a life form dedicated to the frivolous and the superficial; what intelligent man could consider happiness – but at moments like this he comes close. Especially at moments like this, bursting bubbles, looking down at his own face reflected in miniature in the dull wash of light, everything like him including the elongated lobes – his boy.

Linda stands holding the front door open, arms encumbered, keys dangling perilously between fingers, daughter heavy-lidded, leaning against her, Mother Courage. "You can ring your mother while I put the kids to bed," leading the way down the hall.

He doesn't want to. He has heard everything his mother will have to say; he has done his bit. At least the children are sleepy, submissive, will show gratitude if he lets them skip brushing their teeth, will give him dreamy elfin hugs and kisses, no hard time. "I'll tuck in the kids," opening the apartment door before she can.

She gives him a look, but it is wifely, amused, understanding, and says, "Okay."

First, however, she has to put the things away, and then David's clean pajamas are missing, and Patricia can't find her lavender stuffed rabbit with the missing ear (without which she cannot sleep), and Paul goes to get glasses of water but becomes distracted, and Patsy wants to tell her just one story about this boy at school who had eighteen stitches in his head.

By the time she is dialling Rita's number, Paul is already in his study, wearing his old Shetland sweater and faded plaid carpet slippers, a double scotch on a woven raffia coaster next to his typewriter, the radio on ever so softly – an inspirational hum.

In the kitchen, pouring boiling water onto a tablespoon of granulated coffee, Linda says, "Hi? Rita? We just got in. Sure, everything's fine. Paul had some work to finish up . . ." Would Linda have liked to have not come home? Or to have left the children locked in the car? Does she care about the boy with the eighteen stitches, or that Ralph Hoffman (who is in David's nursery class) throws up every lunch time because they make him drink milk? Does Linda want to talk to Rita (who, ten years ago, refused to come to her wedding), to hear, yet again, how much Lillian's dress cost, how Walter would have adored the children, for how many people Rita used to cook?

Steam rises from her blue and white striped mug – but it is only steam, not a puff of magic smoke, not a minuscule cloud formation hovering over her Nescafé. She switched the tree lights (all ten of them) on as she went through to the kitchen, now stands in the doorway watching them blink uncertainly. Everything Linda does, she does for love. One of the bulbs, the purple one (the only one that is not green), goes out.

Doesn't she?

   ★   ★   ★

Paul begins to type:

The old lady has come home to die. For nights outside of the house the bats have flown, wings like dark angels, circling through the shadows. Hovering. Waiting. Summoned by death,

25

retrievers of her soul. The old woman scrubs the floors, fills kettles with meat and broth, polishes the windows to transparent, like God's love, throwing back sunbeams in her eyes, like man's love, ironing smooth as raindrops tablecloths, shirts, scarves trimmed with lace. She waits to die, filling up salt cellars and hours. The house surrounds her, comforting as arms; her home envelops her, the past palpable, having shape and form — furniture, photographs, bolts of purple ribbon, tarnished spoons — all of it unlocking years. Her children touch her fingers, make her tea, sip the soup, saying, not enough salt, too much, noticing without seeming to see the smooth shadows slope out of time; her children's children touch her heart, unlocking tears.

*   *   *

Within the world that is concrete, touchable, logical, rational and clear, lies another which shrinks from tedium and reason, a universe of electricity, ageless passion, deathless meaning and timeless love. This is what Paul believes. It is this that he wishes to communicate, to pass on. This is what his writing is about, his life is about, his love is about. He knows that not everyone sees this, he knows he is special, that he has been lucky enough to find the secret. Some think it is money, or power, or politics, or sex, or knowledge, or revolution – but Paul knows it is love.

What Paul doesn't know is that within the very conjurer's cave, secure in the center of the perpetually miraculous, the boring, the dull, the ordinary and the predictable still exist. And are difficult to avoid.

2

The streets of New York are grey and cold and blown with snow. From the Sutcliffe kitchen window, the little bit that shows above the dingy burlap shade and the air conditioning unit, the storm can be seen as a fluttering organdy curtain, disguising the details of buildings but not the shapes.

Paul sits in the corner, head bent over the *New York Times*. On either side of him sits a child: on the right, a child mashing banana into his cereal; on the left, a child paring the crust from her toast with a steak knife.

David lowers his face into his Peter Rabbit bowl. "Ugh," he says, making a retching noise, "my cereal smells like dog doodoo," and then he laughs at how funny that is. But his father is unmoved.

Patricia tosses the unwanted ends under the table to the cat, who doesn't eat bread, but who instead waits patiently for the scraps of egg, bologna, or tuna fish casserole which often come her way. A wad of toast hits Paul's foot. "Stop it," he says, fascinated by the letters to the Editor; she stops.

"Did you know that if you mix water and flour together and then fry it in butter it tastes just like a T-bone steak?"

"Ulk," chokes David. "It'd taste like Martian eyes."

Paul looks up. "Who told you that nonsense?"

Patricia looks hurt. "Grandma did. She says they did it during the Depression."

"Well, it's not true."

"But Grandma said it was."

27

"And I say it isn't."

"Or camel humps," contributes David, a child who sticks pretty much to his own concept of the universe.

"It doesn't taste like anything but flour and water," Paul announces, his voice a little loud.

David balances a soggy Cheerio on his nose; he thinks it makes him look like a circus seal. "Indians used to eat babies," he continues, catching the piece of cereal with his tongue.

It is not even eight o'clock yet.

"The Indians did no such thing," says Paul, trying to interject the right amount of authority into his tone. "The Indians were very badly treated by the white man. Their lands were stolen, they were lied to, humiliated, degraded and slaughtered."

David sticks another milk–soaked circle on his face, this time on his forehead, and rolls his eyes together.

But his father is not amused. "Can't you listen to me when I'm telling you something important? The way we treated the Indians is one of the most disgraceful chapters in our country's history."

David makes his eyes go up into his head. "Hard-boiled egg," he says. "Look!"

Patsy takes a swallow of juice. "Uncle Jimmy's an Indian," and she looks to her brother for astonishment and her father for approval.

Paul smiles tolerantly. "Not exactly."

Patricia's eyebrows draw fractionally closer together. "He said he was."

Surely the Christmas holiday was never this long when he was in school. "Then he was just teasing you."

She stares back at him, unperturbed. "No he wasn't. He has black hair doesn't he? He said that once his people lived on this beautiful island, and they had all sorts of fruits and flowers and lovely animals and cute little frogs. And then the white man came and destroyed the land and made the Indians slaves and took everything they could get and made everybody unhappy. And now they can't even live on the land any more like they used to, now they all have to work in factories and be poor and have everybody call them names," and she burns her space-eyes into the bridge of his nose.

He would like to dream of his son growing up to be President, but that might mean that his daughter would wind up as God. "Uncle Jimmy," he says, pronouncing his words carefully, "is Puerto Rican, not Indian."

Patricia doesn't blink. "He's Puerto Rican Indian."

"It's not exactly the same thing as being an American Indian." He folds the paper and rests it on his lap. "David, stop doing that. Finish eating."

"Of course it's the same thing," pushing her chair back and picking up her plate. "Don't you remember the play we put on at school for Puerto Rico Day?"

"Go get your things together," he commands. It is not that he dislikes Puerto Ricans, but he would have preferred that his brother-in-law were Cuban.

A few years ago, Patricia would have been wearing a nice little dress and thick wool socks, and would have flounced from the room. But she is wearing jeans and a navy-blue leotard, and so she stalks, jerking her brother's chair in passing.

Linda limps in as Patricia makes her exit. Linda is going to be late for work. She is brushing her hair, and in her teeth holds a large safety pin with a blue Donald Duck head on it, which she would like Paul to use to pin her blouse together in the back because the button's popped. She can't find her other shoe.

"She's goddamn stubborn, that kid." He glares at her as she approaches. "I can't imagine where she gets it from." Though he obviously has a good idea.

Linda feels as though she's been up for days. She has fed the cat, fed the children, made the coffee, found the pompoms for Patsy's ice skates, put a crease in her slacks, changed the cat litter and located Paul's library pass in the inside pocket of his gray tweed jacket. Her shower was only warm, her lipstick broke off from its base (Patricia again) and in the one shoe she could find there was a very very small submachine gun which put a hole in her stocking (also Patricia). She doesn't know what he's talking about. "Huh?"

He takes the pin from her mouth, shaking his head, wondering what she'd do without him, she's so disorganized. "Patsy has got to be the most stubborn kid I've ever come across. She's even thicker than the kids in my ESL class." (English as a Second Language – which everyone is forced to teach. When questioned, Paul always says that he loves his ESL class, that he relishes the opportunity to take on a real personal challenge and that they teach him a lot; he finds them fresh and rewarding. What he really finds them is a bunch of lazy, undisciplined, antagonistic savages, from whom he daily expects violence.)

"Ouch. Watch it."

"For Chrissake, Linda, bend down."

"Why don't you stand up?" But she lowers herself just a little.

"Because I am trying to read my paper and have my breakfast, though it's next to goddamn impossible in this house."

And whose fault is that?

"Thank you," she says, straightening up, giving her hair a few more very brisk strokes. "Thank you very, very much."

He is turning to the book review. "If she's this bad now," picking up where he'd left off, "what do you think she's going to be like when she's twelve?"

Linda pours herself half a cup of lukewarm coffee. "Who?"

"Who were we talking about?" he asks, making note of Linda's continued absent-mindedness. "Your daughter."

There are mornings when the bustle and busyness, the squabblings and catastrophes of the family give Linda energy, make her feel active and purposeful; mornings when she glows and pulses with the joy of being alive. This is not one of those mornings – this is one of the other mornings.

Linda has not yet risen from her depression; has, in fact, squelched down just an infinitesimal bit more. She awoke this morning, Paul's arm flung across her, thinking of the futility of life. This week she three times recognized someone on the street who she knows beyond doubt is dead. She has taken all this as an omen. Now, eyeing her husband as he mutters over the book review, which everyone knows is all lies anyway, she wants to cry. Is this it? she would like to scream at him. Is this it? Paul would be right, she is going to get her period – but that, of course, is only part of it.

She doesn't scream, she doesn't cry; she doesn't even whack him over the head with her hairbrush. Instead she says, patiently, almost lovingly, "You won't forget to pay the nursery, will you?"

Paul nods. "Listen to this, Linda, just listen to this. This guy's got about as much critical ability as an android cheerleader. Just listen to this . . ."

"I can't now, hon, I have to find my shoe."

"Linda, just listen a minute. It won't take long."

Wild of eye, sharp of tooth, eel-like locks spiralling out with electricity, the bewitched woman wails, "My shoe, my shoe, my shoe, my shoe," and shoves the table against his solar plexus as she hobbles from the room.

Her shoe is right outside of the kitchen doorway, with scratch marks on the toe. Miss Molly, the cat, is sitting on top of the bookcase, eyes closed to slits, nodding in her total innocence. Linda jams on the shoe, jams her little rubber boots on, drives her arms into her coat, pulls her floppy wool hat over her head and shouts into air, "Mommy's going now."

"Bye."

"Good-bye."

"Byyyyeee."

They all hate her. They all hate her so much that they can't even be bothered to throw her a kiss, wish her a nice day. "Paul," she says, turning so that she can see him through the doorway and the short hall that breaks off the kitchen from the living room.

"Now what?"

"You won't forget to give Patsy money for the ice skating. And make sure she takes an extra pair of socks."

"Sure thing."

She gathers up her briefcase and her umbrella, undecided as to whether she wants forgiveness or revenge. "Good-bye. See you tonight."

31

"Have a nice day, sweetheart," and he blows her a gentle kiss over the top of his paper. "Don't work too hard."

"You either. It's your holiday, you deserve a little time off."

He gives her a smile which means that he can never have a holiday, that he can never relax, that he is in a competitive, cut-throat profession, and that the only way he is going to fight his way to the top is by producing, by publishing and by never once relaxing his vigilance or his guard. Today, though it is still the Christmas break, he will be working all day on a paper he is writing on the modern Cuban novel. Paul's specialty is Hispano-American literature (in translation – though occasionally he does a course in conjunction with the Spanish Department, the Banana Republic).

After Linda leaves, Paul puts his cup in the sink, zips David into his red nylon snow suit, and together they escort Patricia down two flights to Katie Wilson's. Then he takes David to his day care center, remembering just in time to give them a check for the month.

And so has begun another not insignificant day.

The stairs to the station hadn't been cleared, the man at the token booth had been hostile, the train was packed and the conductor sang *After the Ball Was Over* all the way downtown – and very hauntingly at that. Because of all this she was two stops from her destination before she realized that she had left the manuscript she needed under her desk with yesterday's stockings on top of it. Linda must return home.

Linda, just emerging from the dark, protective recesses of the subway, is surprised to see her car – their car – slide next to the curb in front of her. She is even more surprised to see a young woman – hardly more than a girl – dash out from under the shelter of a shop awning, yanking the door open as though it is her own door, as though it is a door she has yanked open hundreds of times before. Linda can just see Paul leaning out as the girl leans in, and the briefest of kisses being exchanged, before the girl is sucked into the center of

Vera the Volvo. Through the foggy, snowed-upon windows, she watches their phantoms kiss again. Her blood races, the sound of stampeding stallions pounds against her ears. For an instant she thinks that she is going to faint, but it is only her heart dropping. The car pulls away. An upward flow of travellers lands her on the sidewalk, ankle-deep in slush. Bewildered, she waits for a friendly, familiar face to step from out the hurrying hordes and offer her a hand; confused, she waits to wake up in Lynchfield, Illinois, with her hair in plastic rollers and Morning Prayers on the TV. An ambulance flashes down Broadway. Maybe there's been an accident; maybe they've been mowed down by an uptown bus; maybe they've plowed into an empty building, so intent were they on fondling each other, on licking the love from each other's lips; maybe they're both dead and mutilated and she'll have to identify the bodies.

Linda turns and goes back into the station. She will make up some excuse for not having the manuscript; if pushed, she will say that she was mugged by a neighborhood street gang with chains wrapped around their bodies and the teeth of victims dangling from their ears. She can't go back home now. She is afraid of what she will find.

There have been flirtations, there have been friendships that crept to the fringe of discretion. What man does not have his fantasies? And then, of course, there was the affair with Janet two summers ago. Midsummer's madness, he told her; something to do with the moon, man-made satellites and Linda's preoccupation with bi-lingual easy readers. Solstitial insanity, he pleaded; something to do with light fluctuations, humidity and the way Janet needed him.

He told her about it while they were on vacation on Fire Island. Sand in the beds, seaweed in the shower, a longing for someone new in his heart. He came early Friday evening, salty with sea spray, bearing gifts of watermelon, corn on the cob and sirloin steak, scotch, Mateus and Sara Lee Fudge Brownies. He took the kids down for a swim; he yelled at her, for Chrissake, Linda, don't trim all the fat off of it. He kept looking at her as though he expected her to tell him something. He trotted down the shore with David on his shoulders, laughing as the waves broke around them; he told her, Linda, some women are suited to bikinis. He explained things to her as though she only read lips. He played fourteen games of Go Fish with Patsy, letting her win all but two; he asked Linda if she thought she would ever go back for her Master's, as she once said she would.

And only then had he told her, lying side by side in the moony night, sweating, waiting for a refreshing island breeze, voices gliding past the window like low-flying gulls, laughter cutting through the thick, sluggish night. I'm having an affair. A muffled noise: a plane, a boat, a distant bomb? And that's how he told her, touching her hand, enfolding her in his arms, her body as gone to him as in death. I just can't seem to help myself. Oh, yes, you do, you help yourself. I can't live with myself, I am so guilty. Ah. I love her, yes. Ah. Ah. I am so guilty and I love you too, I love you so much. Love me back.

But that was now all over. He had been given his options (Janet, with her horsey laugh, her drive for academic status and recognition, her tiny walk-up; or Linda, with her solid career, her two beautiful children, her half-share in a superb apartment and a country house), and he had made his choice. With difficulty. I do love her, but it isn't worth my marriage, worth my children, worth my home; worth you. They had their second honeymoon: flowers, dinners, plays; holding hands, calling home, one never leaving without kissing the other good-bye. They were mature and sophisticated, he could talk to Janet at work, she could call him about the journal, she could even come to dinner, in a crowd. But nothing more. Promise me you will not love her any more, want her any more, remember any more. Women – the bewitchers, the enchantresses – are also good at the breaking of magic spells, the turning of princes back into frogs. Rititnitit.

Linda rides back downtown, hunched into a corner seat,

scowling. She looks more deranged than bereaved. She looks, in fact, though it is difficult to know how anyone on the subway could know this, very much like Patricia in one of those moods in which she locks herself in her room and pushes little notes under the door: I Hate You; I Hope You Have To Go To Australia And All The Blood Goes To Your Head.

When Paul promised never to see Janet again, Linda hadn't considered that he might still see someone else. Or, and this doesn't occur to her until 59th Street, that he might not have been sincere at all.

Linda is crazed, half dazed. Wall-eyed, she walks through the morning stepping on toes, treading on feelings, answering without hearing, speaking without thinking. Torches of hurt light up her body; torrents of anger put them out. Does she hate Paul or does she adore him? Does she want him, safe in the living room with his shirt off, complaining about Carlos Fuentes; or would she rather he were sitting at some other woman's table, eating curried lentil soup and thinking about how good his life used to be? Only as long ago as early this morning she thought that she would have to tell him to leave; now she is afraid that he will want to go. She stares at herself in the ladies' room mirror. Has she let herself go? Her face shows the effort of not crying, her eyes look as though they're about to explode. There is nothing that doesn't remind her of Paul; thinking of Paul is like having a terminal illness and concentrating on the disease. For God's sake, just cut it out.

Linda retouches her eye make-up, makes her complexion blossom with natural blush. She reparts her hair and clips it so that it looks less severe. She arranges the collar of her blouse. Surely she has been here before: wept these tears, heaved these sighs, let rend her bosom these terrible sobs. She turns on both taps to cover the sound of her hysteria. How often will she have to go through this? What does it mean?

Finally, she washes her face with cold water, dries it, puts on fresh make-up, smooths out her blouse, pats her hair. It is not exactly the same this time. The last time, the first time, she thought it was the end of the world. This time (the last time?) she knows it is not. She shuts her bag, hangs it over her shoulder. With no effort, she can see Paul's face as he kisses his lover, as he whispers his words of love, oh love, oh love me do.

And so it is that that morning when Mark Schwerner asks her to have lunch with him – as he asks her almost every week, solemn and sorrowful – to discuss, he says, the problems of the non-fiction list, Linda accepts. Knowing full well that she is after more than a cold meat platter and a glass of dry white wine. She and Mark have talked around the possibilities of their "relationship" for months now, but always she has pulled them short. And now, of course, despite all of Mark's best efforts at pursuing and wooing, it is revenge and not desire that wins the day.

At about the time that Linda and Mark Schwerner are telling one another, bravely and apologetically, that they have long been attracted, been noticing, been interested – he saying, pouring more wine, that he knows how devoted she is to her family, to her husband; she whispering, accepting more wine, that she would never do anything to disrupt either marriage; the both of them agreeing, as they arrange to meet for dinner, that they will be no more than ghosts in each other's life – about that time, Paul is arriving at the airport. He is alone now, though he won't be for long. Today is the day that Janet returns from her Christmas visit home.

Pampered, pumped and petted, lovingly gorged with the dishes and delicacies she liked so much as a child, red and pink knitted slippers with pompoms on the toes folded carefully into a corner of her suitcase, head stuffed with her mother's interminable lists of the engagements, marriages and births of anyone and everyone she has ever known, met or heard of, and her brain still aching from the effort of avoiding her father's cautious curiosity ("Won't anyone be picking you up from the airport, dear?"), Janet disembarks.

Little winged angels with cherry mouths speed her across the rose-strewn floor, a thousand violins sing softly above the din of jet engines and tired travellers, the sun is blazing over Queens, showering sunbeams instead of cherry blossoms or rice. And he is there. Immediately recognizable in the crowd, more handsome than remembered, more perfect than recalled. They do not fall into each other's arms, they thrust themselves, hugging tightly, kissing hair and collars and earlobes and, finally, mouths.

"God, have I missed you . . ."

"Oh, honey, oh, it's so good . . ."

People walk around them, smiling – remembering, perhaps, a better time, a different place.

"Oh, darling, talk about blue Christmases . . ."

"Jesus, I have missed you . . ."

The sorrows of a weary world seem strangely lightened by their love.

"Merry Christmas, darling."

"Happy New Year."

Reluctantly, they prise themselves apart, and are returned to the impersonal airport terminal on this dreary winter afternoon. "I have to pick David up by six," he says, linking his arm through hers and steering her towards Baggage Claim.

Janet hugs his arm. She is understanding about the children. "Did they have a nice Christmas?" In days gone by she has gone on outings with the younger and not yet verbally reliable David (whom she considers spoiled and lacking in maternal discipline), and has shared some tense car rides and one remarkably unpleasant half hour in Central Park with the younger Patricia (whom she considers precocious if not actually sinister), and, of course, in the long gone by days when they were all friends (when Patricia was still cute and David was still not toilet trained) she has talked to them and cuddled them and admired chubby faces and raw-looking spaces where teeth used to be and teddy bears dressed in drag, and often told Linda that she didn't know how she did it. But

37

things are different now: Linda will no longer speak to her and the children are liable to speak too much. Unable to see them in person – and thus judge how much better a job of raising them she could be doing – she must content herself with always asking about them, always being thoughtful of them, always speaking of them with concern and warmth. On birthdays and Christmas she passes small anonymous presents on to them, as a token of her affection for these children of the man she loves. She knows that she can never claim any credit for these gestures; just as she knows that the presents she gives to Paul himself – the pipe, the ring, the hand-blown champagne glasses – must all be kept in his office, exiled from the rest of his life.

He kisses the top of her head. "I think David nearly OD'd on chocolates and gingerbread men. And Patricia got the most incredible space station I've ever seen. It took me nearly three hours to assemble."

Janet's mouth mocks delight. It is Linda's affectation, she believes, that Patricia is to be given only non-sexist toys – that is, boys' toys; in fact, it is Patricia's own preference, it being David who is more inclined to fill plastic cups with cat litter and pretend that he is cooking. "And did she like the doll I got for her?"

Arms entwined, they watch the chrome merry-go-round revolve, waiting for it to give up Janet's matched red leather luggage with her initials in gold by the locks. He can't remember the doll, perhaps it's still in the back of the car. "She loved it. She's already made a special bed for it," only then realizing that he gave it to Liz for her child.

"I'll give you your present when we get home," she says in the instant before he breaks away to retrieve her suitcases.

A set of her keys is in his pocket. There is Chablis in the refrigerator, Brie on the table, a gold chain wrapped in silver paper on the pillow of the bed. "And just you wait till we get home." He winks, or blinks, not allowing her to help with the baggage, heavy enough to throw his back out.

Janet does not ask what Linda gave him, or what he gave Linda; what they said, or what they promised; what they did.

She is understanding about his life. Has she ever been begging or complaining? demanding or bitchy? She knows that Paul loves her. She knows that he still has feelings for his wife; she knows that he still makes love to Linda – but out of duty, out of the memory of love. "We still screw," he assures her, "but I almost never kiss her." Janet is well aware of the difficulties – the hazards – of loving a married man. Isn't everyone?

Janet's parents aren't. Janet's parents live in a world where that sort of thing happens only in films or on television, or, at the very most, to the wayward daughters of people who, really, don't deserve any better. Janet's parents are very shortly going to be the parents of a Ph.D. in Literature – but do they care? Yes, of course they do; it is something to talk about, it is a point of pride, a vindication of all their years of struggle and sacrifice, pushing and dreaming. But it is not the same as talking about a son-in-law, or a grandchild, or a visit to New York to your daughter and her husband in their new apartment. Janet's parents have had her all to themselves for seven and a half days, and though they are too polite, too cultured, too well-educated and too civilized to say anything directly, they have made it clear that they expected better things. They have also managed to start Janet thinking that that was what she had expected.

As they sway and trundle across the parking lot, the ticket now clenched between his teeth, hearts beating with anticipation, tongues and thoughts just waiting to release the torrent of events and wishes that have only been waiting for this time together, the snow whipping about them, the tiny illuminated hands on their watches ticking on, there is that moment before they finally reach the car – and fall at last into a wet and lingering kiss – when he thinks that he should have arranged the day better to allow him some time for work, and she thinks that they are soon going to have to have a serious discussion about the future.

Rita, thinking that Paul might be working at home, has called him several times throughout the morning. She has even

39

called the operator once to make sure she was reaching the right number since she knows, she explains to the frosty, disembodied voice, that there is sometimes trouble on the line. Sometimes, no matter how carefully you dial, you get the local precinct or a pizza parlour on 94th Street. But the operator only repeated, "I'm sorry, but there is no answer at that number, you will have to call again later."

So far today, Rita has exchanged some words with Mrs Imperatrice on the poor garbage collection and on how cold winters used to be when they were young; has waited for and collected the mail (two leaflets and a Christmas card from a niece she hasn't seen for eight years who now lives in Santa Fe); has held down two cups of tea; has listened to a program of nostalgic music on the radio which had the effect not of making her cry or even hum to herself, but of making her feel that she would, after all, be much better off dead.

She would like to talk to Paul, to hear what the children said or did this morning, to see if he wants her to take them one day during the vacation. If she could get him on the phone, she would tell him that Mrs Lombardi next door received a five pound box of candied fruit from her son in Rhode Island, and that little Mrs Renzulli from across the street was mugged last night, just coming home from up the block, and is in the hospital and not expected to live. She would not ask him if – after all those years when he used to slam doors in her face, when he wouldn't speak to her or visit her or remember her birthday, and all those other years when he tolerated her (for the sake of the children and because Linda made him), when he visited her seldom if dutifully but always with much ceremony and telephoned her only when he needed a babysitter – he has yet found a way to forgive her, if he has yet begun to love her again, as once he loved her and held two of her fingers with his entire hand and promised that he would always live with her for ever and for ever. Rita does not understand that Paul does not forgive her. For what? Rita does not understand that Paul stopped caring about her more than twenty years ago. She tells everyone (everyone: Mrs Imperatrice, Mrs Lombardi, Evelyn, Mary Ryan – but probably no longer little Mrs Renzulli) that her children love her, are so good to her, would do anything for her, but that she doesn't want to be a burden. At other times, of course, she tells everyone how ungrateful her children are, how hard her life has always been, how she has suffered and sacrificed for them, only to be looked down on and cast aside – but that is rather seldom now. Where once she might have nagged or demanded, she now can only whine or ask. Rita has lost more than her teeth, her eyesight and her colon with the passage of years.

Living alone, being alone, Rita lives a lot in the past. Often, she is unaware that she has spent the morning or the afternoon reliving moments that never happened the way she remembers over forty, fifty years before. She hears voices, smells aromas, feels the wind, the rain, the warm sunlight. But these are not ghosts, these are not memories. They are instant replays, over and over, as though Rita's life is on high quality, long-life video tape.

She settles down to watch her soap operas. Even Lillian makes fun of her, says that she doesn't know what the attraction is. "Really, Ma," says Lillian, "you have to be a simpleton to get into those things." Though Jimmy said that he had rather liked them that week he was laid up with the flu. Not that Jimmy's opinion impressed any of them (if Paul sometimes gives people the impression that his brother-in-law is Cuban, Rita has occasionally given the impression that her son-in-law is Greek). Paul does not even comment; he simply makes it obvious by the way he pretends not to hear her that it embarrasses him having a mother who is so crude and so unclever.

She sits in her old brown armchair, inherited from some neighbor who was moving away, and thinks she is sitting in a different chair, in another living room, in a distant year. If only she could press a button and erase whole segments, rearrange entire sequences, edit the dialogue; if only it were possible to freeze frames. But, of course, Rita doesn't think like that. She only wishes that she could have some of it back – and some of it different.

41

Dying.

She can see Paul's face at eight, round and dark, and it dissolves into Walter's face, Walter lying in the hospital, staring up at her with the eyes of a corpse, saying, "I'm not coming home, I'm not coming home," closing those eyes, closing his skin, his lips so dry, saying, "that should make you happy, you bitch."

Dying.

Is he watching her now, laughing a Boris Karloff laugh? Is the first one out the winner? Did he know that all the time?

Her eyes are on the television, but she isn't looking at anything. How can this have been sixty-eight years. How can this possibly have been a lifetime. And the world still so busy.

Her old woman's hands rest on her lap, barely recognized. They should be smooth and white, soft and marbled, with long, passion-red nails. Usually she dances in the past, lips scarlet, eyebrows plucked, seams straight; repeats picnics, dates, arguments and conversations.

In the show, the nurse whose son was killed by a hit-and-run driver has just found out that she is pregnant, but thinks that the baby might be deformed, or, even worse, might be the child of the man who raped her the night she had the fight with her husband and walked out on him to go to a bar by herself. Rita has known people whose lives were just like that. She thinks it's realistic.

Today Rita is gathering no comfort from the past. Today there is nothing; she cannot quite get her mind to exist separately. She is hoping that Lillian will call, or that Paul will insist she go visit, or that the pain will stop. She remembers the winter she lived with her grandmother, waking in the cracking morning in the old house and seeing through the glazed windows, first thing, the sky and the thick trees – making her feel as though she could almost hold sunshine, cupped in her hand, herself a part of the unspeakably beautiful, the perfect. She can still remember feeling that, but now it is like remembering an event in which you took no part; or, more, an event whose significance has been obliterated or transformed (a wedding, after the marriage).

42

How could she have felt like that. Why did she never feel like that again?

The telephone is ringing, though for an instant she thinks that it is ringing somewhere else – downstairs, next door, in the hospital where the beautiful young girl has just lost the baby of the man she truly loved who has been kidnapped by left-wing terrorists. It is all right to let it ring three times, four. Lillian will think that she's in the kitchen, Paul will think that she's in the bathroom.

When she does answer, her voice is casual, comfortable, mom's. "Hello?"

"Hello, Angie? Angie Calavetta?"

"I'm sorry," says Rita, "you have the wrong number."

*　　*　　*

She sits in the center of the night, on the narrow bed of her widowhood. Her room is as small as a cell, gauze curtains like cobwebs stir in the shallow breaths of dark. Her small light glows. Wings beat: phantoms dancing for the moon. The old woman sits with her past spread out before her: photographs and postcards, cracking letters, rounds of old ribbon, velvet and silk, a tiny wooden box of rings inlaid with mother of pearl, a small blue leather folder, her documents. She keeps it locked from them, the key enveloped in old stockings, buried beneath her underwear, smelling of old age. She touches the years: a hot summer morning, jewels damp on the grass, her heart a rose, petals closed, a butterfly flutters nearby; raw sun, first flecks of green, mistake or promise, a face just seen, embossed upon her consciousness, her heart a rose, petals opening, a small insect walks on one rim; snow in her boot, steam mist frost cloud on the platform, everything under water, hands just touching, lips moving, no words, her heart a rose, petals dropping.

*　　*　　*

A small, glossy red ball bings against the wall in front of him, slams into the typewriter, thuds against the ceiling, grazes the side of his head in its final descent to the carpet.

43

"It's a high bouncer," Patricia says from the doorway.

He waits for a second to make sure that his heart hasn't stopped before becoming enraged. "What the hell's the matter with you?" swivelling the chair around, his eyes like marbles, steel ones. "You scared the shit out of me. Can't you see I'm working? Do I have to put chains on the door?"

Patricia doesn't blink. She is not even nine, but she is clearly determined to reach adulthood. "Mommy says to tell you Grandma's on the phone."

Paul studies his daughter's face for traces of fear, remorse or respect. She throws the ball in the air, claps once; throws the ball in the air, claps twice. In all of his considerable experience with women, Patricia is the only one who not only naturally assumes equality but manages to project the suspicion of her superiority. It's a frightening thought. "Tell Mommy I'm busy right now. I'm right in the middle of a scene."

She throws the ball in the air, claps five times; throws the ball in the air, claps six times. "Grandma wants to talk to you. And Mommy's going out in six and a half minutes."

"I know Mommy's going out. I'll call Grandma back when I'm done working."

"Maybe it's important," claps seven times.

"I'll call her back, Patsy."

"Maybe there's somebody trying to break into her apartment and she needs you to go beat them up." Throws the ball in the air, misses.

"Go keep an eye on your brother, and make sure you shut the door after you."

She slams the ball against the far wall, delighted as it ricochets past her. He could beat his head against the typewriter, he could moan and beg for mercy – but Patricia is not impressed by those sorts of theatrics, has not even the most casual interest in guilt. She will be, he knows, a lousy mother. "I am busy now. Get out," voice very normal, tone natural and level.

"Okay."

"And shut the door after you."

She clicks it loudly to. "He's too busy," she shouts down the hallway.

Above the sounds of the traffic on the Drive, above the sounds of the violin concerto on the radio, above the thudding of Patsy's ball as it bounds along the corridor and David's piercing wail because the cat has scratched him, Paul can hear two women sigh: one in the Bronx and one in the kitchen. And in his mind he distinctly hears the first woman say, "Oh, is he busy?", and the second reply, "Yes. He's working", in much the same way that they will say, when David has been summoned to the phone, "Oh, leave him alone if he's busy", and "Yes, he's busy dressing the cat up as an Arab".

Now he can't write; his muse has been hustled away.

He stares at the page and sighs. In a few minutes Linda will be abandoning him for some boring publishing dinner, and then the children will want his attention, and then he will have to put them to bed, read them their story, bring them their water. How is he supposed to work?

Linda pokes her head into the room. "I'm going now."

"Don't drink too much."

"I told them they can stay up an extra half hour."

"Terrific."

In a hurry, she glances at her watch. "They're watching TV, Paul. They won't bother you."

"You know damn well they'll bother me. I don't know how I'm supposed to get any work done with all these constant interruptions." And he pins her to the doorframe with his truth-seeing gaze.

"Paul, I have to go, I'm going to be late."

"So go. What I'm doing isn't important, God knows."

"I'll see you later." She forgets to shut the door, and he must get up and do it, listening warily for the sounds of approaching children. He sits back, eyes closed, arms at his sides, meditating, thinking.

This, he knows, is the most important thing he has ever written. It is the story of his childhood: of his parents; of himself and Lillian (though her part is rather minimal); of their life as a family; most importantly, of Walter's and Rita's love. For it is love, he believes, that held them together, those two very different people, his parents; love that gave them victory in the face of defeat. He is searching for sense and justifications, reasons and meaning. He is questing for the quintessence of love. Some search for truth in money, or religion, in politics, or causes. But Paul is a poet, a lover, an artist – and so he searches for his truth elsewhere.

But he has forgotten the book for the moment. He is thinking of Liz, with her long legs and long hair; he is thinking of Janet and her little girl hugs, her big girl kisses.

From the hallway comes a sound oddly reminiscent of roller skating. There is immediately after it a slamming sound, followed by a wounded scream as David speeds into the wall. The Jr Skateboard. "If you're gonna be a cry-baby," warns Patricia, in a loud and penetrating whisper, "Daddy's gonna come out here and beat you till you stop crying."

Should he laugh or weep? "You go and watch the television," he screams, not moving from his seat, "or you'll both go to bed right now and I'll break the goddamn skateboard in half."

It's going to be a long night, but once the children are tucked in he will call Janet, and wrap himself in her warm, undemanding love.

★   ★   ★

She is too pained to kneel; leans instead against the pillow of her bed, gazes at the ghostlike circle of moon, pure and bright like the eye of the universe, and prays, Oh, mother Mary you have helped me, loved me, protected me, I beg one last favor, one final sign. Her tears shine like ice. I am losing faith. Her heart is gasping. There is a moaning sound from somewhere in the night, a soul dying, her soul being drawn from her unbelieving body. She raises her liquid eyes to the moon. Has her life on earth been nothing? been for nothing? Would her absence never have been missed? Has her presence not been noticed? Have all her struggles, her hopes and her dreams meant nothing? Trees rustle, the skirts of the night. Is life no more than ice falling into water? The old woman sleeps. And in her dreams begins to relive her life.

*   *   *

He once published a story (under yet another pseudonym) in a bi-lingual journal that only accepted things with a pronounced Hispano-American theme. In that story, which was about the time Rita had threatened to leave because Walter had painted bunny rabbits all over the walls of Lillian's room and had had them both packing their cardboard suitcases at ten o'clock at night, he had had to make Rita Mexican. His little ol' Mexican mama. At least this time he can just stick to the facts, can simply peel away the tacky and the mundane from Rita's life to expose the female knight below, the woman searching for beauty and truth.

In her bathroom, still waiting for his call, Rita sits on the toilet, shitting blood into the bowl. In a tiny apartment on Christopher Street, Mark lights candles, checks for the third time that the wine is nicely chilled, checks his watch, wonders if Linda will really come.

Linda, sitting in one corner of the train, surreptitiously opens her bag, pretends to be looking for nothing as she snaps open her compact, checking her make-up. What is she doing? does she know what she's doing? why is she doing it? Her eyelashes look a bit thick, but otherwise she doesn't look too bad. She can always turn back. She can just walk down the block to see what it's like, and then she can turn right around and go home. She doesn't have to go through with it.

Paul switches off his typewriter, turns off the radio. "Come on, kids," he shouts, good-humored again, tolerant and kindly, "you can have a snack before you brush your teeth."

They clamber around him, they hug him and hang on him, they ask for ice cream and Oreos and pink milk.

His children. His kitchen. His refrigerator. His home. His wife. All of them making a happy hum.

47

He is beginning to think that it hasn't been such a bad day after all.

Linda is beginning to think that this has been, and is continuing to be, the very worst day of her life.

It took her twenty-five minutes to walk from the subway station up Christopher Street, inch by inch and foot by foot, each step weighed and weighted, pausing to peer with wonder in every store along the way, stopping twice to adjust her shoes and once to straighten a twisting stocking. She thought of phoning from the diner on the corner, you won't believe this, but I've got an awful toothache, but then remembered that she didn't have the number. She could have put a note through his door, sorry but something came up, but who had thought to bring a pen and paper? In the leather store where she stopped to price a bag, she decided that her behavior was irrational and immature and that no matter what thoughts might be dancing in the brain of Mark Schwerner there was no law anywhere that said she had to sleep with him. She could eat and run. No, she could eat and chat and then say that she'd better get a cab home, her husband would be waiting up for her.

It is a six-storey building and he has two rooms at the top. Whose rooms are they really? By the time she reached his door, she was out of breath and damp around the edges. When he opened the door he was so clean and combed, the smell of aftershave lotion rising from him like the stink of rotting vegetation from a bog, standing blocking her entrance and grinning at her like a salesman, that she almost laughed with relief. The man was just another fool. What possible threat could he be to her? What could he do that she couldn't handle? And she slammed into his hands the cheap bottle of wine good manners had forced her to buy.

For supper they had wet chicken and instant rice, and gossiped about everyone at work. He's really very sweet, she'd thought. After dinner they had coffee and brandy and talked about themselves. He's really very bright, she'd thought.

48

Now he is sitting in the rocking chair by the electric heater ("This place has a lot of old world charm," he'd joked) and she is sitting on the couch, uncomfortable against the lumpy cushions. She hasn't checked the time for over an hour, is actually enjoying herself now that she knows for certain that nothing is going to happen tonight. Maybe, she thinks, some other time. He is agreeable, he is nice and he has no apparent deformities, but he isn't, seeing him in real life like this, particularly attractive. From the way he sits, so straight and stiff, she can tell what he'd be like in bed, boring but quick. Maybe some other time, when she's feeling a little more drunk. Or when he is.

"Would you like some more?" he asks as she swallows down her third brandy.

"Oh, no," Linda smiles. "No. I'd really better be going. It must be getting late." And stands up to go.

Mark stands up, too. He had forgotten about the time, that they didn't have all night, she would have to get home. He hadn't wanted to leap on her the moment she arrived, and now she is going to go. He puts his hands in the pockets of his grey flannel slacks, then takes them out again. "Do you really have to go?"

"Oh, yes," says Linda, moving one step towards him as he moves one step towards her, getting ready to shake his hand. "I really should."

He takes one more step forward and she does the same. "I wish you'd stay a while."

Chest to breast, her eyes just level with his mouth, Linda whispers, "Well . . ."

"I really wish you'd stay," he repeats, and in attempting to kiss her lips kisses her nose instead.

"I guess I could stay a little longer," as he holds her against him, suffocating in the stuff of his shirt. How can she say no?

In the bedroom, Mark undresses with nervous glee and Linda undresses with resignation, afraid to look at his flabby white body and the greying few hairs on his chest.

She lies beside him. He kisses her lips and tentatively touches a breast. His touch is more than curious and more than

49

sure, and Linda feels her body loosen. He holds her breasts together and runs his mouth over them, his fingers pulling at her eager nipples. And then he takes one hand and puts it on her, holding her tightly, rubbing her with some private power that may make them both explode.

Linda moans. Can it be true that no man has ever really touched her before?

3

Cloudy, freezing temperatures and high winds; occasional showers, sleet and snow warnings; early fog, poor visibility and hazardous road conditions. Is this the winter weather, or does it describe Paul's present life? Still strong and courageous, he is trying to struggle through the bleak, barren days of this grim season, but he is finding the going rough. It is only January – will he live to see the sylvan shores of spring, dappled with rainbows?

He sits in his office, the door locked, a note taped to the glass saying "Professor Sutcliffe will return in twenty-five minutes". It has been there for an hour. It is his office time, but he can't face one more crawling or complaining student, one more young woman thrusting her tits at him, one more young man threatening violence or blackmail with his smile. So he sits in the shadows, lights off, trying for an astral projection.

Today he gave the ESL class their essay assignment: The Bravest Man I Have Ever Known. They mumbled amongst themselves, they cast upon him their innocent, imploring looks.

"What do you mean brave?"

"You mean like a war hero or something?"

"I don't know nobody who's brave."

"Professor, what if you don't know anybody who's brave?"

He had taken deep breaths, he had smiled on them kindly,

their friend, their benefactor. Paul Sutcliffe cares about the poor and the oppressed, about the disenfranchised and the victims. He reads the *New York Times*, he subscribes to the *New Republic*, he has once or twice bought the *Guardian*; he has always voted Democrat. He has read Marx, Guevara and Cleaver. He has always been sympathetic to his students, he always does well on the yearly student polls. He cried when Allende fell. He's a good guy.

He tried to explain to them about bravery.

Hector, who sits in the back and is usually stoned, said that the bravest man he'd ever known was his cousin, Tony, who took on three cops one night.

Everyone had laughed; they appreciate a good joke, it is a pleasant, good-humored class. Paul had smiled broadly, a man of the people. "That's not exactly what it means."

The girl in the front row with the fantastic figure and the black nail polish wanted to know why it was the bravest man. "Don't you know about women?"

The boys had sniggered and whooped, yeah, we know about women.

Finally, Yollanda, the sweet one who wants to be a nurse, said that she thought that Professor Sutcliffe was brave because he didn't want to be there with them, but he came anyway.

How did she know?

He dismissed the class early, and since has been hiding, trying to breathe with the passage of footsteps. He does not consider this teaching. Not just because of the ESL class, but because of all of them, including his graduate students. He is sandwiched between the deprived on one side and the depraved on the other; flanked by the drugged and desperate in one direction, and by the Burger King mentality on the other. There is no joy, no zest for learning, no love of knowledge. They have no discipline, no goals that cost under $200, no yearning to stand a head above the common mass. If they can't put it on, put it in, or put it up, then it doesn't exist. And the ambitious ones are even worse, hoarding their good grades like nuggets of gold; quibbling, their little nose twitching, their beady little eyes shining, over the difference between a 95 and a 96, or even a 96 and a 96.5; sitting in little bunches during exams in case they have to cheat off one another; threatening to charge him with discrimination when they don't receive the grade they think they deserved; deciding among themselves the most lucrative professions, suitable environments, beneficial spouses, as though they have blueprints for their lives rolled up alongside the blueprints they have for their future homes, garages and beach houses, tucked away in their attaché cases. They talk about art, music and literature on a high level, but their souls are committed to nothing more than a personal prosperity – if they even have souls, that is. He hates them; he hates the way they look at him, sizing him up, judging how long it will take them to replace him, how long it will take them to surpass him. All he ever seems to hear them saying is but how much does he make, but how much did it cost, but what sort of car does he drive, does he own his own home? Fucking Philistines.

It doesn't stop there. If none of them has either genius or soul, they do all seem to have palsied parents, illegitimate children, problems with alcohol, troubles with the police, girlfriends who wait in the hallway, sobbing, or boyfriends who burst into the middle of lectures screaming "Just come outside for a minute, just come outside and talk to me for one minute". They either have too much of a sex life, or none at all; parents who can barely remember their names, or parents whose hands rest firmly on their shoulders with the grip of death; they are either so simple-minded that a college education is wasted on them, or so aggressively ambitious that the mere act of education pales into insignificance. Is this an institute of higher learning, or a day care center? a sophisticated zoo? a training ground for small-time despots and business guerrillas? Is this, then, what all of the dreamers of dreams, the magicians and the wizards, the poets and the visionaries, the thinkers and the believers, the mystics and the madmen have been striving for through the dusty centuries? Is this the culmination of Western culture? Literature 242.1, where they tell him that they don't like stories without beginnings, middles and endings; Literature 51, which they have to take or they can't graduate, and in which they constantly complain about the lack of relevancy between literature and their lives.

They walk in in the middle of class, eating hot dogs, dripping mustard down their chins, slopping coffee over their books. They unscrew jars of nuts and raisins during crucial points in his talks, passing them around, holding out their offerings to him, would you like some, Professor? At least twice a term someone tells him that they don't like fiction very much, they'd rather read about real things. Not more than two of them are capable of writing a grammatically correct and intelligent sentence; at least one third of all his students think the words "of" and "have" are interchangeable.

Sitting in the silence and the dark, he grits his teeth.

Worse than the young dope fiends and the revolutionaries with chips on their shoulders are the crazy middle-aged women, beginning life again, with their powder and their perfume, their clammy sincerity, their appalling belief in truth, justice and cleanliness. Little Jewish mamas, little black mamas, little Italian mamas, all of them smiling hopefully every time he looks up, all of them taking down every single word he says. "Oh," they murmur, blushing, smiling at him as though they know he's teasing, "I don't like that story, don't you think it's a little bitter? I don't like that story, it isn't very nice about the mother; I don't like that story, it's so depressing." Go back home, he wants to tell them, yell at them, patting puffy hands, go back into the kitchen, lock yourselves to the stove, watch the soap operas – my mother does and look how happy she is. Do the ironing, scrub the floors, subscribe to *Reader's Digest*. What possible use can Julio Cortázar be to you? Go and fill the world with home-baked cookies and hand-knitted chickens. Take care of your children and your grandchildren. For Chrissake, stop wasting my time. But they stay, and he always passes them. Always. He's afraid to see them cry.

Rubber soles shuffle in the corridor, someone breathes on his door.

If only there were some way to rig up a small bomb, not enough to kill, just enough to disable for a month or two. He would call "Come in", and as they opened the door the knob would explode, severely burning a hand.

In the past few years, while he has been working so hard to climb the departmental ladder, to accumulate the points and credits and little gold stars he will need if he is ever going to be Chairman, he has had perhaps as many as eight students who had any real promise. And of that handful the top two have both been graduate students: the first was Janet, the second is Liz.

The footsteps move away, pause, come back, move away again.

Thinking of Janet and Liz depresses him more. Thinking of Janet and Liz reminds him of Linda – which in his present frame of mind could make him suicidal.

The problem is not really the students. They contribute, they do their bit, but they are far from wholly responsible. It is only during those long, dark nights of the soul that the students become so unbearable. Normally he doesn't worry overly about their lack of prospects, their limited intelligences, the smallness and the meanness, the super-ficiality of their lives: if God doesn't care, why should he? It is only in times of personal pain and stress that they weigh on him like the great lumps that they are.

The problem is really women. His women. It begins with Linda – who is beyond any doubt finally losing her mind – and it ends with Liz – who he is afraid is going to tell him to get lost. In the middle is Janet, who has become sulky and petulant recently; who is always calling him at home to ask him if he loves her. Clearly, she is going crazy as well. It's contagious. Perhaps he himself is the carrier, spreading it with his love, pumping it into them with his seed.

He has tried to be sympathetic to Linda. "Maybe you're working too hard," he has suggested. "After all, publishing isn't exactly creative, soul fulfilling work." And, alternately,

"Maybe you shouldn't go out so much. Maybe if you spent more time with the kids you'd feel calmer." And again, "Probably if you lost some weight it would give you a whole new outlook on yourself."

She looks right through him. She pretends to listen politely and then she goes right on with what she was doing all along. She greeted his suggestion that she might take up a hobby with a horse-like snort, and then burned his pork chop. Generously, he thought, he offered to pay for graduate courses at the university of her choice. She replied that it was he, not she, who was obsessed with accumulating degrees. "You wouldn't necessarily have to get a degree," he countered. "Then why go?" she sweetly sang.

"I think that you're in a rut," he hugged her, enveloping her in understanding. "I love you, Linda, it hurts me to see you like this. You need to do something different, something meaningful."

"Shall I hitch-hike around the world? Shall I go to medical school? Should I become a belly dancer?" She'd pulled the clean wash from out of the machine, letting it slop onto the floor. "Should I become an undercover cop, start a home for battered wives? Or do you think that it'd be enough if I just learned how to make my own puff pastry?"

He hadn't missed the note of bitterness, but he was at a loss to explain it.

Up until very recently, Linda has always listened to him, has always taken his advice. It was he who influenced her taste in clothes, music, literature and home furnishings; he who taught her that honey-glazed ham was not the highest of culinary achievements; he who steered her towards the right career; he who has always offered her loving, constructive criticism and selfless concern. And now she mocks him. Now she makes faces when he offers her suggestions. Now she cha-cha-chas out of the room when he is trying to speak to her about serious things affecting their life.

Twice he has returned home, saddened and demoralized, seeking empathy and support, and instead she has gone to bed early. "I'm sure it'll be all right," all but patting him on

56

the head. "I've had an awful day, I'm going to turn in now."
Leaving him sitting by himself, all on his own, unloved and
abandoned. Didn't she even fucking care? How could she just
turn her back on him like that? She has never been tired
before. Up until now Linda has always been interested in
him, always been there to confide in, always been ready with
her companionship, devoted and loyal. On the night that he
first realized that he loved her he had taken acid, and called
her – some sense of preservation in the middle of a bad trip –
called her to come save him. And she had come; has been
coming ever since; it's all right, I'm here. Up until now.

He has a class in ten minutes. Half of them won't have
done their assignment, and of the half that has, half of them
will have done it painstakingly and incorrectly, and the rest
will have done it sloppily but adequately. Their excuses for
late assignments range from "I forgot" to "I left it home";
from "It must of fallen out" to "My mother got mad at me
and ripped it up". There was, one time, a long, involved
story about it falling to the floor of the car, and the car having
a hole rusted through the floor, and the essay falling out
through the hole onto the wet and hostile pavement of
Broadway. Had he thought it was worth risking death by
oncoming traffic to retrieve it? And once the kid had been
mugged and his homework stolen, your essay on Juan Rulfo
or your life.

The excuses, the scenarios, the visions of reality that
emanate from Linda and Janet, Janet or Linda, are no less
innovative and inspired, veritable phantasmagorias flowing
from their fevered female minds. Janet, dressed in her
immaculate, conservative suburban way, can stand in her
kitchen – an ordinary, typical kitchen – chopping peppers,
whack whack whack, sliding them from the board to the
bowl with the knife blade, and while she is doing this, and he
is watching, sipping his wine, and she is working, sipping her
wine, and the music is playing, and he is even thinking that
this wouldn't be such an awful way to live, perhaps, she will
suddenly say, "You just think of me as your whore, don't
you? You never use anything I've ever given you". Or will

57

burst into tears, stumbling from the room, wailing "I can't take it any more". He arrived at his office one morning to find a box, addressed to him, sitting in front of the door, and in it some – though not all – of the presents he had given Janet, all of them damaged in some way. It was unclear as to whether she was returning them because they were defective, or because he was. When asked she simply said, "I will never love anyone but you".

And Linda. Happy, cheerful, humming one moment; stern, miserable and enraged the next. He can leave her light and sunny, to return and find her dark and gloomy. There are times when he pauses to give her a casual embrace that she will wrap herself around him, trying to burn her body into his heart. There are other times when he is afraid to kiss her, in case she's decided to turn him to stone.

The minutes move inexorably on. He cannot stay in here for ever. On the desk is the list of things he is supposed to do this afternoon. He must telephone Rita because he has promised to take her and the children out on Sunday; he must phone Janet because he has promised to read a paper she is hoping to publish; he must call Linda to see if she was able to get the book he needs for the article he's planning for the Summer issue.

When he emerges from his hideout, already late for class, Harvey Miller is lying in wait for him. "I had an appointment with you, remember."

He smiles at Harvey, whom he loathes. "I have a class now, Harvey."

"But we had an appointment. I didn't know you were in there, Professor Sutcliffe."

One of the reasons he despises Harvey is because he's so self-righteous. "You didn't knock, did you? How was I supposed to know that you were skulking around the hall?"

Harvey lopes beside him, unwilling to relinquish his only advantage, which is that he knows he must be in the right. Harvey wants to "get into" computers when he graduates, and Paul can picture him, squatting inside a computer, surrounded by books and an abacus, the little man who actually figures out the answers. Harvey originally wanted to be a plastic surgeon, but has had to settle for second best.

"But we were going to go over my test paper. I really don't understand how you arrived at your grade."

"Make another appointment."

"But I had an appointment."

Paul stops, Harvey goes a few steps beyond then stops as well. "Harvey," says Paul, "you wrote a C paper and a C you got. If you want to waste time that would be better spent learning about literature in going over the unchangeable, then make another appointment."

"I just want to know what criteria you used. I feel that I covered every point you asked for perfectly accurately and comprehensively. I don't see how you arrived at that mark."

Paul claps him on the shoulder, little Harvey Miller, who will some day program a computer to analyze fiction, of that he has no doubt. "You want to know how I do it, Harvey? I take all of the exam books and I toss them into the air and the ones on the left get an A, the ones next along get a B, the ones on the right fail, and the ones in the middle, Harvey, they get a C." He shuts the classroom door in Harvey's face.

Paul walks the length of his desk several times, finally stopping in the middle and leaning against it, balancing his weight on his hands. "Well," he says, "and what have your fevered little brains made of this book?"

Almost everyone laughs except for a few hard cases and the one or two who already are asleep. A hush falls, as half the class stares at him with interest, leaning back in their seats expectantly, and the other half flips through the novel, handy on their desks, as though looking for a scene or character, passage or paragraph they had meant to mention.

"Well?" smiling pleasantly and kindly, like a pal, encouraging them to take those first, shaky steps away from the safety of their knowns – the processed cheeses of daily papers, television, loud noises and bestsellers – and into the shoals of the broiling brain and intoxicating imagination of man. "Have any of you read the book?" he chuckles, sliding up on the desk and crossing his legs, giving them, row by row, a shy smile, showing that he means them no harm, there is no right and wrong in literature, there need be no fear of embarrassment, that all he wants to do is electrify their minds with the empyreal energy of man's boldest visions.

"Oh, sure," say several voices, and most heads nod, with more or less conviction.

"Well? How did you like it?"

The three shyest girls, who sit like monkeys in the first row, almost afraid to breathe, all flash him tiny smiles of encouragement, it wasn't so bad.

Frank, the veteran who still wears his combat boots and whose strongest criticism is to say, "Well, it wasn't like that in the army", clears his throat and pushes his glasses back. "I don't know, Professor. I hadda lotta trouble wit this. This guy's really crazy, you know?"

Paul smiles like a lighthouse beacon on a dark and unfriendly night. "Frank thinks this guy is crazy. What makes you say that, Frank?"

Frank flushes. "Well, you know. All this stuff that's goin' on all the time. It's all crazy. You know."

"It may be different, Frank. But I don't think you could really say it's crazy." Crossing his legs the other way and straightening out the leg of his trouser, wondering what Frank's image of him could possibly be that would lead him to believe that Paul could possibly understand what went on in the lightless, airless, stagnant chambers beneath his short-cropped, greasy hair.

Frank twists his face and narrows his eyes, searching for the words to express his own tortured vision of god and man. "Well, you know. All these ghosts and crazy people and women floating up to the clouds, it's all crazy. That's not real. Is this place supposed tuhbe real? People don't go around like this."

"Certainly not in the army," laughs Paul. "Cathy? Did you want to say something?"

Cathy shifts in her seat. "I didn't like this very much either," she says, in a voice that assumes he, or the universe, might actually care what she thought. "Some of it was pretty interesting, but there wasn't any hero. There was no one person you could really," gazing up at the fluorescent lights, "identify with. It made it all very confusing."

Paul's smile is smaller, but still shines. "Crazy and confusing. That's a beginning. Did any of you actually like the novel?" Although, if they did, what would it mean? that the book was seriously flawed after all? Surely winning acceptance with this gathering of wasteland refugees would be similar to being made poet laureate of Jersey City, New Jersey?

Fabio, who sits in a corner at the back, away from everyone, and in such a way that at no time does his ass actually make physical contact with the chair, nods. "Yeah," he says. "I thought it was terrific. I like books with imagination. That's why I usually only read SciFi."

"Imagination," says Paul, as if from a dream. "Imagination."

"But you know," speaks the luscious Lisa, having just finished checking her make-up, "it didn't really have a middle."

"Excuse me?" says Paul, awake again.

"I mean, it had a beginning and an ending, but it didn't really have a middle. A lot of things kept happening, but it wasn't really a middle." If he gets her meaning.

He chooses his next words carefully. "Did any of you," he asks, touching with one hand this book of brilliance, this masterpiece of twentieth-century literature, this novel that, like no other, encapsulates the human experience, "did any of you think this novel was realistic?"

They all make eye contact with him, scanning the depths of his irises flecked with gold to see what it is that he is really saying. And then they all begin to laugh.

When he finally escapes again, he sees Liz down at the other end of the corridor, talking to Mahler, the department's middle-aged boy wonder. They appear to be quite chummy. They appear to be having a good time. As he approaches, Mahler (spotting him?) moves away. "What were you two talking about?" he asks her.

"Just an assignment."

"An assignment? But I thought I told you not to take that class with him."

Liz starts to walk away. "You did."

Linda is ironing Patricia's flannel workshirt with one hand while trying to keep a grip on the telephone with the other. Since it is not really necessary either to listen to or answer Rita, her mind is on other things: what she will wear tomorrow, whether or not there is enough milk for the morning, if Paul will be able to pick up the kids, how much of a fuss the *Conversations with Chloe* author is going to kick up when he sees the changes she's made to his book, and doom. The thoughts about doom are recurring ones.

Rita says that she saw a really cute pair of red corduroy dungarees for David, and Linda, trying to flatten out the space between buttons, says, oh, that sounds adorable. But her mind is really on sin, guilt and recrimination.

Rita says that they are predicting that this will be the worst winter for years, and Linda, trying to rub those little wrinkles out of the cuff, says, yes, isn't it terrible. But her thoughts are really on loneliness, struggle, poverty and frustration.

Behind her the washer and dryer hum, before her the comfortable apartment sprawls, inside of her her children call out "Daddy". She is a prisoner of paradise: what will happen if she leaves?

Lillian, says Rita, is trying to have another child. Linda smooths at the name tag in the neck of Patsy's shirt. "I thought that she had enough with one. I thought she was going to make Jimmy have an operation."

"Walter would have liked more kids, you know. He loved kids. But two seemed perfect to me. A girl and a boy. It's natural," giving no indication of having heard her.

"What happens if they have another girl?"

"You know," says Rita, her voice sharp, "you know I have a little bit of money put aside for each of the kids. It's not much, but just a little for each of them. For when I go . . ."

Go, go, go, go. If Linda goes the entire world will have to

begin again. If only a family's possessions could replicate themselves – two bathmats where there used to be one, two sets of dishes, two double beds, two vases bought on honeymoon in Mexico City, four children. "Don't be silly, Mom, you're not going anywhere."

The iron hisses a tongue of steam, and Linda sighs.

"I used to say that I was looking forward to the day when I would be all by myself and I would just have one cup, one plate, one knife and fork." There is a pause while all the telephone wires linking the Bronx to Manhattan whisper in sympathy. "And now I have that."

Linda straightens the perfectly laundered and ironed piece of child's clothing on its red plastic hanger; it glows with mother's love. "Don't talk like that. You have all of us," and she moves on to the next item. "The kids are really looking forward to Sunday. And we want you to stay overnight."

Rita is sitting in the dark, blue light from the television flickering across the room. Her pain is extreme. "That'd be nice. I guess I could do that."

"Of course you could. We'll have a really nice time."

"Well," Rita says.

"Well," agrees Linda.

"Remind Paul to call me later."

"Sure, Rita."

"I've got some things I have to do now." In her kitchen, only feet away, a tap drips into a melmac coffee cup.

Linda jerks the plug from the wall, kicks David's wheeled plastic duck under the table, quackquackquack.

Rita holds the receiver for several moments, though it is no longer connected to anything, listening to the water slowly leaking away, dripdripdrip.

Linda folds up the ironing board, wraps the cord around the chunky body of the iron. She suspects that she may be about to cry. For Rita? For herself? For the world?

There are a variety of reasons why she has not confronted Paul with her discovery of his new affair. She tells herself that it is nothing serious, that it might even be other than what she knows damn well it is. She tells herself what Paul would

63

probably tell her, that in some subtle but irrefutable way she is partially at fault, she has failed him. She tells herself that she is getting even, that she is getting even and she doesn't care; that since her lover is no threat to her husband, the correlative must be true, Paul's behavior holds in it nothing personal.

But what is also true is that to confront him is to have to make a choice, to leave him or to accept it, and she is not prepared to do either.

Her tearducts must be broken, for she cries all of the time, sporadically and indeterminately – on the train, staring at the designs of dirt; in the supermarket, staring at the beading of blood under plastic; in the elevator, staring at the little green light, 1234567. She is the spectre that haunted the Upper West Side.

"Patricia!" she calls. "Patricia, it's time to get ready for bed." She leans her head against the metallic coolness of the refrigerator. Will she always be like this? When she thinks of leaving Paul she cries; when she thinks of staying with him she cries even more. Sometimes just folding his underwear can move her to tears; or picking up a small, battered toy; or making a macaroni and cheese dinner, deluxe, the family favorite – a voice inside the normal, rational side of her whispering, you wouldn't do this again, you would never do this again. Is it an omen, is she dying? But at other times she will see a note he has written, a book he has left lying around, his underwear on the floor of the bathroom, and will be overwhelmed by the desire to heave all of his possessions into the hallway, to beat him with his fucking antique coffee grinder until he bleeds from the eyes. This must be insanity.

He has suggested she seek professional help. If it were hormones she would go to a medical doctor, wouldn't she? Maybe he wants to have her put away; maybe he is planning to leave her and he wants grounds for his getting custody.

She pictures her telling him they are through – quietly, after the eleven o'clock news, sipping brandy with their coffee, the special continental blend that he discovered when she was in the hospital having David. It will be a civilized, mature and unhistrionic announcement. There will be no blame attached: she will not cite his lovers, she will not mention hers. She will invoke such deities as space, personal growth and mutual respect. They will always remain friends.

Patricia shuffles into the kitchen in the bedroom slippers Rita made her from face cloths. She is still fully dressed and dramatically dangling a summer nightgown from one small but perfect hand. "I can't find anything to wear."

Linda straightens up. "In your pajama drawer," she says sweetly, "you will find pajamas."

"This is all that's in there, except my Mickey Mouse pajamas with the feet in them and they're too small. They hurt my toes and they won't pull up all the way."

"Then wear the nightgown," pretending to search for something in the refrigerator – mango juice, perhaps.

"It's a summer nightgown."

"That's all right. Just for one night no one will notice." Is it behind the left-over lasagne, under the bread, disguised as grape jelly?

"It's practically snowing out, I bet. I'm not going to wear summer pajamas when it's below zero."

She abandons the snark hunt, stands up and thumps the door shut, gazing unaffectionately on her girl child. Most of the time Linda considers herself to be a good, positive and patient mother, doling out love, encouragement and discipline in prescribed measures, willing to put her own interests and wants aside, to sacrifice gladly for her offspring, the fruit of her womb. "We do have heating," she says, sweeter still. She would like to slap the smile off the selfish little bitch's face.

Whenever Rita is drunk, or yelled at, or her feelings have been hurt, she will sooner or later begin to cry. Whenever Linda is seriously arguing with Paul, or has had a very bad day, or feels that everyone is against her, she will sooner or later begin to cry. Patricia now bursts into tears – is it environment or genes?

As though summoned, Paul appears behind her, carrying an empty coffee cup like an offering, an expression on his face of a man who is above the trite and the trivial. "What's going on here?" resting a hand on Patricia's head, Papa's benediction.

65

Patsy snivels. "I don't have any clean pajamas."

Linda concentrates on breathing. "I'm sure there must be something if you looked in the right place."

"This is all I could find," wiping away the tears with the edge of her pink flamingo nightdress.

Paul gives her a hug, gives her mother a gentle smile. In the last analysis, it is always he who must make the decisions, locate the path of reason, arbitrate, deliberate, judge, settle and, generally, keep them all from falling apart. It is obvious that Linda is in danger of breaking down, of creating a scene, all because of a silly and totally insignificant incident. First she will cry; then she will rage through the apartment, banging doors by brainwaves. Paul once wrote a story in which the plot centered around the fact that all women were actually alien beings, planted on the earth centuries ago by a superior life form wanting to keep human men from ever reaching their full potential, either individually or collectively. As a story it hadn't been particularly successful, but he occasionally wonders just how farfetched the idea really was in itself.

"I'll tell you what," he speaks, resting his cup on top of the stove. "Why don't I let you have one of my T-shirts as a nightgown for tonight?"

Patsy's tears snuffle to a halt. She carefully avoids looking at her mother. "Really?"

"Sure," lovingly turning her around and pointing her outwards. "Could I have some more coffee, I'll be back in a minute," he says to his wife.

Why is he always the one who is soothing and assuring, why is his the voice to whisper it's okay, Mommy's had a hard day, by what law is he the nice guy? Will they hate her for ever if she makes him leave? Will he win their love from her?

She puts on the water, takes out a clean filter. Maybe they would all be better off if the children lived with Paul. He is such a good father: he gives them rides on his shoulders, he knows what to do if they get severe burns or cuts, are suffocating or have a heart attack, he can always make them

66

laugh, he has plans for their futures. While she, she lies awake at nights, worrying about wills, guardians and whether or not the grandparents will force the children to go to their mother's funeral – a preoccupation which could very well contribute to their growing up neurotic. It would never occur to Paul that he might die at some inopportune moment. He is always sure of himself: he offers them structure and security. He accepts the inevitability of his own success as others accept the inevitability of winter snows. He always assumes he is right, unless he is unavoidably proved otherwise: he offers them discipline and the assurance that he will always make the right decision. He can give them protection.

Linda has never told him that she has three gallons of spring water hidden behind the old boot box in the hall closet, in the event of a nuclear war. Three gallons of spring water, her grandparents' wedding rings to use for barter, two boxes of Saltines and thirteen cans of pork and beans, all buried under a pile of old sweaters. Just in case. He would laugh at her if he were to find out, thinking that it was cute. He would laugh at her and he would tell his girlfriend. He would be lying on his side, stroking her young, unblemished ass, admiring the curve of her thigh and the perfect blunt cut of her shoulder-length hair, and he would say, "You'll never guess what she's done now. She's squirreled away some old jars of water and a bunch of canned food that was on sale, probably six for a dollar, in case there's a war". They would both laugh at that, his benevolent, hers sympathetic, poor demented soul.

"She can't find her mouse and David insists on wearing his socks to bed," he sneaks up on her, making her jump. "Where's my coffee?"

"It'll be ready in a minute." She rinses out his cup.

"They want you to kiss them good night."

She stops with the bright red mug dripping in her hand: does she make the coffee for him or go to her babies?

"And I'm to remind you that Patricia needs a brown bag lunch tomorrow for the school trip."

She measures out the sugar, one and a half. Is there bread?

"And you remember that I won't be home till late tomorrow. I've got that meeting."

"Your mother wants you to call her back."

He takes the cup from her. "Later. I'm right in the middle of an important scene. As soon as it's done I'll read it to you. You'll love it."

Even in that he is sure. She watches him stride away. Small but strong voices call to her, "Mommy, Mommy, Mommy. We're ready."

Linda studies the linoleum, made to look like stones. Is this it then? Are these the perimeters of her life? Who will she be if Paul goes away, if he takes away his iloveyous? Who will she be if he takes her children? Who will she be if everything remains the same?

The kitchen light makes a soft popping sound, leaving her in shadow, overcome by thoughts of love. Love, the only necessary ingredient. Love. Even if she doesn't always think she believes in it, will she be forced to live without the sound of it?

Paul types. The children bounce on their beds. Linda remembers Mark.

"Mommy, we're waiting for youooo." Knock knock. Who's there? Little old lady. Little old lady who? I thought you said you couldn't yodel.

Rita has fallen asleep in her chair. She watches her mother getting ready to go out to a party, dressed in the red silk dress she bought the year Rita was nine, crystal earrings winking against her skin, hair piled up to make a crown, her beautiful mother. But just as her mother, arm tucked into father's crooked elbow, steps off the curb – the three kids watching, waving from the front window– an ice wagon screams down on her from nowhere, knocking her away from him, flattening her out on the icy street. Even in sleep, Rita knows that that is wrong, thinks, that's not right, it was Walter was hit by the truck when he was a boy, and then, no, that's wrong, too, it was the cat. It was Duchess, the white Persian, was hit by the ice truck. But that had been in the summer.

She wakes up, mouth open and wet, body burnt by pain. Now she will stay awake all night, waiting for the sun. Rita is convinced that she won't die in daylight.

There is a gunfight taking place on the television, miniature men with tiny toy weapons evening scores, fighting for either truth and justice or lies and inequality, not letting anybody take them alive. If God would take Rita alive, would she go?

She watches the screen without actually noticing what is on. Rita, the she-witch who raged through twenty years of marriage, her voice electrifying the neighborhood, a lonely, legendary figure standing on the corner in her housedress, hands on hips, waiting for the delinquent child, the delinquent husband, has now become the docile old mother. Grey-haired and toothless. Even Lillian – who always got on with Rita better than the others – is sometimes surprised. Where did the other Rita vanish, the Rita whose voice was always thin and loud with fury at a world that conspired to fail her? The nagging, the scolding, the bitching, the complaining, the always warring – what happened to her? Did they bury her with Walter?

Rita squints at the set, unable to tell the good guys from the bad.

She had tried so hard; wanted so little: some love, some respect, some security. That's all. Her children to love her and fulfil her dreams; her husband to love her and secure her fantasies. But always they outmaneuvered her, meeting her questions with silence, her hopes with scorn; always they stood just so much out of reach, whispering and plotting amongst themselves, excluding her from their councils and conversations: you wouldn't understand.

With Walter's death the patterns of Rita's life had become more apparent. Before that, she hadn't thought of her life as pattern and routine. She had thought of it, if at all, as essential: wife and mother. But Walter died and the children left, and there was less to wash, to clean, to buy, to polish, to cook, to occupy her; no one there when she came home; no one to need anything or want anything; no one to tell about the doings of the day. Just work and home, home and work. When the grandchildren began to arrive, Rita thought that she might be needed all over again. But Rita the Terrible has aged into Rita the Stupid Old Cow. She still embarrasses them – but this time without having any power. What do they care now, locked away in their nice homes with their busy, busy lives, for her needs and grievances? Their IOUs are scratched into her face and body, in lines and scars and failing flesh, but what is it to them? How can she ever hope to collect?

A person can choose to die.

She can still remember Walter the first time she saw him. He was sitting on a stoop, waiting for someone; he asked her if she knew what time it was. She knew him from the neighborhood, but she had never really looked at him before. There was an instant recognition; if you listened you could hear the future flop into place. Love or doom? She once told Lillian she married Walter because it was the closest she could get to love – after the one that her mother sent away. There is always one who is sent away, or who runs away, or who dies so young. The closest she could get to love, sneaking up on it with your hair permed and your nails done, crawling as close as you can.

Rita remembers Walter, his smell, the sound of his breathing, his skin. He had defined her life. His death brought her not release, as she had always thought it would, but despair. She was still in the shell but the life had gone.

But still she says "Daddy", "when Daddy", "didn't Daddy", "if only Daddy", "remember Daddy"; still she counts the anniversaries, your father and I would have been married thirty years, forty years today; still she says, oh your father would have loved, he would have been so proud, he always said.

It was an August evening, that day that Walter was sitting on the stoop on 93rd Street. He saw Rita coming up the block and he thought, now there's a real good-looker, and so he asked her if she had the time. And everyone's fate was sealed.

★

Linda is in the bath. The only light in the room is a single white candle burning in a peanut butter jar lid in the corner nearest her right foot. On the shelf Paul rigged up across the tub so that he can smoke and read while soaking off the oily fingerprints of the hundreds of whining students who each day dog his footsteps, there sits a glass of beer. This is the only room in the house in which Linda has ever achieved any real privacy – though often they will stand outside the door and talk to her.

But the children are in bed, and the children's father is still locked in his room. She shuts her eyes and lets her bones droop, the magic Manhattan mermaid, floating atop her rubber lily pads in her pearl-white lagoon, one solitary moonbeam lighting her way to the island of dreams. But what will she find on the island of dreams? The magic mermaid straightens up and sips her beer. Will she find the enchanting prince? Or will she find the enchanted prince?

Deep in his secret dungeon, the enchanted prince bangs away at his typewriter. Once he was the enchanting prince, on whom the sun shone solely, whose words could change lives, whose seed could create a new universe. But now, now an ancient, evil spell has been cast upon him, a curse which drives him on and in upon himself, a charm which makes him restless, dark and desperate, a bewitchment which leaves him distrustful, uneasy, dissatisfied. She alone is unable to reach through the curse to find him again; every other mermaid in the metropolis can, even the ones who've just gotten the braces off their teeth, but not she.

There is a splash. She drinks off half her beer. Every time she thinks about him she either becomes enraged or depressed. Everything she thinks of makes her think of him. Rooms away a phone rings, making her think of her mother-in-law.

She submerges, stretching out, her nose and mouth like islands poking up from the sea. Maybe, instead of a mermaid, she should become a submarine.

There is the other, the enchanting prince. He seems to

think that she's wonderful; her jokes have never been so funny, her perceptions have never been so intelligent, her eyes have never been this blue. He wonders at her clothes, her choice of colors, her taste in hats; his wife, he says, is a bit of a slob. He marvels at the flatness of her stomach, the firmness of her breasts; Marilyn, he confides, has a little trouble with her figure. When she left him the first time, he told her, he sat on the bed with the sheet over his head, smelling her still, lost in the aroma of love. He says that he is jealous of Paul.

But Paul would not be jealous of Mark, she knows. Paul would think that Mark was a jerk. He would criticize his smile, his laugh and his political views; he would find fault with his dress, his car and his occupation. Paul wouldn't think that Mark was creative – and so he might as well be dead. Paul's attitude to Jews is ambiguous at best.

And so, there is a part of Linda that is standing back, mouth in a pout, viewing Mark as Paul would, thinking of what Paul would say, comparing him to the paragon. Mark constantly falls short. His clothes are old-fashioned, his hair is too short, he is too trusting and sincere. He doesn't have the same sense of humor, he only knows about folk music, he has never even gotten stoned. He is always trying to hug her on street corners; he has dandruff. Paul would laugh at him, at her. He would say that he could understand her need for revenge, but that without him to guide her she doesn't even have any taste in men. Linda wonders if that might be true.

Paul doesn't answer the phone, he assumes that Linda will. When she doesn't, he calls out "Linda! Linda!" to remind her. One night when he and Janet were very stoned they came up with an elaborate – and at the time inspired – theory of the voices and cries of telephones. That is, though the average person assumes the average phone to be saying "ring ring", or, possibly, "brring brring", in fact, each telephone has a distinct personality and message. Though he has forgotten most of it, he does remember that what his phone, according to their analysis, is calling demandingly from the kitchen and the bedroom is "bury me bury me". It had been significant at the time: and he had buried her with his kisses, buried his cock in her, buried his face in her cunt.

"Oh, for Chrissake." He starts to prepare to get up, but the tinging has finally stopped. Bury me with aggravation. "It's a fuckin' miracle," he says, "it's a fuckin' miracle that I ever get anything done around here."

He knows, of course, that it was his mother phoning to find out why he hadn't called her; he knows, of course, that Linda, continuing her mystifying but indefatigable campaign to be as unhelpful to him as possible, purposely chose this time to sequester herself in some secluded corner of the apartment, knowing that Rita would ring.

Jesus. Resisting the urge to hurt something, to throw his typewriter on the floor, he pulls out a drawer and shoves it back in. If only they had a dog he could kick it. The cat is too small and fast of foot.

Jesus. It is no wonder, he thinks, that God sent his only son to earth and not his only daughter. She would have really fucked up everything: arbitrarily deciding not to go about her father's business because it seemed too nebulous; refusing to walk on water because she didn't want to take her shoes off, get her feet wet, look like a fool; leaving town before the crucifixion because she suddenly remembered a date she had elsewhere. "Oh, I'm really sorry," she would have said to Him, thunder rumbling over the hills, lightning streaking across the blackberry-colored sky, "but, really, I just don't understand the point of the whole thing. It seems rather senseless, you know, just an empty gesture. Not concrete. And anyway," turning left at the crossroads, "I promised Tamar I'd spend some time with her. She's been all alone and really distraught since her husband went off to spread the Word." Led away into the wilderness by the Spirit to face temptation, she wouldn't have lasted four days yet alone forty. She would have brought children and dogs, goats and pigs and sheep with her, bundles of belongings and stacks of postcards. Within hours she would have been turning stones into bread to beat the band, not even waiting for the Devil

73

to slither up to her. "You certainly can't expect the children to go without eating," she would say, flexing her maternal muscles. "You can't go around living in a dream when there are diapers to be changed." She would probably have had the Spirit out searching for water. "We all have to pull our weight."

Paul is a sensitive, intelligent man – and a kind one. He has always been passionately committed to equal rights, pay, education and treatment for women; he is the first to cry out against sexist children's literature; he has always supported abortion reform and multiple orgasms. Women do not threaten him, he loves them, and sometimes even understands them. And, normally, he convinces himself. But he can no longer remain blind to the fact that though they give the illusion of occupying the same general space and of being part of the same species, the whole lot of them, from Eve onwards, might as well have been moon maidens. Having green metallic skin, silver antennae and eyes that look like fried marbles would not have made the female sex any more bizarre than it already is. At least it would have made it clear that there were problems, given clues as to what to expect. There wouldn't have been the insidious deception, the catastrophic confusion caused by sharing similar physical characteristics and a common means of communication. At least if they moved around on wheels and went "billup billup billup" you wouldn't even try to have serious conversations with them, wouldn't delude yourself into believing that you could attempt reason and logic with them, entertain hopes that they might attain your own standards, constantly search for a woman who was almost your intellectual equal.

Walter always said that all women, when they reached a certain age, went insane – or, to be more precise, more insane. It had certainly happened to Rita, who for several years had seemed a normal and reasonable enough person, and who then, somewhere between his eighth and ninth birthdays, had turned into an irrational, hysterical and emotional shrew, creating chaos and disturbance whenever she appeared, shouting through quiet meals and peaceful evenings, your homework, your shoes, your chores, the bills, money, money, money, why doesn't anybody else ever do anything around here, why doesn't anyone ever do anything for me, begrudging each of them any happiness.

There were years when Paul would sneak into the house like an Indian scout, tiptoeing on his black and white Keds, his cap (one season baseball, one season knitted) pulled down to the top of his eyebrows, defying her to recognize him, Sitting Duck Sutcliffe, skulking on the edges of the enemy camp, evading her white woman rules and rantings. If she was in the kitchen he could almost always get through the front door, down the hall and past the bathroom and into the safety of his own small half of the small room he shared with Lillian, divided by a wall of brown paper that Walter had painted on both sides – space explorers for him and a field of flowers for her. He knew which boards squeaked and which doors creaked. He was so good at it that he could have done it blindfolded, hands tied, feet bare and bleeding. He was so good at it that he could smuggle in up to three other small boys, bars of candy and cans of soda hidden under their jackets. But one sound, no matter how soft, how normal, how accidental, how inconsequential, and her voice would streak through the rooms like a cannonball, "Paul! Paul! Is that you Paul? Paul is that you?", what have you done, where have you been, what are you doing and did you remember, have you finished, have you begun, just where do you think you're going? The mere scraping of a Regulation bat across the carpet and she would be upon him like a crazed creature of the hills, her hair escaping from its curls, her mouth stretched around her teeth, demanding details and explanations. "Do you think the other boys treat their mothers like you do?" she once screamed at him from the kitchen window, her shadow lying doomlike across the pavement, right in his path of retreat. "Do you? Do you?" Paul hunched into his jacket between Charlie Mazotta and Sammy Goldberg, both of them rolling their eyes in their heads. Paul remembers his father as kind and gentle and soft; his mother as pushy, castrating and hard. Lillian thinks that her father was a failure and a shit and that he ruined Rita's life.

Some of Paul's early memories are of arguments and threats; his mother hysterical, his father gliding out the door; his mother frosty and forbidding for days, spinning looks and bouncing plates across the table, get it yourself, his father cheerful and independent, carrying on with maturity and decency, an intelligent adult locked in with a more than slightly loopy child; his mother snuffling in the bedroom, her eyes lined in red, mumbling accusations and recriminations like some secret rosary, reciting the sins committed against her to an empty room while the rest of them watched TV and drank rootbeer, joked together and had fun, Walter holding the family together, going on as though nothing had happened, watching television as though the earth was not standing still. Lillian always stuck up for Rita; Paul never doubted Walter.

Walter in his old work pants and plaid jacket, his fingertips stained yellow, his whole face smiling. Walter telling stories, telling jokes, explaining the world, taking him on trips uptown, or downtown, or across town to see some friend, some relative that Rita didn't like much, some important historical site. Rita talked about her childhood, about how beautiful her mother had been, about how she'd always wanted to dance in the Harvest Moon Ball, about the stray cats and dogs she'd adopted when she was little – animals with names like Spot or Snowball or Frisky; Rita taught you things about the world like brushing your teeth and washing under your arms and never wearing galoshes in the house. Walter, though, even when describing the ordinary and the familiar, managed to make the world seem strange and fragile. When he was small Paul had thought of his mother as being white and brown, red and blue; a figure in checks and floral prints and dark wool coats, in a universe of trees and buildings, parks and buses, days for this and times for that, cans and can'ts. But Walter was walking by the water on drizzling days, all the colors tints, running into one another, his voice fading behind clouds of things he'd read or dreamed or thought he remembered, all the while promising something more, something special, pocketfuls of magic, handfuls of wonder: where? right there, over there. There? Here? That wasn't what I said. Where? Rita said that the world wasn't made for dreamers, it was made for people who did things, who worked all day and paid their bills and always wore clean underwear. Rita said that what counted was what you did, what people thought of you. Walter said that there were times when he could eat sunlight, he could lie down, on the beach, in the park, on the white popcorn spread of his own bed, and eat sunlight, till it would suck him up into the sky, his mind, his body, his clothes, even his old tennis shoes, spread out all over the world, millions and trillions of dancing rainbows only seen through cut-glass eyes. Rita said that if it weren't for her he'd have been in prison, the lazy son-of-a-bitch.

The phone is ringing again. Down the hall he hears the shower running – Linda washing her hair.

Above his desk is a picture of Walter, yellowing now, a young man on a beach smiling into the same sun that shone on Paul this morning, a young man in a T-shirt and baggy trousers, grinning with large white teeth into a perfect day. You can't tell whether or not his socks and shoes are on. Paul looks at it now, wishing that he could reach out and hold that body, touch through time and grab that young man, the way the camera did, clickclick.

Walter disappointed him. It does not occur to Paul that legends always do: disappearing at the wrong moment, getting ill right before the big break, choosing the wrong girl, quitting when you expected them to fight, turning their backs on the wrong person.

Walter could have done things, could have been special, could have made his mark. Instead he seemed to do his best to fail, making it the only thing at which he ever succeeded. Whose fault was that? Was it Walter's mother's, always pushing, pushing, pushing; was it Rita's, always nagging, pushing, nagging; both of them paralyzing him with demands, draping him in responsibilities? Why hadn't he stood up to them, gotten beyond them? Instead of showing them, he had succumbed; instead of rising above their pettiness and mediocrity he had ducked below.

The young man on the wall still smiles, into a sun that will never set.

★   ★   ★

Visions of women on horseback, women braver and stronger than any she had ever seen, their eyes clear and dry, their hair close-cropped, their breasts flattened against their hearts, stampede her dreams, churning up the ghosts of memories, the fragments of dead dreams. The old woman tosses in her sleep, moonbeams throw bars across her body. A solitary walker comes from the distance, dark and aloof, almost humbled by the bearded clouds. Outside of the dream she squints her sightless eyes, still closed to the night, searching for the identity of this one, this man alone. A star falls behind the farthest hill.

★   ★   ★

Linda stops in mid-rub, the towel hanging down over her face. The telephone is ringing again. To Paul it may say burymeburyme, to Linda it is saying hurryhurryhurry. She goes back to drying her hair. And it rings and rings and rings.

She shoves the door open, bangs the door shut, races down the hallway, towel and water dripping from her, her bare feet leaving wet prints on the parquet floor.

It is for Paul, a timid student dialling directly to the heart of his terror, Professor Sutcliffe, please.

It is not the usual wifely, tentative tap, I hate to disturb you, dear. It is strong and deliberate. "Come in." Maybe the call is important.

His wife stands in the doorway, looking red: red towel, red robe, red face. "You fucking bastard," she screams, and her voice is red as well. "You goddamn fucking bastard. Just once, just once I'd like to see you get off your ass and answer your own fucking phone. Just once."

78

"For Chrissake, Linda. You know I'm right in the middle of something. What the hell is wrong with you?"

"You are wanted on the phone," she shouts. "You are wanted on the phone. One of your little fucking lambs."

"You mean fucking little lambs," as always good-humored, trying to make a joke. From the way she watches him it is impossible to tell whether she is going to attack him or to fall to her knees and beg for mercy. "Jesus Christ, Linda, are you drunk or something?"

She turns and leaves the room.

He is still on the phone when he hears the front door close behind her.

4

There are problems in the winter. Small children and old ladies cannot be taken to zoos or seasides, parks or boat trips around the island. Small children and old ladies do not travel well in winter, their feet and hands get cold, their noses run, the temperature makes them have to go to the toilet frequently, their teeth chatter. Some small children ice skate, but most old ladies don't. Some old ladies drink, but most small children get bored in bars.

He took them to a modern ballet for children. It was the first time Rita had ever attended a dance program; she fell asleep. It was also the first time he had ever ventured forth with the kids to something more sophisticated than the dramatization of a familiar fairy tale; David kept asking when it would be over, Patricia kept asking what they were doing and what it was supposed to mean. "It's just a dance," he hissed back. "Now they're dancing because they're happy. It doesn't *mean* anything." "Then why do they do it?" David wanted popcorn. When it was finally over Rita said, "Oh, that was very nice. I always liked dancing."

Rita is nervous and on her best behavior. It is rare for either of her children to actually take her anywhere. Last summer Lillian took her once to the beach, then got angry because Rita had to go sit in the pavilion, because her skin is so sensitive. The year before that Paul took her to the street festival in Little Italy and he got angry because she wouldn't try any of the food: "You know I can't eat that kind of thing"; "Jesus Christ, why did we come down here then?" So today she is trying to be polite and appreciative. She is still wearing her Christmas corsage, which she thinks looks festive and which he finds embarrassing. The children adore her.

He leads them up the avenue, walking determinedly and confidently ahead of them by several yards, a handsome figure in his jeans and army surplus overcoat. The three of them trundle behind, a moving triangle of child-grandmother-child, each one dressed more outlandishly than the next. It is a failing of Linda's that she imposes no discipline on the children's dress, letting them make their own selections; Rita, whose fashion sense was always questionable, has deteriorated to a point where most days she wears her pajama bottoms under her housedress – though not today, thank God. Today Patricia, who has topped off an ensemble remarkable for its mixture of plaids, stripes and clashing colors with a Peruvian knit helmet that makes her look as though she's going out for trick-or-treat, wins the bringing-attention-to-the-family prize.

Except for the period when she was asleep in the show, Rita has been talking incessantly since he picked her up, darting from one topic, one time and one character to another, her mind a giant butterfly, flit, flit, flit, one minute in the shrubbery, the next moment on the lawn. And if the speed and vastness of her conversation aren't enough, they are made even more deadly by the fact that she has nothing to say – or at least nothing he wants to hear.

David began complaining of the cold the moment they left the theater, Patricia is sulking because she wants to go to McDonald's.

"No."

"Why not?"

"Because we're going to a nice, comfortable restaurant. It's Grandma's day out, we're doing things for her."

"But it's our day out, too."

"It's all right with me," cooed Rita. "I don't care where we go."

"We're going to the restaurant." Paul wants a drink, he

wants to be warm and he wants to relax. He does not want to have to sit on hard plastic chairs while his son and daughter dip their french fries into their vanilla milkshakes.

Behind him, his children collide with other passers-by, his mother bumps between them. Outdistanced by him, they continue to talk to him, "Daddy, my feet are frozen", "Do you remember the time we took you and Lillian to Radio City Music Hall and. . .", "Oh, Father, Father . . .". "Come on, gang," he cheers them on, turning to jog backwards for a few feet in his best camp counsellor impersonation, "it's cold. Let's get to the restaurant." Even David scowls.

Thank God, they get a seat in the corner. They all take off more clothes than they could possibly have put on, David loses a shoe, Rita immediately knocks over her water glass, and Patricia's outfit in the subdued interior light looks nearly neon. Though they are reasonably secluded, everyone has noticed them. He has Linda to blame for the entire afternoon.

The waiter brings menus, David and Patsy fighting over one.

"Don't you think Lillian's looking wonderful since she lost so much weight?" asks Rita, not pretending to try to read the menu.

"Um. How about a hamburger, David?"

"I want french fries."

"She's still a very attractive woman."

"You can have french fries, but you have to have a hamburger, too."

"Don't you think so, Paul?"

"Yeah, sure. What about you, Patsy?"

"I want shrimp cocktail."

"Don't be ridiculous. You can have a hamburger, too."

"If anything happens to Jimmy, she'll be able to get another husband. She's still quite young."

"I don't like hamburgers. They make me sick."

"Patricia, stop being a pain in the ass." He removes David's feet from his lap. "What are you talking about if something happens to Jimmy? He's as healthy as he is stupid."

"Most of those people die young, Paul. I read it in the paper. They have special diseases."

"Mom."

"I would like to die knowing that Lillian is taken care of."

"You're not going to die."

"Never?" asks David, whose pet hamster died just before the holidays and who was told at great length and with much patience that everyone and every thing dies sooner or later, that even Miss Molly will die.

"If I can't have shrimp cocktail then I'll have fried chicken." He pulls the menu from her grasp. "Thank you, Patricia, you're a sport. Would you like french fries?"

"Some day, honey," and Rita tucks his napkin around his neck. "Grandma will die some day, but not yet."

The waiter brings his drink, a double. "What would you like, Mom?"

Rita opens her menu and stares down at it, more or less blindly. "I'm not really hungry."

"You have to eat."

"Maybe I'll just have some soup."

"Don't forget my french fries," says Patricia.

"Me, too."

"You can't just have soup, Mom. This isn't a diner. You have to have a meal."

"I'm not hungry, really. I just want some soup."

He signals for another drink. "Just have something light. Have an omelette or something like that."

"Maybe Grandma's trying to lose weight so she can get married again." Patsy spits an ice cube back into her water.

The idea is so ridiculous that Paul is forced to smile. His mother remarry – even if she weren't too old now, his mother would just never remarry. Who could ever have replaced his father?

Rita kisses Patsy on the top of her head. "Grandma's an old lady, sweetheart. Old ladies don't get married."

"They just die," says David.

Paul points out a little boy at the other side of the room who has a jacket just like David's. The waiter comes and

83

takes their orders, including Rita's eggs. She asks for a brandy. If the omelette doesn't make her sick the brandy won't.

"A brandy?" asks Paul. "You don't want to eat anything but you want a brandy?"

She looks at him with something of her old frustration. "I'm not a child, you know. If I want a brandy I'll have a brandy."

"Katie Wilson's mother drank so many brandies on New Year's Eve that she fell into the bathtub and all her nails fell off," and Patricia smiles at her own ability to join in adult conversations.

The food is mediocre. David complains of fat in his hamburger and Patricia claims that her chicken tastes sour. Rita, who does little more than move pieces of cold egg from one side of her plate to the other, chatters on about events she expects him to remember that he suspects never occurred. "But don't you remember that Easter, you must have been about eleven. Don't you remember, your father was so drunk he went to carve the ham and the whole thing landed up on the floor?"

"You sure that was Dad?" He has had four drinks; she has had three.

"You don't think I can remember my own husband?"

"I just think you might be confused." He orders them another round.

"And the Christmas he fell into the tree? I remember it like it was yesterday. I was sleeping on the sofa, waiting up for him. He came in, it must've been about three in the morning. I thought it was a burglar, he came in so quiet. And then he fell into the tree. I just put it up that night, you know, so he didn't know it was there. He just passed out in it. You should've seen it when I put on the lights."

When Rita goes to the ladies' room for the second time Patricia laughs about his father. "He must have been really silly," and she giggles so hard that chewed up potato sprays onto her plate.

"I'm warning you, Patricia, either you start behaving or I'm going to slap you right across the room."

"What'd I do?"

"And in any case, Grandma's a bit forgetful and she's had too much to drink. None of those stories of hers are true." David makes himself a french fry moustache. "You mean she's lying?"

"Of course she's not lying, she's just wrong." And he wonders, in passing, if she isn't going to be too senile soon to be left on her own, and what alternative they will have if Lillian refuses to take her in.

It is already dark as they drive home; dark and damp and cold. There is something wrong with the heater and the window keeps frosting over. The children doze.

Rita would like to doze, to fall into that dreamy, painless state where she can think of how nice it would be to sit and watch TV with the kids, to help Linda with supper, not to be alone. But Paul won't let her.

He has been telling her about his book since they got in the car, and most of what he has been saying she doesn't understand. Rita hasn't read a book since she left school. She has been too busy. She has never read an adult novel in her life; she has been too occupied with brothers and sisters, husband and children, routines and survival. Walter, she would say, was the smart one, Walter had the brains and the talent.

And that is actually what Paul is talking about. "You and Dad had nothing in common, nothing at all."

Rita tries to focus. "We grew up in the same neighborhood. He wasn't any better than me."

He bangs on the dashboard, hoping to get the hot air flowing. "Nobody said he was better than you. I just said he was different. He had more education, he was an artist."

Rita stares at nothing. "He used to draw a little. When he was young."

"He wrote poetry."

"He saw the Virgin Mary once, too. She was standing on the tracks at 125th Street."

"Mom." He tightens his grip on the wheel. "You never understood Dad's imagination, that's all. He didn't mean that he really saw the Virgin Mary, he meant that he understood what it would be like to see her, he could visualize her presence, he could create her in his mind," and Paul himself can almost feel, if not quite see, the fragile female form, passive and chaste, innocent and pure, as it walks in front of the car at the light, robes flowing.

Rita pulls her coat around her. "He was just a mechanic and he drank too much, that was all. I don't know about no imagination."

Hands spring up. "That's exactly what I mean – 'He was just a mechanic' – just a mechanic. You just never saw the whole man. You just saw what you wanted to see, and you tried to push him into being what you wanted. You just wanted things from him . . ."

Rita sits, walled in by her outdated coat and the tinselly corsage, plastic bells and plastic holly, a scarf tied around her head; her profile is the same as it has always been, lips thin and tight, perpetually ready to strike. There has never been any other side to Rita, she has always been right there, wanting what everybody else had. "I just want a normal life," her ghost shouts through the car, "I just want a normal life like everyone else. Is that too much to ask? A normal life like everybody else has?" Her ghost, that young Rita never silenced, never put to rest, hair uncombed, eyes rolling in its head, lipstick smeared, every slack piece of flesh wobbling in rage, the screaming banshee of Flatbush and Corona, running out on the stoop on winter mornings you'll be sorry you talked to me like that, you'll be sorry; she continues to protest, to bewail the injuries of her life. But the body of Rita – not quite left behind and not quite having grown away – says nothing: she has no idea what he is talking about.

"But the thing is, Mom," and his pipe bangs against the door, "the thing is that in spite of everything you stayed together. Nothing could destroy what you had together."

Rita turns to look at him, mottled by shop light and street light. "Of course not," she says. Me and your father; your father and me. "Of course not. We had you kids."

"Love."

"I would never do anything to hurt my kids." She could have married again, she could have had a boyfriend. "It was the love you had together. It was always there. That loyalty."

"When you marry someone," recites Rita, "you stay with them. You have to stay together. Not like today. Not like today when everybody thinks they can do whatever they please."

He turns the car off Broadway. A cat streaks across the road. "It's the love that was important. It's the only thing that matters."

He feels nearly tender towards her; she thinks that he must understand. Patricia wakes up and gives her brother a kick which starts him crying. Paul, trying to park the car, curses. Rita coos.

Freshly bathed and looking rested, Linda sits on the edge of the kitchen counter, the phone cord bent around one shoulder, smiling into the plastic receiver. "I love you, too," she says.

Outside, the winter wails against the fortress walls; three cats howl in the alley by the garbage cans; a star falls. Inside, the children have been washed down and filled up, and are now watching television, snug in pajamas and terry cloth robes. Patricia is eating potato chips. David is eating sticks of cheese smeared with peanut butter.

Behind them, each in a comfortable chair, the mothers sit sipping sherry and scotch. They speak softly, around the sound from the set – and even then a child will occasionally turn and say "Shhhhhh". Linda has asked several times about the day, about the show, about Lillian, Jimmy and Angela, and about the miniature orange tree Rita has been trying to grow in her kitchen window. Every seventeen and a half minutes or so she asks Rita whether or not she would like something to eat. Rita always declines. "I've never been much for food," she says.

Rita's feet are up on a handmade leather hassock, her lap is covered by David's old carriage rug, her thoughts are warm

87

and comforting as well. If Rita were to die now she would at least be smiling.

Linda's feet are tucked under her, her lap is covered by the *New York Times Book Review*, her thoughts are intemperate and chaotic. If Linda were to die now she would look worried.

Paul's radio plays, his clock ticks, his typewriter purrs, and his family ticks over like a well-oiled engine. He lights his pipe and blows tiny clouds across the room. He can lift a hand and make them scatter.

★　　★　　★

When they met they were both young and smiling. Leaves scudded along the gutter, in the alley someone was whistling an old love song. They recognized one another immediately. His eyes were blue, the color of a sea she had never seen, would never know. He noticed her perpetual look of concern, her lack of frivolity. Should he ask her out? should he walk her home? and, later, should he talk to her, touch her, kiss her, entrust her with his heart, enlace them with his soul?

They stood in the doorway, his back against the mailboxes. Good night, good night. Could they part for one night? for a week? for a month? Could a day exist for one without the other? When he was absent, she thought about his dreams and his holding her, the things he said, his meanings and his wants. She worried he would find someone prettier, or kinder, or brighter, or funnier – someone better. She wanted to bind him to her with love. When he was absent, he thought about her kisses and promises, about her trust in him and the way she held his arm when walking and the vision of her rounded with his child, his. He worried she would be swept away from him by someone with money, or ambition, or a car – someone who would easily impress her. He wanted to bind her to him with love.

And that night. The entire city stilled and expectant, every murmur and movement significant, as though the history of man – every battle fought and child born, every disaster and triumph, plague and progress – had been only for this, for their meeting, this coupling, for her to say, his mouth against her hair, his heart beating into her, for her to say I love you.

He pulled them apart. "What?"

"I love you."

He had sworn his love and sung his love and begged her like a woman, but she had said no: no, they were too young; no, they were too different; no, they had no money, no prospects, they had to wait, they must be sure. And then she said "I love you", as though it were something she had been saying all along. And the world was held tight by joy.

But it was days later, holding hands against the ferry railing, the tears of the drowned following the boat, the out-of-towners pointing, oh look, look there, that he said they must marry. "I know I'm not good enough for you," he said. "I know, but you are half of me, part of me, the same as me" – they could not be apart. She cried on to the buttons of his coat. At last her life had begun. At last his life had a center.

They were married on a day like the one on which the world began, all in the universe achieving perfection. He was so nervous he could barely speak. She was so beautiful it seemed like a dream. He slipped the ring onto her finger. Now neither of them would ever need to worry again. Now each had become complete.

★　　★　　★

Rita says that she is happy her children are grown and that she is not the mother of young children at a time when schools are dangerous, filled with riff-raff and don't teach anything except how to join a gang and get doped up. She says she has read some shocking things in the paper, and cites as examples a ten-year-old junky, an eleven-year-old pusher, a twelve-year-old whore. Things were not like this before – though she can't say that to Lillian, because Lillian would snap her head off – when you walked the streets without being terrified and when everyone learned English instead of talking in a foreign language and acting as though there was nothing wrong with that; when in Rome, says Rita. She also says that everyone knows that people are brought up differently and some people just aren't as clean as other people, and some people aren't as smart, not that it's their fault, and just the other day, in Woolworth's, she saw two young men holding hands, as bold as anything, and it made her sick just to think of it. Rita says that the bad winters of the past few years are because of satellites, that the Communists set up Nixon, and that now that she has no man to worry about she hardly ever eats meat.

Linda sighs but does not argue. Sometimes she is bothered by the notion that the world might actually be as simple as Rita believes; that at least the world as her mother-in-law sees it makes some kind of sense. Linda, remembering her afternoon, is confused by images of cigarette smoke, faces over candles, wine sliding down the inside of her glass, Mark holding her hand as though there were electricity in her bones, holding him to her. She is trying to talk to Rita, but keeps hearing him say, "But I love you. I don't know when it happened, but I do". She had thought that he was happy with his wife, and that they were friends – sophisticated, clear-visioned and mature – having a good time, no strings. Have things already gone too far? Why did she say that she loved him?

"Is it all right if I fix myself a cheese sandwich?" asks Rita.

Linda looks up, speeding from the feel of tweed against her cheek and Mark's smell of a public library and Marlboros to the real world of daughterdom and motherdom and wifedom. "Don't be silly, I'll get it for you." Is she starting to be neglectful?

Rita trails her into the kitchen, talking about brands of coffee and the casseroles you can make with Velveeta cheese. Maybe Rita would like to talk about death, about her own dying, about Walter's; maybe Rita would like to talk about birth, about her own birthings, the thing itself, removed from horror stories and anecdotes of forceps, turned wombs and twelve days of labor. Or maybe she would like to talk, just once, about the morning she had been making the little Lillian french toast with cinnamon sugar for breakfast and had suddenly noticed the stained crust of sugar around the

90

rim of the bowl, thinking to herself, oh Jesus, Mary and Joseph. Oh, Jesus Mary and Joseph. Pregnant. And then she had gone inside and thrown up before walking Lillian to Kindergarten. Maybe she would like to talk about how she had prayed and prayed, prayed and prayed that the baby would never be born; prayed as she had never prayed for the salvation of lost or wayward souls, for the repentance of the mean and wicked, for the redemption of the poor sinners who had died without a Catholic baptism, she had prayed for the tragic and untimely death of her unborn infant, for its microscopic soul to be hurled without mercy into the pits of purgatory – promising that she would devote the rest of her life to saying novenas on which it could crawl its way back up to heaven. Balled up in the night, her back against the sleeping Walter, staring out at the ghostly, menacing forms of furniture draped in clothing, she had talked to God. Bargained. I had a lot of trouble with Lil, she'd thought, jogging His memory. Remember all the trouble I had? I almost died. I don't want to go through that again. There was that, that and money. Would she want to tell how she had thrown herself down the stairs, twice, but too afraid to really fall? She would have ridden through Central Park, eyes empty, on either a motorcycle or a horse, but she hadn't known anyone with either of those things. So instead she drank a quart of gin and puked all over the shag rug in the hall. Could she tell her daughter-in-law – or remember to herself – how she had felt: as though she were alone in the world, left clinging to the ledge of a large, ugly hill, and no one, anywhere, at any time, would ever care. Before that there had been times when she had thought that she was lonely – but compared to that feeling it had been like thinking you were starving because you'd missed lunch. She had known that God wasn't above bribes, but she'd had nothing to offer that He might want. Except Lillian – and at that thought a calm, colorless terror had obliterated her awareness of the new child. Would Rita, maybe, perhaps, want to talk about any of those memories?

"It isn't easy to be called mother," says Rita, twisting the plastic loop around the neck of the bread wrapper. And Linda sighs, thinking how true; somehow surprised that Rita should know that.

Rita sits on the bentwood kitchen chair, watching Linda pour boiling water into the hand-crafted coffee mugs. "I always told Lillian, some day you'll have a daughter of your own, and then you'll know what I've been through. I always told her that." Your face will freeze, you'll be sorry some day, what'll happen to you if I die, do you think you can always have things your way, your father won't always be around to protect you. "And now she knows what I was talking about."

And don't we all, thinks Linda, saying, "Milk or evaporated?"

Rita chews her sandwich, pushing wadges of bread back between her lips. "Of course," she says, "they have a hard time financially, with only his income. And they're still payin' for his mother's funeral."

"Everyone's having a hard time," feeling, again, her lover's fingers on her nipples, her lover's lips upon her breasts. "Both Paul and I make good money and we're still always broke."

"Lillian had to hock her engagement ring. Can you imagine that? Because of all the trouble they had with the car over the summer."

In Mark's car there is a St Christopher medal hanging from the dash. He says that he found it one summer in Paris, Maine, and that it saved his life a week later when his car was totalled by a Birds Eye frozen foods truck in New Hampshire. When she thinks about the medal she thinks about his hand inside her slacks. "Maybe Lillian could find some part-time work."

"And who would look after the baby then? It's not like in the city where there are places you can put them."

What am I going to do with you, he asked; let me out at the next corner, she replied. When will I see you again, he called, holding her wrist; but instead of saying I don't know, she said, tomorrow. "Doesn't she have any neighbors she could swap with?"

"Lillian's not the type to take advantage of anyone," says

92

Rita, stirring the water and the milk and the coffee powder around and around.

"No, of course not," whispers Linda, wondering if he misses her.

"Life's not as easy for some as for others. It's luck, I suppose. Some people can work just as hard as others and never get the right breaks." She sips at her coffee. "If you know what I mean."

Of course, hairs grow out of his nose, his sense of humor is not very good and he has confessed to having voted for Hubert Humphrey; he is more enthusiastic than Paul but not as adept; he doesn't seem particularly fond of children. "I guess people can't help it if they're lucky."

Rita's cup goes click as it sets on the table. "Can people help it if they aren't?" asks Rita, not sure of what she means.

"Still," sighs Linda, wondering if he meant what he said about her intrinsic sympathy and generosity, "once Angela goes to school Lillian will be able to work again and that'll help."

"Only part-time. She'd have to be home for when the baby came back." As Rita had always been, rushing through the shopping, passing up trips downtown and visits in kitchens with coffee and prune danish, never lingering and never lacking, when she had a job cleaning or watching someone's child always making sure that she was home by three, waiting, never thinking of herself. "I don't think Lillian would let Angela spend the entire day only with strangers," and she doesn't look at Linda, in whose children the signs of maternal neglect are so painfully apparent.

Linda stares at her own hand, sculpted from some ancient shaman's stone, blue veins and snowflake patterns, thinking about spending one's entire life with strangers only. She knows they are only having fun – but does he really see her, could he really care? "It's the quality of love, not the quantity that counts," she finally replies, but Rita gets up to put the kettle on and doesn't seem to hear.

Rita notices things like slimy soap dishes and grit around the taps, dust on top of picture frames, shoes that should be polished, shirts that should be bleached, colds that should be seen to and acrid aromas in the towels and linens; she notices and she keeps track. Rita's concept of quality is somewhat different from Linda's. "The road to hell," says the old lady, "is made of good intentions." And then adds, "When you have kids you have to make some sacrifices. Lillian wants to live like they used to before the baby came. She's got a lot to learn, that girl." Rita turns off the burner, thinking about all the sacrifices she has made, about the quantity and the quality of her love throughout the years and all that she has always done for everyone, and how good she knows it should make her feel.

Linda runs her fingers through her hair, fingers of hair and fingers of fingers, thinking about her sacrifices, her penances, about the quantity and the quality of her love and how it never seems to be enough, and how it never really seems to come back again, somehow.

Blinking lights, bells and horns, lovers arm-in-arm, kisses in the shadows; screams and squeals and screechings, soft steps in the nightness.

"I've had a very full life," says Rita. Linda looks at her expectantly. "With my family. What more could anyone ask from life?"

What indeed. Linda smears with one finger the ring left by her cup. Champagne in your slipper, silver threads among the gold, freedom for all political prisoners, full bellies for the starving children of the world, crimson hearts tattooed across your soul, no more seal kills, fucking all night long, a return to the simple values and virtues of the past, someone worshipping the ground you walk on, immortality with no strings. "Well," she sighs. "I guess some people just feel that they need a little more."

Rita flicks imaginary crumbs from the table. "Oh, yes, I guess so. Yes." She gazes at the hand-painted tiles behind the sink with her blue blue eyes. "It's television and the movies. That's what did it. I wouldn't go to a movie any more. All it is is sex. If you've ever been married you've had enough of that to last you a lifetime."

94

A few weeks ago, Linda might have agreed – but not tonight. Paul's love-making may put her to sleep, but not so Mark's: his handprints are still hot across her body. She has begun to wonder if anyone else has ever wanted her. "There are still some good movies being made."

"That and violence. If it isn't the one thing it's the other."

"At least they're still making some good kids' movies."

"It's the permissiveness. You can kill somebody now and be out on the street in a couple of years with everyone feeling sorry for you because you were in prison."

Linda blinks. "Uh . . ."

"What do you expect people to do? Do you think people will work when they can get handouts for nothing, for just sitting around? Everything handed to them?"

Rita is remembering her nightmares.

"Well," says Linda, blinking again, torn between what Mark would say – I love you, nothing matters – and what Paul would say – most people will do as little as they can get away with, though, of course, no one should have to starve, especially children – "if someone wants to work but can't, then they shouldn't have to suffer because of it."

Rita is up, rinsing her plate. "Walter never in his life took any charity. Never. No matter how bad times were, he would rather have been thrown in jail than have to take handouts. He always said, as long as a man can pay his rent no one can ever tell him what to do."

And Linda can imagine that family of memories – the young Rita and the living Walter, little Lillian with her hair in pony tails and littler Paul with a crew cut and a too-big red flannel shirt – standing in the deadening cold grey morning of their prison cell, shadows of bars across their faces, waiting, hands interlocked, to be marched down the clanging corridors for porridge, a family who wouldn't take charity. And Linda can picture the tiny tap dancers in satin shirts and short skirts that Walter saw one New Year's Eve, tiptapping across the kitchen counter, over the stove and up and down the refrigerator, gold pillbox hats a-tilt, the landlord shouting at the door, they'll be no tap dancing by four-inch-high Kewpie dolls in my building, Walter yawning, pouring himself another drink, yelling at Rita, worried about eviction and insanity, for Chrissake, I pay my rent. "I know what you mean," she says, never having been poor, never having missed a meal unless she was dieting, never having prayed for someone to happen along who could change bread into meat and water into milk. "Pride is important to people." Remembering now snow, like rice, being showered over the car in which embraced the kissing couple.

"To most people." Rita's eyes burn into nothing. "But not all. Some people don't care about anything. They don't care what people think about them, or what happens to them." Rita is thinking about Negro hop-heads and Puerto Rican street gangs, about Welfare mothers with their children in the same bed as their lovers and Communists with thin lips and narrow eyes telling people not to work. "Dignity. People gotta have dignity." Like her, like Walter, like her children and her parents, shutting doors, drawing curtains, keeping out the world always ready to see you make a fool of yourself, always ready to help you fail. Keep yourself to yourself. "Otherwise you're just a bum. A man with no pride is just a bum." But a woman is different. Women are proud of their hair, of their homes, of their children, of their figures and the absence of lines on their faces and hands; women carry it with them, inside of them; proud of their husbands, their grand-children, their carpets, their extravagant sacrifices and their maternal martyrdom. A woman with no pride is just a whore.

Rita turns her wedding band around its finger. She has her snapshots and an old card or two from the kids – I love you, Mom, with hearts and crosses – she has the lace tablecloth she got when she was first married and silver dessert spoons from when Walter's Aunt Mimi died; she has her husband and her children, easily retrieved from their hideouts in the past, to walk again through her kitchen and her hall and down the stoop where the old ladies sit on their plastic folding chairs in summer, re-creating decades. Rita's ring is wide and plain. No one would ever call her a whore.

Linda chews a nail. She smiles and mumbles something

about ethnicity and cultural roots, trying to find reasons why Rita's accused should fulfil her hobgoblin prophecies. Tutored by Paul, Linda believes in justice and equality; unlike Paul, the poet and visionary, the only universe she can imagine is the one she can see. Linda has so little. They have closets of clothes and shelves of books, cupboards filled with pots and drawers filled with stainless steel cutlery in a modern design; they have dishes and couches and beds and patterned sheets; they have records, pictures, two electric typewriters, a washing machine, two children, one cat and a dishwasher. She has coats and scarves and stockings and jewelry, a high school and a college year book, a battered dustbin and her grandmother's rocking chair; she has two toothbrushes, one vibrator, an electric shaver and a hair dryer with three speeds. Unable to understand why the poor, the victimized and the dispossessed don't try harder to live up to the standards of their critics and their patrons, she often believes in a concept of inevitability. Linda wonders if she would have been a whore if Paul hadn't married her, and if she will be one if she leaves him. She glances over at Rita's blue blue, watery blue eyes. And then she remembers that Mark loves her.

★   ★   ★

Without him her life would have run through time like slight, dissolving silvery arteries and capillaries. With him her life remains fixed in firm and perfect patterns, indelible and infinite, ancient and for always, back and forwards, forwards and back – an intricate tattoo on the breast of eternity. She irons his clothes, cooks his food, bakes his bread, makes his bed, washes his floors, and dies in his arms each night. He adores her but can find no way to say it. He thinks of her as being part of him, a twin designed by destiny, washed up on the shore of his secret self, an invisible birthmark the only clue. When he is with her he is almost alone, so completely is her soul sucked into his, so total the communion. He does not have to woo her, or please her, or pretend; he does not have to be polite, or cautious: she breathes with him, feels with him, thinks with him. She feeds him, holds him, envelops him. His arm is always held, his toast buttered, his back rubbed. She is his balance and his shelter. He is her shelter and her sail.

Without her his life would have interrupted infinity like several sudden cracks of thunder during a dry and blazing summer: crackle birth and crackle puberty, sex, awareness, working, friendship, crackle crackle death. With her his life is fixed to the heart of the universe by slender silken strings of truth, held back from the black holes of fear and uncertainty, aloneness and despair, held flat against the hot and yearning breast of destiny, held high in jubilation and conceit. He pays her bills and paints her rooms, sees her safely to the shops, notices her absences, compliments her cooking and births himself again each night in her succoring wetness. She believes in him and so is obedient, surrounding him like a moon: she wants everything she does to say I love you. She thinks of him as being more than she, the better self regained, all that was missing replaced, the whole made whole. With him she is never alone. He stands beside her, his coat spread over his arms like wings, held over the curls and ribbons of her head, protection from the bloodied rains of life. She pleases him, he guides her; she comforts him, he provides for her; she arranges stars, planets and asteroids for his convenience, he lays his world at her feet. He cherishes her, he longs for her and holds on to her. Her days are always full, her nights contained, some things are certain. He is her guard and her god. She is the priestess to whom he offers his life, and in acceptance blesses it with meaning.

*   *   *

Paul has had a good day. The streets of Manhattan are glazed with slush, the sky hangs low in dark grey billows, and passers-by are muffled in coats and scarves and still faces – but in Paul Sutcliffe's heart the sun shines down on lascivious, lean brown bodies with big breasts and small black bikinis on a beach where palm trees pray and fisherchildren play along the shore. Paul has been invited to go to a conference in California for a week, all expenses paid. Paul is taking Janet.

He will take Janet and call Linda every day; he will come back rested and missing them; he will bring the children T-shirts and ceramic models of the San Francisco trolley and send Liz a postcard; he will enjoy himself and long for Linda's familiarness beside him. He will also make some valuable contacts, perhaps get someone interested in his novel, and say a few meaningful things about contemporary fiction in the Americas.

As he nears his block he thinks about his family and he misses them, drawn around the dinner table without him, the play, as it were, continuing without him, and decides on wine and Brie for supper, and a bottle of Linda's favorite liqueur as a present – I'll miss you.

Paul is whistling as he waits for the elevator, thinking that one's life is easily arranged for maximum comfort, really, *and so will I stretch my world for you.*

Linda has not had a good day. From David's nose drip snakes of pale green mucus, he is grumpy and complaining and, the teacher said, may have been exposed to chickenpox; Patricia ripped her new jacket but can't remember how and wouldn't speak on the way home because her mother yelled at her in public. There was a series of crises at work, she has burnt her hand turning over the hamburgers, she is getting her period and she and Mark had a fight over her inability to arrange her time so that they could have a weekend away together. "I don't think you really want to," he said, smiling, weary and hurt. And she had slammed the car door in his face, "Goddamn men. I hate all of you".

Heartsick, she tests the potatoes and tosses the salad with android perfection, smiling with her motorized mouth and just-like-real eyes at her children, her human masters, who are waiting without patience for their dinner and who have a lot to tell her about their day. David sniffles; the android mother sighs with concern and hands him a green tissue. Patricia complains that Kevin, the one with the curly dark hair not the other one, pulled her chair out from under her during art and nearly made her fracture her knee; the android mother examines the scars and wonders what Kevin's homelife must be like.

Her life in ruins, she makes the children lemonade from a packet, remembering who wants which glass, and puts the tomato catsup on the table. David says that when he grows up he is going to be an astronaut so that he can watch everybody on earth and no one will be able to shoot him before he can shoot them. Patricia says that Timmy Lewis wrote "fuck" at one corner of the blackboard when Mr Tripp was out of the room and he didn't notice it all afternoon. Linda says that she thinks it would be exciting to be an astronaut but not to hurt people and that Timmy Lewis, whose mother is a psychologist and head of the PTA, should know better than that.

Her happiness shattered, she organizes the evening in her mind: bathe the children, read a book about a family of trolls who get stranded on Staten Island, wash her hair, do the *Times* crossword, have a stiff drink and go to sleep. It is not, after all, as though she and Mark have anything truly special together. She throws the cutlery in a heap onto the table. If this is the beginning of the end, then sobeit, she's not a teenager, God knows, she can easily go on as though she'd never known him. David is accidentally whacked in the head when she turns to lower the flame under the meat. Everybody knows how many letters there are in the word love.

It is just as Paul is leaving the elevator that the phone rings, Linda saying to Patricia, "If it's Katie Wilson, you tell her you'll call her back after you eat."

Patricia makes a face. But the call is for Linda, Mark's "Hello, Linda?" harmonizing with Paul's "Hey there, everybody" as he steps through the door. Paul holds up the wine and mimes a kiss. Mark says that he is sorry he was such a fool, but can't she believe how much he wants her. Linda smiles on Paul with what she hopes looks like affection, and says to Mark, "Everything's all right now, thanks. I'll let you know what happens with it later in the week. I'm afraid I have to go now, my husband's just come home."

Paul kisses his daughter and hugs his son. "Someone from work?" as she hangs up. "I bought a very nice wine, to celebrate," he croons, coming up behind her and rubbing her ass.

She pours the dressing over the salad. "Oh, what are you celebrating?"

He floats his hand around and cups a breast, marvelling at the wonderfulness of woman. "The West Coast conference. I've received a special invitation. I've even been asked to give a talk." He pinches her nipple and kisses her cheek. "Isn't that wonderful?"

"How long is it for?"

"About a week. But I might stay a day or two longer to check out some people."

All that Linda says is "Mmmm", occupied with organizing babysitters and overnights, a visit to Grandma's and perhaps a trip to the zoo to make up for her neglect.

"And I have something special for you," he whispers, producing with one hand the liqueur and with the other rubbing her between her legs. She leans her body towards the knotty pine cupboards, trapping his fist.

"Would you mind putting the potatoes on the table?" and she smiles at him with her old friendliness, as though he might, indeed, be still adorable.

Linda is in the bathroom adjoining their bedroom, red tub and sink and bowl, white walls and plants at the window. The shower is running. Paul is travelling, midway between the kitchen and their room, bearing a silver tray with golden goblets, humming to himself, a lover's song. When she emerges from the steamy warmth, he is lighting a candle by the bedside table, a priest of shadows, smoke flowing from his fingertips. His voice is thick with secrets and heavy with promises, pitched low, sent gently to reach her. "I thought you would like a drink," he says.

Linda rubs her head with a towel. "I can't see in this light," stopping beside him to switch on the lamp. "I have to dry my hair."

What, now? This is not what he would get from Janet,

who would let him take her wet and soapy, cold and helpless on the blue tiles of her bathroom floor. "Let me dry it," he whispers, not discouraged to realize that she is already dressed in pajamas and robe and fuzzy pink slippers.

She smiles at him, nearly with affection. "It's all right," sliding from his lover's touch, "I meant with the dryer," disappearing once more into the other room, trailing the cord of the hair dryer behind her.

Paul drinks his drink, pours another and drinks that as well. All he can hear is the night and passing cars, the sound of a piano drifting through the airshaft and the whirring of a tiny motor. Paul sits on the bed, thinking of Linda's vibrator. Should he have mentioned it when he first found it? Should he have bought her one himself, surprise surprise? He drinks her drink, then refills them both. Is she purposely avoiding him, or is she merely teasing him? If he asks her about the vibrator, will she quote *Cosmopolitan* or the Boston Health Collective? Will she tell him it is an everyday sex aide, ignoring his protests that it cannot be considered an aid to sex when he was never told about it? Did she go into the store herself to buy it? He tiptoes across the room, casually, and opens her sweater drawer, but the vibrator is no longer there. He could have been holding it when she returned to the room, he could have spread her across the bed and used it on her himself, watching her nipples rise and harden, watching her engorge and swell, her clitoris emerge and retract, her wetness gleaming on the plastic shaft. He searches another and then another of her drawers, the only object of interest being a small, plastic dinosaur. Perhaps she has simply hidden it from the children: his eyes scan the room, closet pictures rugs and curtains. Or maybe she simply grew tired of it, bought on the spur of some feminist enthusiasm, and has passed it on to a manless sister or one whose man is less rather than more. He tucks a runaway pair of stockings back into its space. If none of those things, where could it be? Thrown away? She wouldn't be stupid enough just to throw it away. What if the janitor found it, draped with limp lettuce and hardened spaghetti. Would he know whose it was?

102

Linda snaps off the dryer, shakes her head, studies her face in the mirror for signs of untapped beauty and unsuspected age. She wants to believe that Paul is asleep by now, gentle and vulnerable, a book collapsed on his chest, his face heartbreakingly attractive in his sleep, prince sweet. But she can hear him singing now, "Green grow the rashes O, green grow the rashes O, she mows like reek thro a' the week, but finger-fucks on Sunday, O". She brushes her teeth, rubs cream into her cheeks. Under normal circumstances, Paul loathes Burns, the drunken bumpkin.

Linda has refused Paul only twice; then waking to find that he didn't take her refusal all that seriously anyway. It is not a sense of duty but a sense of futility that keeps her giving. She could lock herself in the bathroom and sleep in the tub, one foot wrapped around a tap, but the gesture is melodramatic. Paul believes that his wanting her is the same as her wanting him. Linda flushes the sink with warm water, dislodging a blob of toothpaste. So simple is the world for some.

He is still dressed, but sitting on the bed, the pillow puffed behind him, rolling a joint. He has noticed the resistance. She takes an extra second in shutting bathroom light and door, noticing how handsome he is and how little it affects her, wondering why they can't be friends, why they can't accept the mellowness and maturity of their relationship now, after all these years. Sex, really, is so unimportant when viewed against the totality of one's life. Why should they be jealous of one another? Why feign desire when they have respect; why sham lust when they have a deep and well-established love for one another? Would the world end if she said to him – in the same voice that has soothed him through writing blocks and interdepartmental feuds – that she had no interest in him tonight? What is she trying to prove?

"Come let me see your carrot cunt," he whispers, wreathed in ritual smoke, his eyes heavy-lidded, his lips looking very kissed. "Come spread yourself for me."

Linda stands with her back to the closed bathroom door, slipping the robe from her shoulders, as though entranced by the force of his voice, hypnotized by his desire. Slowly, she slides her pajama pants down, unbuttons the top.

Paul is a practised and expert lover; his body is beautiful, his touch sure; he is never dull and never shy.

She walks to where he holds the cigarette out to her, a peace pipe, piece pipe.

But it is Mark who always makes her want him.

She takes the joint, coming close to him; he dips her nipple in his drink and sucks it off. She pulls at his hair.

He has always told her that she is the best woman he has ever had.

And she believes him.

5

Liz lies comfortably on Linda's side of Paul's and Linda's bed, sipping a Bloody Mary from a green tinted art deco glass. Beside her lies Paul, pillows propped behind him, holding a tumbler of straight bourbon. Janet, at this moment, is preparing for the evening ahead: she is soaking in an oily, fragrant bath, reading a book Paul recommended to her the week before, and on which he is sure to expect some response, and she is thinking about the weather in California. Linda is at the country house with the children, filling her body with crisp, clean air and her mind with thoughts of peace and solitude: he told her he thought she needed a break, was working herself too hard.

There was a time when Paul's sex life was confined to his marriage and his private madness. On dull days, he would imagine the little cutie in the front row, freshman English, the one who always looked so bored, splayed across the oversized desk in his office, jeans in a heap on the floor, her striped gym socks and Adidases still on, her breasts exposed, nipples yearning: he could hear her moan, oh, fuckmefuckme. And other fantasies, too.

There were dreams of pure, virginal desire, such as his wordless adoration of the tall blonde in his graduate seminar. Handing her a book he would imagine her naked and warm and wet, sweat glueing their bodies together, face buried into neck, arms tightly encircling, a gentle, soft murmur, a purr, coming from her, more a love song than a cry.

105

There were the dreams of a pure and putrid hatred, such as his unspoken loathing for the youngest woman on the faculty, the Bryn Mawr bomber. With the exception of the very old – who were too senile to care – and the very young – who were still too smug and secure in their visions of their futures – every man on the faculty felt the whoosh whoosh of a razor graze their balls when she approached. She wouldn't flirt with them, and she wouldn't let them tell her what to do: they all dreamt of getting even. But especially Paul. Bending her over his bed, her face pushed into a satin pillow, her round round ass waiting, open like a kiss, rubbing her, priming her, teasing her, what do you want, youwantyouwant . . . not until you take back what you said about James Joyce.

But now there are no confines: the magician seeks but magic; the poet seeks but love. To limit your love is to limit your vision of God. To plant your seed only in one plot uses up the land and wastes seed. If all the world were to concentrate on fucking, then no one would ever get fucked. Although, as he once explained to Lit. 79F, there is a clear distinction between screwing someone and having an affair. The latter assumes love and commitment, seriousness, depth and grace. Paul only has affairs.

"I just don't know what's gotten into her," he says now, watching the ice bob around in his drink.

Liz nibbles on her stalk of celery. "How old is she?"

He stretches an arm above her head and rubs her toes with his. "She's only thirty-seven. It can't be menopausal yet." Though it might be. He's heard of women who went through it in their twenties. Paul runs one finger over Liz's breasts. She is the sort of woman it is difficult to picture as ever being anything but twenty-three or -four. Born that way, with straight, thick hair, clear, clean features and near-perfect teeth. The sort of woman who comes into the world knowing how to give herself a vaginal examination, how to lace up high boots, the best place to have an abortion and where there is this fantastic jazz pianist in Jersey. She will never have stretch marks, put on weight, make a scene in

106

public, or send letters to your home. She is never above average in bed, but when you walk down the street with her other men notice.

"It's unlikely, but it might be." She puts down her glass, rolls over and begins to nibble his nipple.

He starts to stroke her hair. "I just don't understand it. She's never been like this before. It's driving me crazy. I can't even get any work done, because I never know what she's going to do next." And he gazes at her with a face that is torn by compassion, distrust and desire.

She ceases licking circles on his chest. "Maybe she's just tired. You can't be much fun to live with."

His hand halts. "What?"

Liz lifts her pretty little face to him, smiling kindly. "I said that I don't think it can be easy living with you," licking his earlobe, teasing.

"Why not?"

And so she smiles. "I was only kidding."

And so he doesn't quite smile. "No you weren't. Why did you say that?"

"Oh, I don't know," shrugging, looking for the best way to put it without actually starting an argument. "You're pretty, oh, you know . . ." selfish, demanding, egotistical, insensitive, uncaring, domineering, sexist, condescending, immature, neurotic bordering on the clinically psychotic . . . every adjective that Linda has ever used, in the heat of the moment, to describe him, he now sees whizz through his lover's eyes . . . "busy."

"Busy?" Paul swallows deeply, wondering if she thinks she's lying.

"Yeah. Busy." She sits up level with him, reclaiming her glass. "You know. With school, and the journal, and your book, and your research, and extra stuff at work, advising and everything . . ." Liz is about to add "and your women" but, glancing at the line his lips are making, decides against it. If she mentions women he will go on for another fifteen minutes on love and adult relationships, and she has to pick up her son by six. "I just mean that it must keep you busy all of the time, so you really can't pay all that much attention to her, or help out with the house and the kids and all . . ." she rubs his knuckles, meaning "the way you would want to if you were able".

"There's nothing at all wrong with my and Linda's relationship." He grips her fingers between his, onetwothreefourfive. "We are partners, equal. We both do our share . . ."

"I didn't mean that you didn't."

He stares down at her bright red nails. "Most of the time I'm the one who picks the kids up from day care and after school."

"Um."

"And I take them both out on Sundays."

"Um."

"And I spend a certain amount of time each evening with them."

"Um."

"I read David his bedtime story. I tuck them in."

"Uhhuh."

He downs his bourbon in one swift swallow. "I am a terrific provider."

"Sure. Providing she doesn't come home unexpectedly."

"What the fuck is that supposed to mean?"

The lovely Liz smooths the sheet around his knees. "Nothing, Paul. I was just joking. I don't know what you're getting so upset about. All I said was Linda's probably tired."

"The implication was that I am somehow failing her."

Liz makes a face for him, that he is not to see. The sigh she sighs is for herself. Liz has already had two husbands of her own and a number of other people's: she knows when not to joke, and she knows when to keep quiet. This moment is obviously both of those things. "I didn't mean that."

"What would you like me to do, alter my career so that Linda can nap in the evenings?"

"Paul, I . . ."

"I happen to make a hell of a lot of money and I work damn hard for it."

"Paul . . ."

108

"Do you think I do it for myself? Do you think I enjoy working till two, three, sometimes even four in the morning on some paper that only a handful of people will ever read? Or correcting some essay by a moron who would be better off cleaning latrines in the army? Do you?"

She watches him from behind a fringe of hair. How risky would an honest opinion be at this point?

"Do you? Is that what you think?"

"Of course not . . . I . . ."

"I do it for Linda. For her and the kids. If it were only me I'd be just as happy living in a cave . . ."

"Living on spring water and berries."

He allows her the smallest of small smiles. "Okay, not a cave. But you understand what I mean. I want the best for my family."

Liz leans over, leans back, dimpled ass, pouring herself a fresh drink from the pitcher on the night table. "Of course you do." She has a beautiful spine.

"What, exactly what, is a man supposed to do? How much can one man do? Tell me that. Just tell me what more I should be doing."

"How the hell do I know? I only see you once a week, plus in class. How should I know what you do and do not do?"

He is pouring himself another drink, forgetting that he only likes bourbon with ice. "I thought you knew everything. I thought you were rapidly becoming one of New York's leading feminist thinkers."

She smirks. "Hardly."

"What?"

"Why do you ask me for my opinion if you don't really want it?"

He covers his eyes with his arm, breathing in his own aroma. "Of course I want it. But instead of giving me any useful advice you criticize me." He takes his arm away, leans towards her on one elbow. "You're so damn cynical, Liz. What about love? What about my love for Linda? Don't you think that counts for anything? Do you really think that anything else matters?"

109

This time her sigh is for him and is close to weeping. "Oh, love. Of course."

Tenderly, he touches her ankle, encircling it, a bracelet of flesh and bone. "I don't want to argue, honey. This whole thing just has me so tense." He kisses her knuckles. "She walked out the other night. Just got up from dinner and walked out. Didn't say where she was going, came back and didn't tell me where she'd been. She was gone for hours."

Liz smiles at him warmly, touchingly runs a hand across his forehead, strokes his haggard face. "Maybe she's having an affair."

You could have heard a butterfly breathe.

"Don't be ridiculous."

"Why not?"

He takes his hand from her arm. "I'd know. She'd never be able to hide a thing like that from me."

Up until now, Liz has been fulfilling her role of sensitive female confidant beautifully, even brilliantly. But now it begins to fall apart. It begins as she registers his saying "I'd know"; by the time he has finished the next sentence she is laughing rather uncontrollably.

"Is something very funny?"

The tears are making her eyeliner run; she swipes at her eyes with the back of her hand. "Oh, come on Paul, you can't be serious . . ."

He has moved his body miles away from her though touching. "You don't think I'd know? I've been married to Linda for twelve years, Liz. You don't think I'd know if she were having an affair?" See it, hear it, feel it, touch it, smell it.

She smooths a design on the hairs on his stomach, trying to bridge the space. "I don't see how you could possibly be so sure."

"Liz." His tone is close to the one he uses for his forty-five-minute lecture on Hemingway. "A woman can't hide that sort of thing from a man – not from the man she loves. Not," his wedding ring glinting in the glow reflected from his drink, "from her husband."

110

Totally serious, not even the memory of a smile lingers on her lips. "Why not?"

"Because she couldn't."

"But why couldn't she?"

How can he explain a woman like Linda to a woman like Liz? He plays with his moustache, making him look pensive. "First of all, because she would feel much too guilty," as he had felt that first time, with Janet, driven to blurt it out, forced into confession by his own sensitivity, oh, darling, darling, I couldn't help myself, oh, darling, darling, I do love you so, love you still. "She couldn't bear it alone. Besides, she loves me."

Liz's eyes flash closed, flash open. "But if she loves you and she was having an affair, then surely she wouldn't tell you."

He hides his face behind his hands. "But, Liz, because she loves me she wouldn't have an affair. Unless it were for revenge, and she'd have to tell me about that."

She raises herself against her pillow, thoughtful and concerned, and curious. She is trying not to laugh again. "Paul, you love Linda and you're having at least two affairs."

"Two."

"Well?"

He stares back at her, innocent and in peril. "But I'm in love with Janet." He looks away, down at a mountain range in the geometric patterned sheets. "And I'm in love with you."

"But, Paul . . ."

"I can't help the way I feel," the tiny dinghy of his soul wobbling out on a sea of tears, a sea of heartbreak, transversing the stormy currents of love.

She is saved from responding by the telephone. He always answers – or almost always – in case there is an emergency, in case one of his children has just been hit by a drunken kid in a fast car, or found doubled up and bloodied in a garbage can in some alley.

It's Janet. His voice drops, sounding almost musical and benignly sweet. His Liz voice is flatter, more straightforward and worldly; his Linda voice more certain and unguarded.

111

He whispers, "Hello, honey."

Liz lights herself a cigarette, crossing the room for an ashtray. She has a blue star tattooed on one ankle, wears a silver bracelet around the other. Returning to him, she sits cross-legged on the bed. He strokes her thigh. The conversation involves much discussion of food, a small amount concerning traffic, a nominal mention of The Late Show.

"I love you, too," he soothes. "Yes. All right, I'll see you later. Yes. Love you." He pulls on Liz's pubic hair. "Yes, of course," kiss kiss. As he stretches to put the phone back in place, he gently falls on top of her. "And I love you, too," he drawls, his tongue already between her teeth.

It is snowing in Upper New York State. It snows on road and field and town, candy coating the world, and especially it snows on Linda. It has been snowing since the afternoon before. Patricia is refusing to go outside, convinced that she will get frostbite and her hands will fall off. David is refusing to remain indoors, shuttling back and forth, out and in, in and out, caked with snow and red of cheek, ice water sloshing around inside of his Snoopy boots.

Linda is sitting in front of the fire, drinking Irish coffee, reading a book about a hippopotamus that wants to be a ballerina, and thinking about her husband. Why hadn't she always known what he'd become: her bright, bubbling boy now a moody, broody man? Why had she ignored the symptoms of his childishness, his antagonism towards women, his sexual insecurity, his selfishness? Had she thought they were cherishable weaknesses, had she thought they were endearing signs of his need for her? A hiss, a crackle, a miniature meteorite shower over a landscape of stone and ash and a half-devoured cookie carton. Hadn't she really been half-pretending when she'd said she was in love with him; when she told her friends she loved him, that she'd never known anything like this before? Deep down, hadn't she truly known it was just a phase, a cycle, a part of the intricate life pattern, so rich, so intense and so bright? Who had she been kidding? From where had come the notion that her life must hold him or else be incomplete?

The new Linda – who needs no one; who believes in friendship and equality but not in falling in love – recrosses her legs as she lies on the sofa, wondering why a woman would compromise her instincts and her uniqueness for the sake of being part of a couple. Who in their right mind would want to be half of anything? The old Linda – who dreamed of quiet dinners, sharing the *New York Times* on a Sunday and family picnics in the park – she touches up her make-up the way he likes it, wondering why anyone would choose anything else in the world over love.

Linda now watches the fire – in every woman waits a Joan of Arc – knowing, as she does, that people need sex and affection, friendship and support, just as everyone needs food, air, water and a reliable system of excretion. There are no mysteries, no grand commitments, no destined pairings: you eat with Tom, you talk to Dick, you fuck with Harry. It is harmony and simplicity which lead to happiness, not finding a mate for your soul. It is concentration on the self that leads to fulfilment, not absorption in someone else. The Linda of now, who has been there and knows, will never put herself second to some man, even if he can walk on water and likes to cook.

But the Linda of then, shadowing her, worries that she has done something to make him stop loving her, or that someone has done something to make him love her more. She plans her days around his schedules and her dreams around his moods; she relaxes in the security of his decisions. The Linda then has peeped out of her burrow, checked the wind and the weather, and ducked back in. Why struggle and sacrifice? Why take risks? Why dedicate your life to being all alone? Why not have a joint bank account, a nice house, a car and summers by the shore? Is there anything wrong with doubles for bridge? The single man is strong and romantic – unless, of course, he's an accountant with dandruff, a mother and a stutter; the single woman is desperate and pathetic – unless, of course, she's a stunningly beautiful heiress, with an endless string of lovers and does charity work. To be cherished, she knows, is the rarest of life's gifts; to be understood and cared about the ultimate happiness. Is not having to wash someone's socks more important than caresses; not having to sit through a boring ball game more significant than always having someone to talk to? Independence, the Linda then thinks, seasoning the stew the way he likes it, is all right when you're twenty-two and can still see the future. Every refuge, the Linda then thinks, washing the cup he left in the sink, ignoring his coldness and the jibes in front of guests, has its price.

Outside of the picture window a branch bends.

"Errgat."

"What?"

"There's nothing to do." Patricia, on the opposite couch, flounces, prone, first one way and then the other.

"You could build a snowman or go for a sleigh ride."

Knees bent to her chest and Dracula teeth curling out from her mouth, Patricia gives her mother a contemptuous look, whistling through the left tooth, wheee. "It's too cold."

"Not if you dress warmly."

"My mittens will soak through and my nose will go numb."

Linda stares down at the hippo in its pink tutu. "Then why don't you draw a picture?"

The little girl, so agile, rolls back her body and becomes a headstand. "I've already drawn six pictures. Including the one David threw in the fire."

"Make it seven."

"I don't want to."

Both the Lindas sigh: the one wanting true communion, mother to daughter and back again, the other wanting to be left the hell alone. "What do you want to do?" The hippopotamus in the pink tutu is in love with a mouse in a green velvet doublet – a mixed marriage.

Patricia has the ability to make her eyes very very small, so that they appear not only beady but calculating as well. "I want to watch cartoons."

Patsy was once a delightful infant, gurgling and good-natured, sleeping on schedule, eating all her food, smashed plums and pre-digested meats. She walked on schedule, talked on schedule and never had really bad teething. Linda gazes upon her one daughter, whistling through one plastic tooth, jaw set. She is now just like her father: stubborn and lazy, self-indulgent and spoiled, expecting Linda to do all the hard work and take all the blame. "Why don't you make up your own cartoon?" Seldom do little girls snort. "I want to watch cartoons, not draw them. Why couldn't you leave me home with Daddy?" The hippo is too fat to get over the wall which divides her from her own true love; he is too small to climb to the other side. "Because Daddy has to work this weekend."

"You're working."

"I'm not getting much work done with you sitting around moping. If you can't find something to do in the house, then get dressed and go outside and play with your brother."

"I hate him."

"Patricia."

"I do. I hate him."

If Paul were here, he would discuss this sensibly, kindly, using the knowledge gained from all of his own years in analysis to deal maturely and objectively with what he would easily diagnose as nothing more than a very ordinary case of sibling rivalry – all kids go through it. If Paul were here, he would make his little girl laugh and tell her a secret, bundle her into her orange anorak and take her out in the snow with her baby brother to scream with delight and giggle uncontrollably as he trotted them through the softly twinkling snow – bringing them together. If Paul were here, he would gather them all in his strong, capable arms, firm but gentle, explain to each his or her mood and behavior, then whisk them all away on his brand new snow tires for a Chinese meal. But Linda simply says, "You don't mean that."

Patricia looks slightly puzzled. "Yes I do."

"He's just a little boy. You can't possibly hate him."

She kicks her feet against the sofa, leftright, left right, leftrightright. "Yes I can. I wish somebody would steal him."

"But he's your brother."

"I always have to play what he wants to play. He never has to do what I want to do."

"That's because you're bigger and you understand more. When David's older things will be more even." She gets up to throw some more wood on the fire, starbursts in the hearth.

"And when will that be?"

"Soon," dusting her hands on her jeans.

"Soon like tomorrow or soon like when I grow up?"

Linda feels as though she's shrivelling. "Oh, Patricia. Not tomorrow but before you're an old lady. Okay?"

Face frozen, Patsy Sutcliffe stares at her mother, peeling her back, layer by layer. She has a face that could sell cough medicine and chocolate bars, and eyes that can see through walls. Her father likes to joke that she has the soul of a pool shark, which he half believes, but which is totally inaccurate. Patricia is merely cautious. And who could blame her? "No, it's not okay," she says, and she watches her mother's mouth to see what it will do; glances at her mother's hands to see if they will hit or hurl or scratch the air.

But her mouth doesn't move, her hands are still. "Patricia," Linda says softly, regaining a bit of her poise, "Patricia, it is just too bad. I can't make David disappear just to suit you. In time to come you'll be very glad to have a brother, believe me. I wish I had had a brother or a sister," sighing a sisterless sigh, trying to show her daughter by the look in her eyes the long lonely hours she has spent as a child, adolescent and adult, having no sister or brother to share with or confide in, to lean on or turn to. "It's very, very lonely being an only child. It may seem like it's really nice not having anyone to bother you, or borrow your things, and not having to always share things with someone else, but it isn't so much fun at all," kneading her hands together as though rubbing out the pox-like scars of her only-childhood.

"Oh, yeah?"

"Yeah."

Patricia chews on a strand of her hair, unpersuaded. "He always gets the best present."

116

"That's not true, Patsy, and you know it. You both get the same."

"It is true too. He got a football, didn't he? He still wets his bed sometimes and he got a football."

Longings and sighs. "Patricia." Beyond the house the river is frozen, ice sculptures where once there was a waterfall and giant, flat, slimy rocks from which to swim. "You don't even like football."

She removes the wet braid end from her mouth. "How would I know? How will I ever find out when I'll never in my whole entire life have a football?"

The little mouse, in his dapper outfit with the pointed cap and red feather, tries scaling the wall that is keeping him lonely. "I think you'd better go outside."

"And I heard Daddy say that someday David would be President."

"He was only joking, Patsy, for God's sake."

"He wasn't even smiling."

"It doesn't mean anything, honey. It's just something daddies say. All daddies say things like that."

She hangs backwards off the couch. "He didn't say I was going to be President."

"You'll find dry mittens in the kitchen."

"It isn't fair, you know. Why can't he come in here and play with me? Why can't he come in here and play backgammon?"

Maybe they aren't really brother and sister. Maybe one of them was stolen by the gypsies right after birth and the hospital put another child in its place, some infant left abandoned in the kitchen among the onions and potatoes. But which one? "David is too little to play backgammon."

The little girl shuffles from the room, kicking at the leather hassock as she nears the door. "You see."

Linda flips a page, or two, or three, as doors bang through the house. True love finally finds a way when the dancing hippo accidentally careers into the wall and brings it crashing down around her. She lays the manuscript aside. The little mouse and the big hippopotamus have, after so much exquisite

117

yearning, finally embraced, hearts dancing happily above their heads.

Linda thought that by taking a lover she would improve her life. She thought that it would calm her anger and her hurt, buoy her spirits, salve her ego and stop her from over-eating. She thought that it would make her feel better to have someone wonder at her body, get high on just her smell, advise her on what to do. Since the advent of Mark, her temper has mellowed, her sense of humor is sparkling and her complexion glows. She feels loved and desired: a serene earth mother drinking love from the morning dew and a horny goddess sucking in the steaming seed from the blistering night, both. But she still cannot bring herself to leave Paul.

It would be like abandoning a child. She momentarily expects to be struck down by angry, blood-lusting gods, simply for allowing the thought. She imagines herself forced to wander, wild of hair, distraught of eye, ripping with bony hands at her shrivelled breasts, for ever an outcast and stranger in a land populated by couples, by people living two-by-two, hands held, monies joined, the mortgage shared, he good at mixing drinks and she at the making of paella, their children sure and secure, their weekends booked days in advance. In an unfair world, the singles must needs make room for the doubles. Shit.

Will she wind up like Rita, all alone in the Bronx, linked by loneliness to other abandoned souls, gossiping about the manager of the corner supermarket, dissecting the details of the lives of the famous, congregating like pigeons on the stoops and sidewalks, their memories plopping like soft shit onto the stony pavement? Will she wind up like Rita, phoning Patricia every day for news, to see if she needs some advice, a recipe, wants a babysitter, phoning David to be given his wife to talk to instead? Why doesn't Rita blow her brains out instead of sitting there, in the shrunken remains of her home and her life, waiting to die? As they all wait for her to die; dreading the day when she becomes too ill to live alone, and, being reasonable and practical, they agree to send her to a nursing home, everyone worrying about the expense.

The fire crackles, cackles and glows; the snow glances against the glass, turns the world into a crystal chandelier. Linda strokes the hair back from her eyes, thinking of Sunday afternoons, stretching emptily and endlessly, the whole world at a family dinner, watching the afternoon movie, riding their bikes together through Central Park, where old people, stranded, loveless, sit on broken benches, fold papers and blink into the shade. Where do all the single people stay? Do they get drunk at lunch, sleeping through the afternoon until it's dark and the bars are filled again? Do they listen to records, entranced by the humanity and passion, while weaving their own blankets, dyeing their own wool, sheared from sheep kept in someone's backyard in Jersey, with beet juice and bark, re-reading *Finnegans Wake*? Oh, love, love, love, what will Linda do all by herself with only a part-time lover? A log falls, snapping at the silence of the room.

Where would you hide a tree? In a forest.

Where would you hide a lonely person?

She stares, entranced, at the big hippo and the little mouse: he with his sword and swiftness, she with her candy-red mouth and dancing shoes.

If the world is just a giant ark, what will happen to her when she is finally by herself? Linda leans her head against the rounded back of the sofa, like a shoulder of the strong and silent, sighing. She is being foolish, she knows. She would not be alone, not really, not yet: her parents would still be snugly secure in their large white house with the sunporch at the front; her children would still call her home, glue their paintings on the wall. Even if she had no resident man, she would still have her job and her friends, people to visit and places to go. Linda studies her hands and thinks about her face, her eyes, her hair, her breasts and her wonderfully rounded knees. With Paul gone, she would have time and space for Mark.

Linda studies the shadow of her hand across the cushion and thinks about Mark's wife, his sailboat, his career commitments, his yoga class and his community interests. With Paul gone, she would have time and space for other lovers.

119

Linda not quite laughs. Lovers in the house with her children? Less-than-lean and no-longer-young these men, rushing naked through the hallway to use the bathroom, tripping over fire engines and stepping on talking dolls, wheeewheee, I love you, Mommy, I love Daddy too; mature and sophisticated, experienced and smooth, ass in the air and flesh melting, as a door opens and a child asks for water. Lovers rushing to a house filled with children? To a woman whose chin sags and whose stamina is less than what it might be? Do women who have to be back by midnight so that the babysitter won't get mugged on the way home often get wined and dined and lured into dark corners where kisses seem to shimmer in the magnetic night? And what good, in the end, is a lover if there is no love? Is the movement of a penis in a vagina, the pressure of a hard and hairy chest against a soft and willing breast enough to still the demons of the universe, to shut out the immobile and perfect image of death? In Paul's arms she has known both happiness and boredom, satisfaction and sometimes (though not so much lately) joy. But it is Mark's kisses that have burnt across her brain, it is Mark's desire which has melded her orgasms into the breathing of eternity, it is his love which has shattered her with ecstasy. She knows that she is deluding herself with girlish fantasies, drugging herself with sentimental dreams. She knows that it is better to stand alone as a whole person, to need no one, to fulfil yourself rather than another. Linda pulls her hair around her face, making her look like her daughter. She knows all that – and still she thinks that, maybe, it is love that makes a person strong and generous, honest and alive; that with no one to give to, you dehydrate and shrivel, you become little and empty. And how lonely and how deprived she had been before Mark; how little she had had and little known. Her soul had been small and worn, bowed and bitter. There had been no joy in her, no passion and no pride. She had been mumbling, stumbling and miming her way through life, the daughter of, the wife of, the editor of, the mother of, the daughter-in-law of; she had impersonated the person she thought she should be, she had imitated the life she'd been told she should have – and all of that had stopped her ears from hearing, her eyes from seeing, her mind from understanding and her heart from loving. She had given Paul everything – her youth, her dreams, her time, her empty spaces to fill and form – but she had failed to understand what was really wanted, she had failed to grasp the nature of her gift. It is quality, not quantity, Linda now knows, that counts. She rests a hand on the pastel image of the ardent mouse. If Mark really loves her, she thinks, if he really does love, then as long as he exists in one veiled and buttressed corner of her life she could live alone. And Paul, Paul too would come to understand that he should himself find love, real love, to suck him dry and fill him up again.

There is screeching in the hallway and the icy wail of a little boy whose sister has just jammed a snowball down the back of his striped turtleneck. Patricia's laughter rolls into the room. "Oh, Jesus, David, you're such a crybaby," she yells above his outrage, marching towards the fire with him writhing behind her, the footprints of infant abominable snowpeople melting on the hand-hooked rugs.

"Patricia, I will not have that language. I mean it."

Patsy drops her mittens, caked with cracking snow, cupcakes coated with old icing, onto the stone hearth. "What's wrong with saying Jesus? It's not a four letter word. It's not dirty." She pulls off her boots and rubs her toes the way her father does when he comes back from one of his winter country walks. Her eyes are bright, her cheeks are ruddy. "Jesus. It's just a name."

"Stop it, Patricia."

"Jesus."

David flops across his mother's knees, snivelling, his nose dripping onto her trouser leg. He watches his sister as she takes off her things and Linda pulls hat and boots and mittens from his limp body. "Drop dead," he says, quite dispassionately.

"Come on, honey," bending him backwards and upwards. "Help Mommy take your things off you and I'll fix you and Patsy some hot cocoa and cookies."

121

David scowls. "She burnt a hole in my back. My shirt's all wet."

His mother hugs him, fishing out from the top of his pants the still frozen remains of Patricia's weapon. "You go put something dry on and by the time you're ready the cocoa will be, too."

Impassive, David stands before her in his stockinged feet, nose running and face flushed, his belly round and his chin, because of the way he is pushing his head into his neck, nonexistent. "She broke my snowman."

"You don't think that was a snowman, do you?" Rolling her eyes at the ignorance and horror of it all. "That little lump with a couple of rocks stuck in it. You don't think that was really a snowman, do you?"

"Yes." He looks into his mother's eyes.

Linda stands. How do others cope, is it easy for everyone else? "How would you two like me to read you a story?" trying not to sound too enthusiastic since it only makes them suspicious.

"What about?"

"Jesse James?" asks the young girl. "Jesse James got shot in the back."

"He was a legion," contributes the young boy.

"A legend, stupid, not a legion."

"No, not about Jesse James. About a mouse and a hippopotamus."

Patricia holds her nose, but David smiles. "Oh, I know that story," he says. "I know that one."

Linda pats his lovely little head. "No, David, this is a new story. This one was just written. I'd like to see what you and Patsy think of it."

He shakes his head and kicks her in the ankle. "I know the story about the mouse and the hipotamiss. I already know it."

Linda's voice is tolerant and tender. "Sweetheart, this is a different story than the one you know. It hasn't been put into a book yet."

Prostrate in front of the fireplace, her hands clasped in

122

eternal prayer, her eyes closed in timeless sleep, Patricia speaks. "All the books you bring home are exactly the same," she says. "You never bring home any adventure stories or anything like that."

"There's plenty of adventure in this one. It's all about how the mouse and the hippo fall in love but how they can't be together because there is a big wall between them and all the things they have to do before they can finally be with one another."

Patricia rolls onto one side, opening her eyes suddenly, like a baby doll whose eyes have just come unstuck. "That's what I mean," says Patricia. "You never bring home anything real."

And it is just then, as the afternoon begins to close down and the fire to look small, as David slumps off to change his shirt and Patricia rolls across the rug because her back is hot, as Linda hears the wind and remembers how alone she really is, how really alone, that the phone rings. Patricia and David both scream, "Daddy!" racing to Linda's side as she lifts the receiver. But it is not Daddy – at least not theirs. It is Mark phoning from a phone box on Broadway, a pocketful of change chilling on the counter, his dog, whose walk this is, sitting outside the booth, tied to a parking meter.

"Hello."

"Hello. Hello, Linda?"

Four eyes watch her face, four ears listen to her heart bang. "Hi."

There is laughter on the street, horns honking and doors slamming, shouts and chatter, the low lament of Mark's dog as it stares into the early evening blur and has slush sprayed in its face by passing traffic. Mark Schwerner smiles at the writing on the wall, *Suck Cock Come Come Come Eat a Beaver JM&TS4ever.* "Are the kids still up?"

She doesn't accuse him, as she would have accused Paul, or Paul's mother, or almost anyone else in the world, that he is an idiot, of course the kids are still up, it isn't even their supper time yet; she says, "Yes. Yes, I was just going to fix them a snack."

123

Someone has urinated in the corner of the booth, and there are three empty bottles – two beer, one wine – on the floor as well, but he doesn't notice. "Are you busy? You want me to call you back?"

Linda makes signs and faces to the children, go away, and go away they do, but slowly, Patricia's eyebrows raised. "It's not Daddy," she hisses as, slowly and largely backwards, they leave the room. "It's a friend of mine."

"Linda? Linda? Are you there?"

"It's all right. I was just saying something to the kids."

The receiver is cold, the coiled metal covering of the wire as it bangs against his neck is cold, the ledge on which his change rests is cold, his breath like tiny smoke signals is cold. "Should I call you back later? When they're in bed?"

"No. They're gone now. I think there are cartoons on or something." She wants to say oh, darling, how I love you, how I ache for the feel of you inside of me, how I long to hold you like a shield against the starless night, to lick the sweet sweat from your body, to offer myself as the earth offers herself to the sun, to bury all the sorrows and pains of life beneath the timeless wonder of your wild tongue in my mouth, your bedevilled fingers pulling at my breasts. "Where are you calling from?" she asks.

"I'm walking the dog." Sometimes he is jogging, sometimes he is buying a newspaper or taking a walk because the apartment is too stuffy or too noisy, sometimes he is walking the dog. He's never walked the dog so much in the six years that they've had it.

"Is something wrong? Have you had a fight with her?" She used to think that Mark and Marilyn got on very well together. She would see them at dinners and parties and think what a normal couple they seemed, married, together, friendly. Now she knows the truth; now she's been told.

"No." He stamps his feet, squelching into something odorous and soft. "She's fixing dinner. We're having people over. Boring people." Her friends. There is a banging on the booth door, but he doesn't look around. "I just missed you, Linda, that's all. I wanted to hear your voice."

She whispers, "I miss you, too." She looks around, expecting to see her children, the private Sutcliffe police force, watching her from the doorway, taking everything down, accusing her of treason against the state. "I really do, you know."

"I can't wait to be in bed with you," he sighs. The thought of her can almost make him cry: she is to his life like a pearl among the barley.

The door opens, squeaking. "Hey, mister, you wanna get your dog? Your dog's shittin' all over the fuckin' sidewalk."

As Linda says, "It's just a couple of days," Mark turns to face the short, the dark, the bearded young man in the tan leather jacket and green scarf who is pointing to Oliver, shit steaming around him, who seems to be having the runs on the curb.

He motions bewilderment with his hands, whispers, "Long distance."

"What?" asks Linda.

"I don't care about no long distance. There's a law against that, you know."

"Look, honey, I'll call you back later. Will you be up?"

"Mark, what's wrong? What's going on?"

"You gonna do something about that dog? It's shittin' all over the place." There are two or three people watching by now.

"Look, Linda, there's some misunderstanding. I'd better hang up."

She frowns at the phone. Is he with someone? A woman? A girl? Is he really calling from home, has Marilyn caught him, coming in with a taste of the dip for him? Is she trying to hurt him, to kill herself? Is she laughing in that loud, almost gauche, way of hers, you don't mean Linda Sutcliffe, the one with the round face, oh, you've got to be kidding? "Mark, what is going on?"

Oliver howls. "This is just ridiculous," Mark says, to no one. "I can't believe I live like this."

"Mark," and now she is screaming, "Mark, what is happening?"

125

"I can't believe I live like this either," says the young man, putting his hands in his pockets.

Is he going for a knife? Is he going to be mugged? "I love you, Linda," Mark calls into the phone. And hangs it up.

"Mark? Mark?" She shakes the phone, trying to relink them, bring him back. When she turns she nearly collides with Patricia, standing at her side looking like an owl.

"Is the cocoa ready?"

"No, Patricia. No. The goddamn cocoa is not ready."

Patricia picks her nose. "Oh." Patricia pulls one braid. "Well, call us when it is."

Paul can't sleep. He lies flat on his back watching the shadows cast by the welcoming lights of the shops across the street, his own soul hunched inside a trenchcoat, standing beneath a pink neon sign that flashes Hot Corned Beef, the lonely footsteps of his soul echoing in the black and open-ended night, isolated but never alone, hardened but never heartless. Okay, angel, have it your way. Sweetheart, I like you, but I don't have that much to give. He doesn't move, he barely breathes, he is the only person alive; no hands wave for him, no phones ring, no fires burn, no candle flickers.

Next to him Janet snores.

It is ironic, if nothing else, that having spent the entire evening ruining his happiness and peace of mind, having squandered their solitary, rare-beyond-belief evening together on petty female bickering and complaining, she now sleeps, swathed in dreams, caressed by her psyche's angels, while he lies awake, furious and frustrated, wanting to punch her in the head.

Wake up you stupid bitch. But to wake her up would be to get involved with her again, her and her convoluted logic, her and her fucking parents and their bourgeois morals and shallow, materialistic aspirations.

He had arrived in high spirits, bearing wine, roses and the last few pages he'd written. He had kissed her softly but deeply at the door, smiled (in that way he has) at the pains she

126

had taken with her dress, her hair and her gypsy eyes. The glasses were already chilled. Her first words had been, "Oh, darling, I've been looking forward to tonight." He had kissed her right breast through the sheer silk shirt.

And then he had opened the wine and told her how he would sally forth in the morning for bagels and the *Sunday Times*, describing how they would lie in bed and do the crossword together, how he would lift the minuscule crumbs from where they fell between her ice cream breasts with his lascivious, longing tongue. She brought in black olives and chunks of feta cheese dribbled with oil. She had seemed to think it a good idea.

They had stretched out on her imitation goatskin rug and lain in a bubble of silence, the way lovers sometimes do. He had run his fingers along her scalp line, twisting a strand of her hair, smelling like honey and wheatgerm, around his bone like a ring. "I wish we could always be like this," he'd whispered.

Her voice, when she spoke, was not her own. It was the voice of generations of Hansen women, her mother's mothers, women with tight hair and mouths and unlaughing eyes, women with the imaginations of accountants and hearts the size of spider shit.

"Why can't we?" yelped, not whispered. The entire Lower East Side shut down for several seconds. She didn't breathe, she didn't stir, he could hear the building sigh. Outside, he knew, traffic had stopped, people frozen as they brought a hot dog to their lips, or pressed a silver knife blade to a screaming throat, or raised a giggling infant in the air: all stopped, all held suspended in the grasping hand of Janet the She-monster, risen from the seas of her middle-class, puritanical past.

Paul had taken his hand away and placed it across his eyes. "You know perfectly well why we can't."

"No, I don't. You say you love me . . ." her breath breaking in half. "You said your life would be meaningless without me."

And he had rolled on one side, draping his arm across her,

kissing her eyelashes, already starting to mist over. "It would be, Janet. I'd be nothing but a prisoner of time without you, just waiting for it all to be over."

In her young and vulnerable voice she had said, "Then why can't we get married?"

He sat up to take a drink. "Because bigamy is against the law."

"You know damn well what I mean."

"I couldn't do it to Linda, it would destroy her."

"You said you hardly ever see each other any more. You said you never have anything to say." The neck of the bottle clinked against her glass. "You said the only thing that keeps you together is the children."

He helped himself. "That's true. But aside from that you just don't abandon someone you've lived with for nearly fifteen years. You don't trade in wives like cars, Janet. I have a moral responsibility to Linda."

"And what about your moral responsibility to me?"

He picked a piece of olive out from between his teeth with his tongue. "What about it? You've known all along, Janet, all along that I was married and that I was going to stay married. Anything I've promised you – any love or time or friendship – I have given. And you can't deny that."

He thought she might spit at him. "You've taken over my whole life: all my time, all my emotions, all my ambitions. I work with you, I sleep with you, I dream with you. I make everything else fit around you. Everything. Everything moves over for you." He thought she would squeeze her glass to shattering. "And all I get from you is crumbs. Fucking shit piss crumbs."

"That isn't true."

Head shaking, eyes melting, words slipping into his heart like daggers. "Oh, isn't it?"

He stood up, reseating himself in a chair, away from her, the wronged woman. "No, it isn't. And you know goddamn well it isn't. From what you've told me about your lovers, if I walked out of here right now I'd still have treated you better than you've ever been treated before."

"You're a real bastard, aren't you?"

"You should be the expert on that."

"We're not talking about my old lovers, Paul. We're talking about you. What am I supposed to do, spend the rest of my life hoping that your wife is killed in a car crash on the FDR Drive? Is that what you want?" It was then that he had slapped her and the fight had begun in earnest. She wasn't going to go on like this much longer. She wasn't going to throw away the best years of her life on a man who, in the end, would probably retire to teach creative writing part-time in Arizona, where he would spend more time on his fucking magazine, the only thing he really cared about, and Linda could devote more of her time to the plants she was so especially good with. It wasn't the being married; she wanted to be legitimate.

"You'll have to talk to your mother about that." She had thrown the olives at him, still in the bowl.

He explained, yet again, that he could not live without his children, who needed him and adored him and who would, should he so brutally reject their mother, be warped by Linda's bitterness.

"I'm tired of crying," she had cried. "I'm tired of sleeping all alone while you go home and sleep with her."

"How do I know that you do?" She had gone for the dish of cheese, but he'd been too quick for her this time.

"I want us to have a home together. I want us to have a baby." Sobbing against him, pouring her tear-soaked love into his chest. "You said once you wanted to stand on top of the Empire State Building and shout to the world that you loved me."

"And I meant it."

"Then do it, damn you. Do it."

Pushing her tenderly away, caressing her hair, comforting her as he would have comforted Patricia, bruised and violated by a crashing bike, he had said, "I would only fall off and then where would you be? You look awful in black."

But now she sleeps, balled up upon herself, looking gentle and innocent. She cried herself to sleep while he sat in the living room, drinking her Christmas Port, which he hates. She didn't beg him to come to bed with her, she said she didn't care if he slept on the Bowery and woke up stinking of Gypsy Rose and desolation. "And you're not such a terrific lover," she had shrieked at him from the doorway. "You're not so fucking good, you know. It's just because I love you. That's why."

He would have gone home, but the loneliness would have driven him insane. "I love you," he had said, over and over, "I love you. What more do you want?" Prove it, proof, approval, you are breaking my parents' hearts, prove that you love me.

In the muted night-time light, in the room filled with shades and shadows, she looks as though she's made out of satin: satin hair and satin skin and breath like rustling silk. What would he do without her? Go back to being only half alive? Go back to feeling like an automated man, his life defined by its limits – you can have that, do that, reach this, own so much. As though we all live on a cosmic dole: you can have passion, but then you can't have security; you can have children who continue you, but then you can't have romance; you can have money and success, but with it you must take the boredom, the futility of being a fragile mouse in a rusting and squeaking wheel going round round round. What is he supposed to do? go back to his checkerboard game of marriage with Linda – to whom he holds no mysteries, to whom he offers no wonder – as with each year passing they become smaller and smaller to one another, the possibilities of themselves shrinking till all they are is "hello darling, good morning dear, how are you, fine, and you, oh fine, thanks, doing anything interesting today, no, nothing special, why don't we go out for dinner, oh, wouldn't that be nice, did you phone the kids, should we go to Florida during the winter break, I never did like sugar in iced tea".

What is he supposed to do, just drop dead? Just stop living, just throw away his paints and jars of iridescent colours, his shimmering cloths of rainbow hues and gold and silver threads as bright as the center of the sun? Is that what he's supposed to do?

Paul slides like moonlight from the bed, tiptoeing into the tiny kitchen for a drink of apricot nectar, all there is. Should I forget that I am a lover, that I can love? he asks the Ché Guevara poster on the wall by the stove.

The shelves of Janet's refrigerator are shining clean and methodically neat and well-stocked. In the compartment labelled "cheese" there is cheese, in the section labelled "butter" there is butter. Eggs nest contentedly on the egg shelf, vegetables crisp merrily in the vegetable crisper. Nothing is unwrapped, or left with crumbs and a fork on a used plate. There is a jar of ice water and a Tupperware box containing cut onions, wrapped in foil, hot chili peppers and pale-skinned cloves of garlic. Order and safety: that is what she wants from him, not the tempestuous turnings of the universe. Women. He carefully removes a slice of hard salami from its clingwrap protection. Conformity and security: that is what she wants from him, not electric excursions into the self's unknown. Marriage. Women always want marriage, especially the ones who say they don't. A female invention, to ensure that the young didn't die during those long winters when it might be difficult for a nursing mother to scrounge for food.

In the past few weeks – since when? he wonders, cutting himself a slice of English Cheddar cheese, moon sliver – in the past few weeks he has been making, or trying to make, love not to Janet but to her parents. To the Kodachrome couple who gaze out at him with tight smiles and narrowed eyes from within the antique silver frame on Janet's dresser. What has happened to his wood nymph, to the witch-woman who so totally ensnared and enchanted him on that first afternoon so irrevocably passed?

He had been courting her for weeks, encouraging her in her work, exclaiming over her papers, telling her, over coffee after class, about the time he'd been arrested in a Civil Rights march, about his writing, about the semi-illiterate background he'd struggled so hard to overcome, and then one afternoon she had been crying over her boyfriend and he'd taken her to

131

a bar instead. He'd made a pass at her when they got back into the car, but though she'd let him kiss her fiercely he had, in the last analysis, been refused. But still he had pursued her, though she tended to stay in crowds. And then, on what had seemed a perfectly ordinary afternoon, she had stayed after the others shuffled out to ask for the handout from the week before. "I have some in my study at home," he'd said. "We could drive there and get one now." She had shrugged her nymphette's shoulders and smiled her slightly buck-toothed smile. "Okay. I'm free for the afternoon." He had parked across the street, unfastened his seatbelt and said, "Do you want to wait here?" sure that she would. "No," she said, her seatbelt already undone, "I'll come inside, if that's all right." "Oh, sure," running into traffic to lock her side. "We can have some coffee without having to share a table with a bunch of speed freaks." He had made the coffee, gotten her the handout, and even found the book he had been promising to lend her, and then they had stood together, looking at the paintings and photographs on his wall, so close that strands of her hair had clung to his shoulder, like elfin ribbons joining them together. That time, when he kissed her, she kissed him back. That time, when he had reached for her breasts she had reached for his crotch. He had made them drinks and brought them to the bedroom.

Later, as he poured himself from the wet and perfumed sheets to refill their glasses, he had laughed. "I didn't know I was going to get laid this afternoon." She was still in the bed, sitting up, the sheets and blankets across her feet, her breasts luminous against the duskiness of her Easter in Florida tan, and in a voice he had only heard in films had said, "I did," and had moved the gold chain around her neck so that it sparkled against the forest of her hair. She had laughed when he'd said that he didn't think the sheets would dry before Linda got home, and offered to lick the smell of her from his body; she had told him that to have his cock inside her was the most perfect feeling in the world. And later she had said that to lie beside him was the only thing that mattered in the world.

Where had that woman gone? What had demolished that boldness and life?

Now she no longer skimmed the surface of his skin with her searching tongue, begging him to touch her. Now she pushed his hands away, smiled at him indulgently, asked him if he thought he was ever going to grow up, asked him when he was going to start treating her like a real person, when he was going to show her some respect.

It is respect, not love, that she now craves. It is her parents, rolling on towards death in their white Cadillac with no grandchildren to strap in in the back seat, who concern her – not he. He is just a lover; they are emissaries from some joyless, stingy god who, having given her one of life's longer straws, now exacted payment in kind: you are healthy, well-off and wise, therefore you must suffer the boredom of marriage to a respectable man who will give you two children and an all-electric kitchen. They had once been a "we, darling" and now they are a "he" and a "she", a "me" and a "you": the she is her parents' child, born for the sole purpose of reaping the rewards and prizes of life as they see it, and the he is the enemy, the educated savage, the barbaric ingrate in denim and corduroy who wants to take take take while everyone else is forced to give give give.

In the cupboard he finds half a bottle of good red wine, not yet beyond drinking. Paul doesn't need a glass. Janet's parents are concerned about her future. The present they see as not only temporary but unimportant. It is clear from what she tells him that Mom and Dad do not think their daughter's life has yet begun, she is still merely waiting in the wings. They tell her that her future is important to them, that worrying about it is the only thing that keeps them alive. "Where is my future with you?" Janet asks him, is asking him still, in her sleep, as she lies curled up in the other room, as he sits on a bar stool at the pine counter and swills his wine from the bottle like a gunslinger. Future, he has often answered, in a world like this you want a future? Yes, she does.

And she, she who once traced his life with her fingertips, who once stared into his eyes as though the answers to the universe lay there, now asks him what he really thinks of nuclear disarmament, the chance of a world depression, natural childbirth and God. She who once told him he was the most intelligent man she had ever met, now wants to know, seriously, what he feels about juvenile delinquency, crime and the real divisions between women and men. She is also interested in his finances, his retirement plans and his views on fate.

In unguarded moments she asks him about his childhood and his youth, not as a lover wishing to explore and absorb the details of the loved, but as a sociologist doing a survey for her parents, the human computers. Does she call them when he's left, to tell them that he never went to church when he was a kid, that he considers himself a humanitarian and closet Marxist, that he hates synthetic materials and he would rather die than vote Republican? Where other women might say, "He is strong and intelligent and good", Janet would say, "He is a hard worker, he has no expensive habits and he is devoted to his children, though they don't really eat much". Her mother probably has score cards for prospective sons-in-law, and he, Paul, has probably lost 125 points per marriage, wife and child. He blows across the top of the bottle, pretending he is nineteen and drunk in the college bar, playing the kazoo. If only he had known then the immense and pervasively painful things he knows now. If only someone had told him. He puffs out the tune to *San Francisco Bay Blues*, but his heart is humming *Why Don't They Make Love Like They Used to?*

There is a sudden shower of light. "What are you doing out of bed?" A solicitous friend? a nagging wife? a soliciting female?

"I couldn't sleep."

"Why not?"

He puts the bottle down gently, shrugs his shoulders like a child, gazes at her from afar with the eyes of a begging puppy. "Thinking about you," he does not say but breathes.

As Janet moves across the room to wrap her arms around Paul, she says to herself that she never meant to fall in love with him, that it's not her fault he's a married man, that she never wanted to hurt anyone and that it is useless to fight against your destiny. As Janet puts her arms around him she says, "I'm sorry I behaved so badly, darling. I just can't help it. I love you so."

"I'm just not ready now," he says. "I love you more than anything, Janet, but I can't give up my children. Not even for you."

Her head nuzzles into his neck. "I know, Paul, I know. But I can't live without you, I just can't go on like this."

He embraces her back, rubbing his hands in soft circles over her ass. Is there no one true and perfect love? When he thought it was Linda he had gotten it wrong; has he gotten it wrong this time as well?

Janet's building is quiet at this time in the morning, the street deserted. They are the only sound-makers, theirs the only hearts beating. No matter what happens, he knows, this moment will always exist in time, will always be happening, the two of them alone and suspended, being electrocuted by love.

"Let's go to bed, Janet," he whispers. "Janet, let's go to bed."

Uptown, Rita sleeps and dreams a dream that is not really a dream but a memory composed of many memories. She is sitting at the kitchen table with her best friend when she was four, Susan Huttenmeyer. She and Susan are drinking tea from plastic cups like the ones Lillian had as a little girl. They must be playing house because they are talking about things like spring cleaning and what to serve for supper. Susan says that she wants four children, two boys and two girls, and that they are all to have blonde hair and blue eyes and to be well-behaved. Rita says that she wants at least six children and she doesn't care what they are, as long as they are not all the same. They eat toast and strawberry jam and wipe their mouths with handkerchiefs, not touching the lips but just the corners. Susan says that she is worried about her babies

135

having the colic, but Rita is worried about scarlet fever. The sleeping Rita is not sure, but she thinks that they are in the country, even though the kitchen in which they sit is the one her mother had in Brooklyn just before the war. It is a good day, there is sunshine and there is plenty of toast and tea. And then Walter comes in. They are four, but he is forty. He is wearing his old plaid shirt with the patched elbows and one pocket missing and his fingers are stained an orangy-brown from twenty-five years of smoking Camels. As soon as he enters, Susan gets up, hurrying to go. "I was just going," she says, and Walter says nothing. Rita, so short next to her already greying husband, offers him tea and toast but he wants none of it. "Isn't there any supper?" he asks. But it is morning, it is morning in the countryside of Brooklyn, off Flatbush Avenue, and there is no supper. "You mean you've just been sitting around all day and you haven't fixed any supper?" Rita begins to cry. She cries so hard that she starts to grow, stopping when she reaches twenty and Walter's hand is up her dress. "Don't," she hisses, not sure whether she should mean it or not. "Don't." "Don't worry," Walter whispers, his hand hot against the cotton of her panties, pressing as though with enough pressure she would pop out, ripe, into his palm, "don't worry, I'm not going to hurt you." "I really have to go," sings Susan, "I really have to go." And Walter, without moving, screams, "Get out of here you old bitch! Get the hell out of my house! Go back to your husband where you belong!" Rita, now thirty, pushes him off of her, starts throwing little blue plastic cups with white handles at him, crying that they have no life, that she knows he has another woman, crying that he hocked the ring her mother had given her for her eighteenth birthday. "You lousy son-of-a-bitch! You lousy son-of-a-bitch!" And then he is punching Susan, who is not Susan any more but Rita's mother when she was thirty, calling her whore whore whore, dirty castrating bitch, while Rita screams for money, why isn't there ever any money, why can't we live like everybody else. As Rita wakes into the stormy dawn, she is running down a side street in the Bronx, looking more lovely than she ever was, and though her eyes are dry and her mouth is hard she is mourning Walter, a blue and rubbery infant in her arms, searching in every house for the coffin in which to lay him. But there is no small wooden box for the keeping of trinkets or broken babies, there is no incensed altar with a priest before it, chanting to the hosts of heaven, linking the unknown with the unknowable; there is only Rita, so young and so beautiful, so depressed and so deranged, stumbling through the blind blocks with her dead child, her husband, Walter, in her arms.

At first, Rita doesn't realize that she is awake. She thinks she might be dead because she feels no pain – but then her eyes pick out the landmarks of her room, the door and closet, bureau, mirror and hope chest. And then the pain begins, and Rita remembers her dream, and forgets it again as the pain begins to steadily chomp its way through her body. Someone else, someone like Paul, maybe, might liken her to Prometheus, bound on a mountain top, having her liver eaten every night. It would work well in Paul's book, as an image. But Rita's body won't be healed in the morning, nor will she have to do this for hundreds of years. Rita thinks of her illness as some sort of divine punishment, some pre-salvation cleansing, which at least gives her the consolation that this won't go on for ever. Rita's sins were little ones.

Does Rita believe in hell? She has believed at times that she lived in hell. She believed, when he died, that Walter went to hell. She pulls the blankets around her, closing her eyes against the memory of her dream, of the carcass she carried just moments before. But there had been a funeral for Walter. A funeral where everyone was very kind, friends and family not seen for decades, squeezing her hand, patting her black shoulder, gazing into her clear blue eyes with earnestness and sympathy, honesty and concern. If there is anything I can do, if there is anything that you need, you or the kids, anything, just say the word. How brave she had been, they had said, how brave and strong, not crying, for the sake of the children, not breaking down, an almost-white handkerchief balled up in her fist, her hands plump and useless on her lap or hanging down in front of her searching for the heart of the world. Rita, Rita, Rita, voices without bodies, faces without voices; Rita, Rita, Rita, so sad, sad, sad. Grief. They had looked at her and looked away, talking to one another around her, about high schools and colleges, jobs and vacations. You should come and see us, come up for a weekend, you and the kids, get some good clean air in you, vegetables from the garden, they had said, these people with whom they had once gone to bars and clambakes, these people who still remembered the time Paul burnt a hole in the dining room table. Yes, she had answered, her muscles locked in something not quite a smile, yes, that would be nice, wouldn't that be nice. They had brought baked ham and roasted turkey, loaves of bread and bottles of wine and whiskey. Whiskey for Walter. Cans of beer for the dead man with his polished shoes pointing towards heaven. Offerings of food for the final homeward haul. All of them looking at him with gentle faces, glad not to have been going with him.

And they had plied her with sandwiches, with cake and potato salad. Not hungry but you have to eat. Putting mouthfuls in, not remembering five minutes later whether or not she had eaten anything. Answering questions, carrying on conversations, not remembering five minutes later whether or not she had heard anything. They had brought her cups of coffee, glasses of liquor, coming up to her in spaces and saying in hushed voices, are you sure you're all right, do you want to lie down, do you want to go for a walk, don't you want to cry, to cry, to drown away the night? No tears. Lillian weeping, scars of mascara, rings of eyeliner dripping tragedy down her cheeks; Paul contained, eyes glazed. Everyone had said that Rita was in shock; the veteran widows, the mothers who had buried babies in cigar boxes, all had agreed. She's in shock. It'll come later.

How many times had Rita said to him, "I'll see you rot in hell, you bastard, I'll see you rotting in your grave"? And just before he'd died, when they thought he would be coming home, she'd said, "Don't worry, Walter, I'll bury you yet".

138

And she hadn't cried. She hadn't wanted to give him the satisfaction.

She lies still on her bed, in a room made eerie by night, in a room patrolled by ghosts, and thinks that maybe she is crying for Walter at last – crying for being so alone. At the funeral someone had said, hand patting hand, "I always think that in some ways Death is like a messenger of peace". Rita suddenly remembers that now, something she barely heard at the time. And she remembers her reply. "Messenger of peace?" Rita had asked with her dry, empty eyes. "Messenger of Peace is the name of a racehorse."

*   *   *

He placed the fragile, gilded angel at the top of the tree. Is it straight? he called. Standing in the doorway, she tilted her head to one side, mumbled, mmmm, wiping sugar from her hand onto her apron. He climbed down, standing beside her, beautiful, beautiful, the tree and her and them. She held his hand. First Christmas. The new lights glimmered, bubbled and glowed, a personal penny arcade, a miniature magic show. The voices of carollers stretched through the snow-dulled streets. Ice patterns grew on the windows. The singers passed the building, their words filling up the spaces of the night, oh, joy to the world, the Lord has come, let Earth receive her King. A perfect Christmas, she thought. A perfect Christmas, he whispered, hugging her to him, and every other dream of joy and peace, every memory of wonder and love melted beside their union and that moment when the silver ball reflected them, head to head, so safe, so strong, so sure. For on that night the world was a Christmas card, where the snow was always snowing and the carollers always carolling, someone always winking. That night everything was laughter and memories of laughter; hope and promises of hope. Beautiful girls were being kissed by handsome young men, and old women were reliving their pasts. From just the way the red light near the top of the tree shone against the gold, bead-wrapped ball it was certain that the couples would all be happy and the pasts had all been good. That night they made love in the living room, beneath the rainbow lights.

The old lady wakes into the hole of the night. There is no sound of breathing. Can she still feel him?

And then returns to her sweet, her dreamless sleep.

★   ★   ★

6

The apartment is darkened and hushed. The radiators hiss, the electric clock in the kitchen whirrs, the cat purrs in its sleep, dreaming of slick fish swimming straight into her mouth. No children laugh or chatter, no news is announced, no music squirms between the spaces. The children are spending the weekend with Rita and their father is in California. In the master bedroom, their mother sits astride her lover, his penis inside her, leaning back against hairy legs, sipping champagne and smoking hashish from a hand-carved silver pipe. He holds the glass towards her, she passes back the pipe, grazing his white, unmuscled chest with her newly hennaed hair.

"We'll have to get up soon," she chants. "We really must."

"Why?" He speaks from within a magical cloud of smoke, Alice's caterpillar, unconcerned with the daily logistics of living. "Today is a holiday. Today is a celebration." He exhales puffs and kisses.

"What are we celebrating, then?" pressing down on him just enough to make them both cease from smiling and thinking and talking for a second. He fills his mouth with wine, rises towards her, pulls her to him, empties his mouth into hers.

"You tell me," tell me tell me, licking teeth and lips and tongue, tell me tell me tell me.

"That it's Saturday."

"What else?" biting lip and tongue and neck, oh, more more more.

141

"That we're alone."

Kissing jaw and neck and opened lips, "What else?"

"That we have two whole days together and we don't have anything we have to do and we have two more bottles of champagne in the fridge."

He can rub her breasts and make her sigh, he can pull at her full-moon nipples and watch her open to him, coming through the centuries, pushing through eternities, with mad lips and crazed cunt dismissing everything in time except the impact of their meeting. He can do all that. "Is that all?"

She is soft, nearly coy; she is a member of a sacred, a secret sect which gives her special benedictions, immunity and quality; which not only permits the foolish and the trite, the pompous and the smug but infuses them with timelessness and truth, encapsulating in the all too human the ultimate fruits of humanity. "Isn't that enough?"

"There's no such thing as enough," time, peace, life, love.

"Let's see . . ." daubing his unused breasts with wine and sucking it off, smearing her begging teats with wine and sucking it off. "We can celebrate the avocado we had for lunch, the Moo Gai Pan we'll have for supper, the day your parents met, the night I decided to stay in New York, the judgment shown by one and all in sending Paul to California, your wife's skiing weekend, and we can celebrate the sun for shining on the vineyards and on California and the revolutionaries for making this the kind of country that the Schwerners would want to forsake their potato crop for."

Linda laughs, liltingly, blissed by the belief that she can do nothing wrong or empty or silly; blessed by the knowledge that the entire history of man has happened to provide her with this happiness. And Mark laughs, grandson and greatgrandson of bent and beaten peasants whose survival was never so much a testament to life as a sort of vengeance on it, son of silent Elliot and schizophrenic Rose, who, after thirty years of hiding out in Brooklyn, waiting for the world to end, are now in Florida waiting for doomsday under the palms, Mark, descendant of pray-ers, mourners and sufferers

142

whose lives could only be released by death, Mark laughs and gently bounces the lovely shiksa on his prick.

"Oh, yes," he giggles, "we'll celebrate America, America, America."

"I love you."

"I love you."

"Love."

"You."

"Love."

"Marry me."

She rises up and stretches out, sucking him in and in and in. "I have nothing to wear, nothing to wear."

"I'll cover you with honey and flowers that shine like jewels. I'll fill you with sweet white wine and drink until you're dry and beg for me to clothe you with semen and kisses. Marry me."

Nurturer, she stops his mouth with nipple; nymph, she teases at his teeth. "Where would we live, we have nowhere to live."

"We'll live in a white room with glass tables and satin cushions on the floor – and no TV. Just we, just you and me. Marry me."

She rides up and down, down and up on his screaming cock. Rides him up and rides him down, pushing her lips open against him, oh darling darling darling him. "Mark," she shoves the words out, pushing them to him with her tongue, lifting and shifting so that it is just the tip of him being circled and encircled by her. "How many angels can dance on the head of a pin?"

"Just one," pulling her to him. "Only one."

Janet is happy. She is the happiest she has been since the day she first arrived at Columbia University, ten years ago, with a foot locker, two suitcases and a tailored red wool suit for sorority teas, knowing, as she sat on her new bed in her new room in her new college in her new city, that the world would never be the same again. Then, she had felt, for the first time, an adult. Now, she feels, for the first time, a wife. Mrs Sutcliffe, signed on the register, introduced at cocktail parties, walked arm-in-arm along the healthy, happy, sunny California streets, kissed on the forehead in foyers and doorways, called "honey". Mrs Paul Sutcliffe, privy to familiar and secret looks across rooms, ordered for while in the ladies' room, answered casually as "dear". Yes, dear, okay, honey, shall we go now, what do you think?

Janet does not look on this as a holiday, but as a sample. And to prove that, she has written to her parents, a hotel postcard, smiling, well-cared-for couples by the pool, saying that she and Paul are here on a mixture of business and pleasure. She has never mentioned him by name before, she has never let them know he has either a constant identity or a job that would enable him to fly to California and work in the sun with their daughter. Hitherto, he has always been described with shrugging shoulders and brief generalizations, as though he were not one man but ten, not a man in her life but a series of tiptoeing lovers. Her parents, fearing the worst, have always suspected that there was something really wrong with him; that he was a legless veteran (Janet was always the sort of child to bring home strays and sick cats) or black (Janet always was impressionable and idealistic – easily swayed by big city trends). Now they will be reassured; now they will know this is real, this is serious.

She is so happy, in fact, that she is not even bothered that, while she bathes and creams and scrapes the stubble from her legs with an orchid-colored razor, he sits on their bed talking to his other wife, Linda the loser. For Linda is losing, of that Janet is sure. Linda has been left behind in the barren wastes of winter to look after the children and the cat and make sure the mail is answered and his study dusted, just another mother in the life chain, while Janet has been chosen as friend and woman, companion and cohort. Janet rubs scented oil onto her lovely legs and rolls deodorant under her arms, having forsaken sprays because of Paul's concern about the ozone layer. Linda is losing at love, and Janet is winning; Janet began as an obsession, and now Linda is the omission. Janet

144

plucks at her eyebrows and examines her nostrils. She would feel sorry for Linda if it were not for the knowledge – which only Janet has been clear-sighted enough to gather and which she has been far too generous and tactful to ever pass on – that Linda has never really been good enough for Paul. He has outgrown her, he has left her behind – she was never really his destined mate, but merely a youthful diversion; she was useful, perhaps even necessary, in the formative years of his talent and career, offering domesticity and stability, but now, like bellbottoms and meditation shirts, she no longer fits. She puts pearls in her earlobes. The boy Paul was needed Linda; the man he is needs Janet. Janet doesn't view the life of the world as a beginningless, endless, constantly connected saga, but as a haphazard collection of short stories – when one is done another must be begun.

She wraps a rose-colored towel around her and flips off the bathroom light. She knows what the working title for those new stories is: Paul and Janet. And it's going to be not a collection but an omnibus.

"So everything's all right?" Paul is saying into the white Princess phone, miming as she drifts past him that he's only just gotten through. "How much did he say the brakes would cost?" making his hand into a cup, pouring air across his lips. "Oh, for God's sake, Linda. Did you remind him we only had them done last fall? Did you make him itemize it for you?" He shakes his head and lowers his eyelids; he sighs and wipes the sweat of suffering from his brow.

She smiles sympathetically from across the room, making it a double. The towel slips just a little.

"Yes, I know. I know. I'm not blaming you . . . Of course I'm not . . . Linda, for Chrissake, I don't think you're in league with the garage. I just want to make sure that you followed my instructions . . . Well, you've never really had a head for details, have you? All right, Linda, if that's what it'll cost, then that's what it'll cost. And you remembered my suede jacket, right? I'll need it when I get back. Linda." He turns only inches away from her as she approaches with his bourbon. He lowers his voice and she pretends to be looking for clean underwear. "Linda, you don't have to shout because this is long distance. It's all done electronically these days. It's not two cans and a wire, you know." He smiles at her profile, eyes grazing, a sad and wistful smile, the smile he normally reserves for students who disagree with him. She smiles back, reassuring, a port in the storm of mediocrity which daily threatens to engulf him.

"Put on David. I want to tell him the surprise I've gotten. He'll love it . . ." There is a pause not of rest but of seizure, and in that pause the towel drops and the white bikini panties begin to move up her newly tanned and silken legs. "What do you mean he's not there? It's nearly his bedtime . . ." She comes to have him hook her bra, sits docilely, almost obsequiously, in front of him. "At my mother's? What the fuck are they doing at my mother's?" Instead, he slides the straps down along her arms, pinching first one then the other teardrop tit. "I really don't believe you, Linda. You know she hasn't been looking well lately. What if something happens while the kids are with her? How can you be so inconsiderate .·. . I could understand if you had her come down to keep you company . . . but why you should foist the kids off on her the minute my back is turned . . ." he turns, he twists and pulls the straining nipples, like putty in his hands. "No, Linda. I'm not suggesting any such thing. I just don't understand why the first thing you do when I go away is to stick the kids with my mother . . . You don't even have the car. What if she has a stroke, God forbid? What if there's an emergency? You planning to take the subway to the Bronx? By the time you got there she'd be buried and the kids would be in foster homes . . ." he pours half of his drink across her breasts, knowing how it trickles down her flesh, staining not like rain the rayon and acetate briefs. "All right, all right. I don't want to pay a dollar a minute to argue with you. I know you deserve some time for yourself . . . just don't pretend you're doing it because you're such a goddamn altruist." She lies back,. waiting, his hand resting on her belly like a frog sitting on a log. "Yes, of course I got something for Patricia . . ." hand pushing down, springing up, landing

146

on the receiver as he changes ears. "Are you accusing me of favoritism now, is that it?" From an awkward angle she gently massages his chest in its Fruit of the Loom cocoon, radiating her trust and loyalty and just a touch of lust. "Linda. What the hell is going on with you? Are you having some sort of crisis? Are you getting your period?" Janet smirks, though not the way Liz would have. "Here I am, stuck in some god-awful hotel room, locked all day long in smoky rooms with a bunch of mincing imbeciles who couldn't analyze a Classic Comic if their lives depended on it . . . I am nearly bored to tears, Linda. You seem to think I'm having some sort of holiday . . . but I'm not, I'm working. I am tired and lonely and I miss my children and I miss my wife and I call because I want to hear your voices and tell you all how much I love you and what do I get? What do I get, Linda?" She has turned now, nibbling his undershirt into a bandage around his chest. "Shit, Linda, that's what I get. Shit. My kids aren't even there . . ." and his voice cracks, much as his image of the burning home-fires has cracked, the image he had of the three of them sitting around the table, his place empty, talking about what Daddy must be doing at that very moment. "I know, I know. I'm sorry, too, honey. I've had a very long day . . ." she is moving downwards now, tenderly undoing his button-fly Levi's. "Linda, there's a waiter here who's the brother of the one we had in Miami that time. You remember . . . the one whose neighbor asked him to babysit and then didn't come back for three weeks . . . yes, that one . . . he even walks into things the same way . . ." by moving slightly he permits her to slide down his pants without disturbing the chuckle in his conversation. "I'd better go. I'll call tomorrow, will the kids be back? What do you mean you're not sure? Have you taken them out of school? Okay, okay, I'll call tomorrow . . . in the evening, of course, I'm busy all day. Right. You're sure there aren't any messages you've forgotten to give me? And you're all right? Why don't you take yourself to a movie, it might cheer you up . . ." and up and up and up he rises, swelling into her sweetly dripping mouth. "Good night, honey. Get an early

147

night, indulge yourself a little as long as the kids aren't around . . . I'll ring you tomorrow. Night." Just before hanging up, he might have heard another voice call "Linda!", faintly, but he is more concerned with dissolving his worries in the whirlpool of her cunt; with banishing the fanged and horned devils of doubt that are trying to destroy his freedom with the force of his orgasm.

When he enters her it is with such strength that she misses a breath, yields to him like grass before a singing scythe. She will always think of this as the moment of the transfer, formal, of power. He will always think of it as the moment of the proof of his power. But then, he always does.

Linda is feeling guilty. "I didn't even ask him how his talk went," she says, sitting herself in a chair.

Mark yawns. "Maybe he hasn't given it yet. He would have told you if he had."

"That's not the point," almost forgetting not to scowl.

Several speeding thoughts streak across his face. "What is the point?"

She takes a handful of the popcorn that he has made as a treat, wondering if it will get stuck between her teeth as it always does. "The point is that I could at least have asked him how his talk went. It's important to him."

"Is it important to you?"

Their eyes engage, then disengage, then engage again. "It has nothing to do with me. There's nothing wrong with showing a little interest in someone else."

He does his one trick of catching three pieces of popcorn in his mouth at once, then stretches as he chews. "What interest does he show in you? The only things he's interested in are his laundry and his car."

"That's not true, Mark, and you know it."

"How do I know it? If he shows any interest in you he does it by telepathy."

She simply stares.

"Well. How does he show all this interest in you? By telling you to go to bed early? If he didn't need you to run his errands and earn half his income he'd probably chain you to the bed while he's away. For your own good, of course. Because he's so concerned. Wouldn't want you to run around loose when he's not here to protect you."

Still she stares, but she is not seeing Mark in his jeans and old sweater, fragments of popped corn clinging to his chest, his presence filling up the chair in which he sits and the room which once belonged to the Sutcliffe family but which now belongs to no one. Instead she sees Linda, at twenty-two and twenty-five, at twenty-eight and thirty-one, at thirty-two and twenty-three: click clack, saved from the seductions of a jazz guitarist by a passionate Paul; click clack, bringing him coffee, sandwiches and sympathy while he sat up all night studying for his exams; click clack, caressing his head as he leaned his ear against her belly listening to their child; click clack, waking up that first night he didn't come home until late with him penetrating her from behind, his penis rhythmically shattering the dark warmth of her dream. Click clack click clack, Linda running, Linda walking, hurrying, resting, working, playing; like a one-woman chorus line she steps and kicks, plumber in one scene and whore in the next, and always, there in the center of the stage stands Paul, a charming smile on his lips and the determination to fire anyone who tried to up-stage him in his heart. "Don't you see, Linda," Mark is saying, "don't you see that he's never done anything for you – just for you as the sort of person you really are? The only time he's really shown any interest in you is when he's been remodelling you into the woman he thinks you should be. Linda, I've watched you for months and months now. Even before we really met. You've been living on your nerves for God knows how long. I can remember, Linda, I can remember seeing you walking down the hallway and thinking to myself, that woman's absolutely exhausted. She doesn't know whether she's coming or going." His hands are spread out on his knees, his body tilts towards her, his eyes scan hers for some sort of response. "You've been going through life like a zombie, Linda. I can remember seeing you at a party one time and thinking to myself, that's

149

one of the most unhappy women I've ever met." She blinks, and almost smiles. "Really. You were worn out and wound up – and, you know what else?" there is a small space in which she doesn't nod, or shrug, or say, "No, what?", "you lacked any possibility of joy. That's what I remember most: a total absence of joy."

And still she stares, and he stares back, his face contorted with compassion, while silently her brain screams, so what so what so what, so what does that prove, you supercilious bastard, so what do you know, you with your boring wife and your epileptic dog, you with your tired little projects and hobbies and weekends in Hoboken with one of the secretaries, who the fuck do you think you're kidding? where the hell do you get off, patronizing my life, feeling sorry for me, telling me what a crummy life I have, what about you, huh, what about you, there's nothing wrong with me, I have everything anyone could want, just look around, tell me what you think I don't have that you have besides your goddamn precious cock, just tell me, so what you don't like my husband, you jealous jerk, so what so what so what?

Miss Molly, who has been sleeping quietly on top of Mark's jacket at one corner of the couch, now wakes up, blinks slowly and stretches her furry little legs across the corduroy, catching her claws into the leather patch of the left elbow. Miss Molly, fully awake now, listens to the sounds in the air and decides to go see what's happening in the kitchen. Her tail is just clearing the doorway when everything goes smash – Linda's face and Linda's voice and Linda's heart – and the room is filled with the not unfamiliar sound of earthly wailing, the gasping sobbing that can drop the moon from the sky.

He goes and leans over her, arms encircling, and soon they are both on the floor, she slumped against him as he strokes her hair and coos "honey", holds her shaking bones and dying flesh against his own, whispering below the slamming of their hearts, "It's all right, it's all right, it's all right, you aren't alone any more."

★

150

The children have been bathed and dressed in cuddly pajamas and terry cloth robes, and their hair, dried by Rita's old electric dryer, the one Lillian gave her when she got her new beauty shop model, fluffs around their small heads like fairy auras. They sit side by side on their grandmother's sofa, eating potato chips and drinking the blue cream soda their father says will rot their teeth out before they're ten. The children are having a very good time, and so is Rita.

They have gone shopping and come back with cheap toys that will be lost and forgotten before the week is over; they have had double-scoop ice cream cones from the luncheonette down the street where the man calls Rita "dear" and them "darling" and he and Rita always say things to one another like "remember when yours were little?", or "not like when we were young", or "they're all I have left, I'm just waiting to die"; they have gone to the park and fed the pigeons while Rita sat on a bench and watched them, the cold making her eyes water. They have visited two of Rita's friends, also old ladies with, for some reason, tissues sticking out of the necklines of their housedresses and a medicine smell clinging to them like veils, and everywhere they have gone they have been pinched and patted, told they were sweet and beautiful and given candies and change. Neither of them has understood more than a fraction of the conversations which have gone on over their heads or behind them while they sat on worn hassocks and watched the kids' shows they are always assured they will love – but they know that they are not only wanted guests but that they are safe here, among the old women, wrapped in childhood and protected by memories and dreams of which they have no idea. At home they have to steal attention from creatures called "work" and "for grown-ups", from demons called "tired" and "depressed" and "busy", and they must scurry and whisper beneath the adult chantings of "not now, not now", "later, later, later" and "in a little while". But here, down among the old women with their stories and pictures of vanished babies and their simple songs and comforting rhymes, all they have to do is smile and remember to say please and thank you.

Rita says that she is in love with the tough cop in David's second favorite program, the one who shows no sympathy for any criminal whatsoever and who would rather die than take a bribe or follow an order he didn't like. "Yuk," says Patricia. "You can't mean that, Grandma, he's ugly."

"He's not ugly to me," says Rita.

"He's the toughest cop in the world," says David.

Patricia squinches up her nose. "He's an old man. Who would fall in love with an old man like that?"

"He's younger than I am," says Rita. "He may be an old man to you, but he's younger than I am."

"But he's fat. You're not fat, you're skinny," leaning her own slim body against the old woman's bones. "Daddy says that there's something wrong with people who are fat. They're not normal."

Once upon a time, when men liked their women with a little meat on their bones, Rita was plump, plump and pink-skinned, a good-looker. And once upon another time, not so long ago, when her body was normal, she was not as skinny as she is now. "He's a real man, fat or not," says Rita, "and there aren't many of them left."

"Bang bang, ptooie ptooie," chants David. "When I grow up I'm going to be a policeman, and I'll shoot anybody I catch doing something wrong. I'll have lots of medals and a gun hidden under my coat."

"Daddy won't let you," dipping a chip into her soda. "Daddy doesn't like cops."

"What nonsense," laughs Rita, ruffling Patricia's fine fine hair. "Everyone likes the police."

"Outlaws don't," corrects the boy. "Outlaws and gangsters hate cops. They kill them dead."

"Everyone else likes them. What would happen to us if we didn't have laws and policemen to make sure that people didn't break them? You wouldn't be able to walk down the street."

Patricia sighs. "Daddy says you can't walk down the streets

now. He says you can't even walk in your own building any more without getting mugged."

Rita shifts uncomfortably between the two children. "Then how can he say that he doesn't like policemen?"

"He says they're all crooks. He says they think like soldiers and they're dangerous. He says it's like giving guns to chimpanzees."

"He certainly didn't learn that sort of thinking from me," says Rita, still defending herself against the unspoken charges of bad mothering.

David says, "Bangbangbangbangbang."

"And what does your mother think?"

Patricia shrugs. "She always agrees with Daddy."

"Everyone agrees with Daddy," adds David simply.

"Your daddy's a very smart man," and he is her son, the college professor, a man who writes books and gives lectures, and whose articles she has never read but has had shown to her, and whose father would have been proud of him. "He takes after your grandfather. He was a very smart man, too." She pats a knee of each. "He would have loved you too, he loved kids." The children breathe and chew. "He was quite a character, your grandfather."

David frowns. "Like in a story?"

"No, like interesting." The wild and winning Walter, with his lopsided smile and crazy charm; he might not have been somebody, but he wasn't just anybody. I am your husband, you are my husband, I am your husband, you are my husband, the unbreakable circle of demands, then give me, then give me back, then give me, then give me back, a dead-end deal, but laws are laws and rules are rules – and if he were here now she wouldn't be alone, it would all have been worth it. Though that isn't quite the way that Rita thinks; thinking it, her life – which at times has seemed so torturously long and now seems to have been no longer than a child's night – must have been worth all she has put into it, she hugs her child's children and decides that in the morning, if she is feeling up to it, she will make them french toast, the way Paul and Lillian used to love it.

153

"If I'm not a policeman," David goes on, reminded, now that the commercial is on, that there are other things in life, "then I'll be a truck driver."

Rita brushes potato chip crumbs from the front of his robe. "A truck driver? Why a truck driver?"

He stares at her through his empty glass. "Because I like trucks."

"Truck drivers don't know anything," snaps Patricia, who is – after all – her father's daughter. "Truck drivers are dumb. I'm going to be famous when I grow up. I'm going to be a famous space explorer. They'll probably name a planet or something after me."

Rita thinks it's funny that when she was a child they all wanted to be nurses or teachers or secretaries and now here is her own granddaughter wanting to be a space pilot. "What'll you do with your family while you're out exploring space?" she teases.

Patricia doesn't smile. "I'm not going to have a family," and her tone is one of certainty; her look is that of one who knows.

"Everyone has a family."

"Priests don't have families."

"That's different. Everyone else does. Don't you want to have a little girl like you?"

"No," says Patricia. "I'm never going to have children."

"For heaven's sake, why not?"

"Because I'm not," and she straightens her robe tightly over her knees. "Children are a pain in the ass."

"Patricia! That's an awful thing to say. We all love you so much, how can you say a thing like that?"

David burps, then, intrigued by the sound, burps a few times more.

"Stop that disgusting noise," she commands, but her eyes are on Patricia, time-warp changeling, dropped from some copless, childless universe where two blood-red suns boil over an argentine landscape of skeletal mountains and skeletal trees and android nomads with micro-chip minds shuffle from non-sunset to non-sunset, not looking for an answer

154

to anything, programmed to know that there has never been any question.

"Oh, can't we stay up for just one more show?" pleads Patricia, eight again and normal, as normal as any of them. "It's a comedy."

Later, sleepless on the couch, Rita listens to the nothing, mechanical noises of the night and remembers the summer she went to a charity camp on Long Island and her parents had to come and bring her back to the steamy city, she had been so so homesick, so homesick that she had thrown up the vanilla ice cream they gave them every supper for dessert.

Mark has returned home from Linda's; Oliver has returned home from the kennel; Mark's wife has returned home from the Catskills. Mark is depressed because he can no longer endure living a lie; the dog is stuffed with the liver he was given as a bribe because of Mark's irrational fear that the animal will somehow contrive to tell Marilyn where he has been all weekend; Mrs Schwerner is in high spirits because she always enjoys herself when she gets away from her husband for a few days – considering him, as she does, one of the most boring humans on the face of the planet.

Patricia and David have returned home, toting between them a garish plastic shopping bag filled with junk and opened boxes of cookies. Patricia and David are also in good moods, happy to have been away and happy to be back. And Linda, of course, has also returned. Guiltily and dutifully, she has set the washing machine to washing, the beds to airing and herself to bustling through the apartment with something approaching, though never quite attaining, riotous good cheer.

It is as she is changing the sheets of their bed that she discovers, miraculously clinging between the headboard and the mattress, one small, golden hoop. Even had she owned twenty-four pairs of earrings exactly like it, she would have known at once that it wasn't hers. And it isn't.

155

Now she kneels on the floor by David's bed, helping him into his pajamas. The golden earring is burning a hole through the pocket of her jeans. Patricia has been allowed an extra half hour of television, because Linda doesn't feel she can cope with her just yet: Patricia always fills her with guilt, confusion, ambiguity and rage; David makes her feel confident and sure.

There was a time, in fact, when he was very small, that she thought he held the secret of the universe; that between his chubby little hands he grasped, firmly and sticky with peanut butter and jelly, the key to the meaning of life. He would sit in his stroller and she would push him up and down the streets of Upper Manhattan, past junkies, bums and winos, past teachers, bankers and poets, and he would sing to himself the entire time. Sometimes he would sing one word over and over (green, or cookie, or shoe) and sometimes he would sing several words, either related (like happy day or smiley sun), or unrelated (like floor, or bird, or milk). Through smog and snow and pouring rain, through humidity, sun and whipping wind – she pushed, he sang. People might keel over beside them, brakes might squeal and lives crumble, victims of hatred and victims of neglect might stagger or shuffle across their path – but still David would sing, hands embracing angels in the air, face euphoric with inner delight, his little voice lilting into the wind. Linda always knew that it was because David Knew. Behind him, she would push, her arms draped with purse and shopping and an old Greek bag bearing emergency diapers. When she looked before her she saw a battlefield of ghosts to be gotten through; a mined war zone to negotiate before she reached the safety of her home, four locks and alarm on the door. When he looked before him, sitting in his wheeled throne, he saw the wisdom of the universe spread out between the all-night groceries and liquor stores; the glories of heaven and its minions fluttering diaphanously above the mutinous multitudes. She looked before her and saw the streets coated with pigeon shit and tin cans; he looked before him and saw the streets of Manhattan paved with gold. It was like being the mother of a prince or a prophet.

But these states of knowing are often transient. He might, at thirty or so, regain that early level; at four, however, he is happy not because he knows All, but because he knows nearly nothing. Patricia, on the other hand, has never known, has always been a querulous, suspicious and wary child, waiting to have her toy taken away, waiting to be given stewed prunes, squinting up at the sun, waiting for the deluge. Patricia takes after her mother.

Linda plays train with the plastic zipper on David's sleeper, chugchugchugchug, chooo chooo, rushing the zipper up with a whooshing sound, snapping the top flap to. David laughs hysterically, and she hugs him, kissing his shiny clean forehead, quacking near his ear. He won't always be this easy to please.

He hangs on to her shoulders as she tries to straighten up. "Read me a story."

Gently, lovingly, she disengages his rubber-doll arms. "Not tonight, sweetheart, Mommy's tired."

Storm clouds threaten the sunshine child, his caterpillar eyebrows inch closer together. "Just a short one."

"Tomorrow, David," pushing him with a mother's caress towards the bed. Her body is weak with weariness, her knees ache, screams rise from her throat – she touches, without being aware, the earring in her jeans.

He flops onto the floor as though his bones have collapsed. "I want a story. Now."

Sometimes David speaks in a syrupy, baby voice, more slurred than lisped, which requires full attention and quiet to be clearly understood. At other times – like this – his voice has the distinctness and clarity of a good church bell ringing through the deep valley on a cold, crisp winter's day.

"Get up, David."

"I want a story. I want you to read about the baby Jesus."

And it isn't even Christmas.

She lifts him up by his arms and swings him onto his bed, a scowling baby ape in yellow pajamas. "Wheee."

"I won't go to sleep till you read the story." He wraps his arms around himself, crosses his legs and locks his eyes. "I'll sit here all night, just like this, and in the morning you'll find me dead and blue and you won't be able to get my arms unstuck."

There is a second when it could go either way. She could slap his hands down, force his writhing body under the blankets, the two of them sobbing and screaming, she slamming from the room with much banging and turning off of lights, then standing in the hallway, holding the door shut, her tiny, defenceless son on the other side, howling in terror, hanging his whole weight from the red ceramic knob, fighting off the green and purple demons of the dark with his pitiful baby moans of MommyMommy; or she could take him in her ever-ready arms, kiss his damp cheeks dry, rummage under the bed for the book and read to him by the light of his space lamp, their heads bowed together, looking like an ad for fluoridated toothpaste. She is about to slap that look from his round, red-cheeked face when something stops her: the thought of all those nights when he will have to stay with his father; the possibility of a custody trial; the realization that she might very well be hitting the wrong male member of the family.

Linda sighs, that signal sound of motherhood, and falls onto the bed. "Okay, you win. I'll read you about the baby Jesus. Where's the book?"

Together, they fluff up the pillows and lie back, his one small arm entwining hers as she holds the book in the light.

Her voice soothing and suitably serious, Linda begins to read, "'And it came to pass in those days that a decree went out that everyone should be taxed. And for this purpose, Joseph had to travel to the city of David, called Bethlehem, with Mary his wife, who was expecting a child . . .'"

"Was it snowing?"

They both look at the illustration of Joseph leading Mary on the donkey. It is hard to tell. "It doesn't really look as though it's snowing."

"But I thought it was Christmas."

"It is Christmas, honey. It's the very first Christmas. But it isn't snowing. Not in this book."

"In my song book it's snowing."

158

Linda sighs once more. Some day she will be an old, sighing lady, wandering through the supermarket, picking up packets of single lamb chops and slabs of beef liver, and sighing; watching young mothers wheeling their infants through the aisles, allowing them to open boxes of cookies and bags of potato chips, and she will sigh at the pass that things have reached – sadly sighing her way through senility. And this is how it all begins; this having children and having husbands, people who can't be talked to, forcing you to substitute the squeezing of breath for words. "In your song book it may be snowing, but in this version the sun is shining."

"I thought it was night." He makes what he knows is his cute face – the one his father thinks makes him look intelligent; the one which his grandmother generally responds to with Tootsie Roll pops or chocolate mints.

"Not yet. We haven't got that far yet."

"Oh. Mom," and he snuggles closer, stroking her leg with his dimpled pink foot, "Mom, tomorrow night will you read me the story about the kangaroo?"

"I haven't finished reading you this story yet."

"I know. But will you read me the story about the kangaroo?"

"David, do you or do you not want me to read this story to you tonight?" She shuts the book, staring down at the cover picture of the Holy Family – Jesus, Mary and Joseph – warm and safe, all the powers of the universe hovering about them, heavenly voices singing from the rooftops; Jesus, Mary and Joseph, the model family, united in love and devotion, never a cross word between them – except maybe later on, Jesus telling them to all leave him the hell alone, but even then you could understand; a son, after all, is a son.

He clamps together his pearly teeth, lips wide apart and locked in a leer, "Yeeesss. Yeeesss." He rolls his wide-eyed eyes, lids stretched open, a baby monster from the bowels of the city, a tiny, yellow-clad creature living with all the deformed turtles and alligators that inhabit the sewers of New York. "Yeeesss, but tomorrow night I want the story about the kangaroo."

159

This is not the first time in his young and hope-filled life that his mother has wanted to kill him. She would like to make him cry; she would like to take all of his books away and make him wail; she would like to burst into sobbings herself. But instead, still rehearsing for her future role as sighing woman of Broadway, she says, "All right. Tomorrow I'll read you the story about the kangaroo."

And so they settle down, the light from the spaceship lamp glowing above their touching heads. " 'And so it was that she brought forth her firstborn son, and wrapped him in swaddling clothes, and laid him in a manger . . .' "

"Because there was no room for them in."

"Because there was no room for them in the inn."

In their very building, an old man, alone in his apartment, sitting on the toilet seat where he will remain for the next twenty-two and a half hours, dies; across the street, a kid named Fred ODs; two blocks over a wino walks into a speeding cab; on 94th Street, a stabbing is about to take place. But in this apartment, a baby has just been born – and no deaths count; in this room, the light glows and the steam hisses. A siren moans, a voice screams, in the hallway is the sound of something heavy falling . . . and the world begins to breathe again. David pulls the pages back and forth, looking for the part where Santa begins.

Patricia comes in as David is finally being tucked in and good-night kissed, chuckling to herself. "You should have seen it, Mom. It was really funny, you know. I almost couldn't breathe."

They exchange a look out of almost identical eyes, and for the first time all day Linda also smiles. "I'm sorry I missed it. I could have used a good laugh," and she kisses the top of Patsy's head which is leaning against her shoulder.

"Oh, you would've loved it. Next week you can watch it with me, okay? I bet next week's even funnier."

Linda gives her a hug, overcome by a sudden desire, unusual for her, to squeeze Patricia's body so tightly against her own that they would melt into one another and never come apart. "Oh, yeah, Mom," says Patricia, giving her

160

mother a little squeeze in return, "you know that big box of papers Daddy had on that table in the hall?"

Linda snaps on the television and pours herself a large glass of wine. She could take a perfumed bubble bath, rub oil into her knees and elbows, set her hair in a soft, becoming style and try creaming the tell-tale lines of age away. She could bake a cake or a batch of cookies, homey offerings to stink the house with care. She could begin work she brought so long ago from the office – the work Paul tells everyone she does so well. She could vacuum, hem Patricia's new dungarees, read a good book to flex her mind, do some yoga to flex her mind and body, scrub out the toilet, or even begin to pack Paul's things for him – there are endless, countless, numerous things that Linda could be doing. Instead, she sits by the light of the silvery screen – much as Rita sits, night after night – her eyes opened, her heart beating and her lungs breathing. She knows that she is wasting time. She can hear Paul say, "But, Linda, you're wasting time. There's so much to do and you do nothing". The children of the world cry out to her for books, the laundry of the world cries out to her for sprinkling and folding, the women of the world cry out to her for leadership and guidance, her brain cries out for balm. But Linda just sits, a glass of expensive wine in one hand and a cheap, gold-plated hoop in the other. She considers calling her mother, but can't think of what she could say. "Hi, Mom, I was just sitting here in the living room, thinking about the meaning, or lack of it, of life, and I thought I'd give you a ring and hear what you have to say." Her mother would say, what, are you crazy calling at this hour of night, what's the matter with you, are you drunk, are you taking marrywanna, what's the matter with you? where's Paul?

Good question.

Paul is sitting on a terracotta patio in a red and white director's chair, in a decidedly green and growing garden set against a red and blue and purple sky. He is sipping a Margarita from a lovely, long-stemmed tinted glass, he is wearing a short-sleeved floral shirt in orange and purple, and he thinks he is at peace with the world. Janet sits next to their hostess, on the other side of the redwood picnic table, grinding potato chips against her paper plate. They have only been here an hour and already it seems like days.

Across the wide and raging waters which separate the table's benches, Paul and their host, the poet Barry, a small and quiet man whose greatest charm has always been his gentle sensitivity, have been discussing the states of literature and culture in the last decade; while on Janet's side, the girls' side, the wife, Nancy, a small and far-from-quiet woman whose greatest charm has always been that she doesn't seem to have any, has kept the conversation going on the recurrent and apparently inter-connected themes of ecology, birthing, pollution, abortion, inflation, vasectomies, and the advantages of organically grown fruits and vegetables and making your own bread. Twice she has asked Janet if she has any children, and having been told "no" has twice asked whether or not Janet planned to have children and has she read Le Boyer.

Janet's back is to the luxuriant backyard and to the belligerently blazing and setting sun and she faces, instead, the kitchen window, with its half café curtains made from what looks to be tablecloths from a bankrupt Italian restaurant and its pots of herbs hanging from intricately macraméd and beaded string holders. Janet knows as much about contemporary culture as either Paul or Barry, and yet they have less than no interest in her opinion; though not a poet or even a prose writer, she is surely as well-educated in literature as either of them, as well, and still they don't seem to care. When she attempted to give her views on women's writing in the past twenty years, Barry smiled with all the sweetness and understanding of Mother Earth and suggested that she was segregating feminist fiction from the universal human experience; Paul, unsmiling and unbendingly just, judged that she was trying to analyse what was quite clearly the work of a special and segregated minority by the standards and techniques that were only applicable, really, if you looked at it honestly, to a much more profound and broadly-based experiential literature. Nancy, confessing that she didn't have much time for reading but that she had certainly enjoyed *Fear of Flying*, asked if she didn't think it was very negative to view men as the enemy. Janet asked for another of those delicious drinks and said that she wasn't always sure. Neither of the men seemed to hear her.

Janet is feeling like a visiting ghost. She can see and hear and smell and even touch, and yet she cannot be seen or heard. Her heart sings and her head buzzes at hearing familiar voices and words, at seeing the place she has always occupied – there, with Paul and Barry, with the professional thinkers and teachers – but when she looks that place is not only vacant but evaporated, and the bright and respected woman she used to be is no longer there. Look at me, oh, look at me, she wants to scream, beating her phantom hands on the still still air. I remember, don't you remember, she longs to shout, her wraith's eyes rolling in her skull. At any moment she expects to feel – or not feel, as the case may be – a fleshless hand on her shoulder and a toneless but gentle voice whisper, "You know, they cannot see you, my child. They do not know that you are here".

Instead she feels Nancy's feathery fingertips, odorous from some exotic Californian handcream, pressing on her temple, pointing out the pressure points for easing severe headaches and migraines. "It really works," says Nancy, "just ask Barry. He always says that he would never leave me because he would never be able to find anyone else to cure his migraines like I do," and she gives a little smile, both humble and proud.

"Oh," watching a tiny, winged creature flit over Nancy's hair.

"Of course, you know what the pressure is like. Especially for men like Barry and Paul. It's bad enough just being an academic, but being an artist as well . . . well . . ."

Janet shakes the fingers free. "Oh, yes. I know."

"Sometimes when Barry comes home from a really full day, he can barely see straight."

Janet can barely see straight herself. "There certainly can be a lot of . . . a lot of . . . pressure," she agrees.

"That's why I think the home is so important. Especially for someone who's creative, like Barry is. Or Paul." She bites a taco chip in two. "They have to be able to escape from the real world – to be free to find themselves."

"Isn't this real?" encompassing the house, the yard and the people in the movement of her eyebrows while fishing a stray leaf from her drink.

Nancy's laughter tinkles, tingles. "You know what I mean. The outside."

"Oh, I know," sighs Janet: but outside of them there is no one and nothing; you go to return; you return to return again – not for escape, for the real arrival. "Outside." She looks to Paul, who is chuckling, if such a thing is possible, over something Barry has just said. He sees her looking and ignores her; he hears her call him and he shuts his door. She forgets, for a second, that Nancy is talking to her. "What?"

"Would you like to?"

"Like to what?"

"Like to come inside and see my weaving. And I'll show you the house." She drains her glass, licking salt from her lips, and climbs out from the picnic table prison. In Nancy's world, no response is as good as a yes and a no is as good as a maybe. "It's the most ambitious project I've done so far."

Janet struggles out and follows, noticing that no one is noticing their departure. "What is?"

"The tapestry," sliding open the sparkling glass doors. "It's sort of a tree of life motif, you know. I got the idea from my women's group, really. It's full of earth symbols."

Janet slides the doors behind her, so that when she looks back it is at a picture of two men sitting at a table beneath a dying sun. "What is?"

"The tapestry. You know the tree of life, don't you?"

Janet says yes – but she is no longer very sure of that either.

★   ★   ★

She cries in the night, every night, until the birds of dawn pick away the debris of darkness, the droppings of the cavern-eyed creatures that flock around her, echoing her pain, screaming out his name, chanting her memories back at her, remember, remember, him walking away and you turning to see him go, remember, remember, his hand against your face, his coat across a chair, him coming in and saying that smells good, him laughing laughing and the universe aflame with joy. She cries every night in the night, held taut by the things she never said and could have done, until the scavengers of day beat away the whining demons of her emptiness with their prismatic wings and there are, once more, at least once more, there are things to do and things to say and sense to be made and she can pretend to forget the price she has paid for paradise. In the light she can afford to remember, to mention him by name, husband, to repeat events and incidents and years – he did that, we did that, there was that time, that problem, that fight, there was this and there was that – as though facts are essence, as though details can congeal to make substance. As though it is possible to define the soul by the shape of the body; the being by the design of the life.

In the oh so white light of day, her mind is owned by the world – she is the same as she was when she was young and younger. She had been such a railer then, wanting so much, counting all she had not; pushing at him, digging at him, pulling his soul through the pores of his skin, I only want, I only want I want I want. But in her nights without distractions, when there is no one from whom to hide and nothing hidden, not a thing to hide – then, now, she sees only what she had, remembers only what he taught her, feels only what she felt there in the serried center of her exploding heart.

★   ★   ★

"All right," he says, stretching himself on the bed. "I give up. What's wrong?"

She removes first one earring, then the other, sliding stud into lock, placing them just-so into her lacquered jewelry box. "Nothing."

"Janet."

"Nothing. I'm tired." She kicks off her shoes and rubs the lipstick from her mouth. "You would be, too, if you'd had to spend the entire evening talking to that dizzy blonde."

Paul yawns. "Oh, I don't know. I thought she seemed rather nice."

Her hairbrush bangs onto the dresser. "How would you know whether she was nice or not? You barely spoke to either of us all evening."

He watches her like an animal trainer who has just recognized a familiar sign of danger. "What do you mean I barely spoke to you? We were all together, weren't we?"

"Were we?" and she jerks her nightgown over her head. He didn't know she even owned a nightgown.

"Where the hell else was I?"

"You tell me, Paul. You tell me where you were. You tell me why you refused to have anything to do with me all evening. Why every time I said something that you managed to hear you made fun of me or acted as though I were joking."

"Jesus." He shuts his eyes, but when he opens them she is still there, standing over him, transmogrified from the beloved blessing of his dreams into the timeless termagant of his nightmares, her eyes accusing, her voice accusing, accusation implicit in the way she holds her body and one hand on a hip. Never before has she reminded him of his wife. "I don't know what you're talking about."

"You know damned well what I'm talking about. You know exactly what I'm talking about."

He reaches for her, managing to grab hold of one limp hand – permitted him not as a gesture of yielding but as one of resignation. He has the impression that he is holding a very dead fish, swollen with pollution; she looks at her hand in his

166

as though he has, in fact, taken one of her feet and she is waiting to see what he plans to do with it. "You're being about as cold as fucking charity," he says – though there is little enough of that around.

"Oh?"

"Oh yes," pulling gently, jerking her towards the bed. "Janet, honey, you can't condemn me if I don't even know what it is I'm accused of. A man is innocent until proven guilty." He kisses her knuckles. "Isn't he?"

She sits, stiffly, on the edge of the bed, afraid of falling in. "Save your rhetoric for your students," removing her hand from his lying lips. "I have never been so humiliated in my life. Never."

"Humiliated? What are you talking about, 'humiliated'? I take you everywhere with me, I introduce you to people you should know, people I know you're interested in, and you tell me I've humiliated you. What would you like me to do? Leave you in the hotel by yourself, playing solitaire? Should I shower you with expensive clothes and jewels and only appear with you in public on special occasions, like some nineteenth-century whore?"

Her bones snap. "That's exactly what I mean."

"What's exactly what you mean?"

"You treated me like I was your whore. Just some tart you go around with to show everyone how attractive and worldly you are."

He takes back her hand. "For Chrissake, Janet, no one uses the word 'tart' any more."

She takes back her hand. "Don't correct my usage. You know exactly what I mean. You take me around with you, and you hold my hand and call me honey, and make a big show of what a happy couple we are, but when it comes down to what you think is important I can just sit and rot with some stupid housewife and talk about bean sprouts all evening. I'm not good enough to discuss anything serious with you and your friends. I'm just part of the background."

Again he takes her hand, holding it a bit more firmly this time. "Janet, you're being ridiculous. You are here as my wife. If you don't talk to other people's wives, who will? What was what's-her-name . . ."

"Nancy."

"What was Nancy supposed to do while we discussed the French influence on early-twentieth-century South American literature? Fill the glasses and pass around the guacamole?"

"I don't care what she does. I want to know what you think I'm supposed to do."

"I think you're supposed to behave like the intelligent, sophisticated and educated woman you are. I think you're supposed to know how to mix with people, to understand that there are certain social conventions . . ."

"Such as not talking to me when we're in public?"

"Such as making sure that things are balanced. For God's sake, sweetheart, you're a woman. Do you think she'd want to talk to me about her blessed bean sprouts? You're supposed to have things in common with other women, you're supposed to like them."

She gets up so quickly she nearly pulls him from the bed. "I do like them. At least women are sensitive. At least they don't try to exclude people. You could have talked with us, you didn't have to set yourselves apart as though what interests you is important and what interests anyone else is shit." Lips begin to quiver, tears begin to roll.

He forces himself to his feet, standing ready to embrace. "I never said that. You're the one who said that."

Janet sniffs and gurgles. "You don't have to say things to say them. You made your feelings quite clear."

His hands are on her shoulders, holding her both from him and to him. "Don't you love me any more, Janet? Is that what's wrong?" his voice so soft with suspended pain, his touch so gentle with expected loss. "Are you sorry you came?"

Around them the night stands still, the entire West Coast paralyzed by their presence on its shores, the only sounds their momentous breathing and the rhythm of her sorrow. "You don't love me any more. It's you who don't love me," she somehow whispers. "You don't love me."

168

He holds her now, spinning in a city of stone. "Ohhh. Ohhh, darling, I love you more than anything in the world. You are the world," his eyes blurred with tears, his voice steamy with desire. "How can you say a thing like that?"

"You don't," she repeats. "You don't," but she is losing conviction as his hands begin to stroke her, the heat from his touch dissolving material and flesh and burning bone.

"I do. I do love you," his hands pulling up her gown, his hands riding across her rump like a seraph sliding through space.

"Oh, Paul. Oh, Paul, I love you so."

"Then let me come in you. Let me come in you, love."

7

It is Paul's homecoming. He called Linda from his and Janet's favorite Chinese restaurant, where they had gone for a final meal, telling her he was at the airport and was getting a lift from someone he met on the plane. He has timed his arrival so as to avoid having to greet his children when he is too tired and too high to have any interest in them. Now, as he speeds uptown in a yellow cab, driven by a young man with a beard and a bandana around his head who has been regaling him with stories of all the times he has been robbed, Paul feels pleased.

For years he has struggled – winning scholarships and fellowships and grants, begging for monies for this project and that idea, to this fund and that fund, even teaching night classes to the illiterate and the terminally moronic to earn enough to live on, to pad out his résumé – and now, as the magic carpet cab glides through the park, he can see that it is all about to pay off. The clouds of frustration and boredom are clearing, the tears caused by the tedious and the trivial are drying; he can feel it in the bones of his feet. His career has been revitalized, his foot is wedged in between the gates of fortune, and he is about to be carried uphill by the tides of luck and perseverance, straight up. In California he received interest and possible offers, admiration and respectful inquiries. Who knows what the future may hold; what gifts may be laid at his booted feet – travelling fellowships, special chairs, special programs or assistantships, heads.

The one problem with going up – as more than one person has noticed – is that at some point one is bound to come down. Probably.

But Paul's thoughts, at this moment of his time, are not concerned with the eccentricities of life. As he ascends in the elevator, walks across the checkered pattern of multi-colored tiles in the hallway and puts his key in the lock of the black enamelled door, his head is filled with images of kudos and applause, his soul is sopping with poetry and the nobler impulses of man, and his heart is swelling with love and lust, though not necessarily in that order. He gazes fondly on the tiny peep-hole and the metal number. It is good to be home. It is good to know that when the door opens he will be engulfed by the familiar, encircled by the things he loves. Travelling, even with Janet, makes him feel lonely and vulnerable. Sometimes it makes him wake in the night, missing his books, his pictures, his own bed where he can sleep against the wall. Home is the sailor, home from the sea, and the hunter, as it were, from the lush but treacherous fields of academia, his blood diluted by too many cups of instant coffee in Styrofoam cups, his spirit folded in upon itself, accordion-like, to fit neatly into his attaché case. Home. Roller skates in the hall, the over-sized amber ashtray he stole from a movie house in Kankakee in his study, his favorite cookies in the Little Red Riding Hood cookie jar his mother gave them. Home. And in half of a blinding instant he realizes what a drag, what a nag Janet has been to him, how tense he has been, how he has overworked himself, pushing pushing pushing pushing pushing pushed . . . and the door opens on an entryway that is just as it should be. Exactly.

"Linda! Linda!" he calls, as he has called a million times before. "Honey, I'm home!" he shouts, just like Robert Young. There is even music in the background, though it actually comes from next door. He puts down his suitcase, puts down his briefcase and folds his coat on top of them. Lights burn brightly in either direction, beckoning. "Linda! I'm home!"

Linda is sitting in the living room, totally absorbed in

nothing. There are several ways in which she could open the conversation – or series of conversations – that is about to begin: she could ask him where he's been, for she has already talked both to his hotel in California and to a very charming young man at La Guardia who is working his way through film school, and knows where he hasn't been; she could ask him if Janet had managed to get a good tan in the time they were away, for though she never called her mother, Linda did once call her husband – and was surprised at how unsurprised she was to hear Janet's voice slide out of the sunshine and dagger-like into her heart; she might even – since he is something of an authority on modern thought and literature and the use of language to express the essence of human experience – ask him the question she has been asking herself very recently, which is whether or not everyone else's life is as much a travesty as theirs. And, if so, why do any of them bother?

"Linda," he says loudly and with a certain edge of impatience, "Linda, I'm home."

She doesn't smile. She rises from her chair like a maiden in a trance. She floats towards him. She gazes into his beautiful, soulful eyes as she has gazed into his eyes a trillion times before. "This is yours," she says, not without a certain transcendent sweetness, and holds out her hand to him. "You can sleep on the couch tonight. Tomorrow you can move out," and she drops the slender hoop into his open palm.

He assumes that she has finally freaked out. Staring at the tiny object in his hand, he sees not the symbol of the shallowness and hypocrisy of his marriage, but a cheap earring, and he can't begin to imagine why she's given it to him. He had assumed that his home would have been held in something akin to a state of suspended animation while he was away – but instead he has walked in at the wrong time, through the wrong door and quite definitely into the wrong scene. Is this what they mean by parallel worlds? "Linda," he says, "Linda, what's going on?" but the woman he has known as Linda has already drifted past him like a satellite, humming and flashing, her course pre-programmed and

172

impossible to change. "Linda! For Chrissake, what the hell is going on?" He waits for her return. "Linda? Linda?" and only when he begins to feel foolish, standing like a stranger in his own living room, does he notice the bed things dumped unceremoniously onto the sofa: two old sheets of David's, the pillow the cat puked on that never really came clean, and the old blanket they used to use for picnics, in the days when they did things like go on picnics. And a letter. Typed on his typewriter – a fact which he doesn't notice until later, but which he will always think of as being shot with his own gun. Bang. Bang.

Now it is Paul who sits in the living room: man in chair with heart breaking, man alone in house that sounds like ten minutes after the end of the world, his blood congealed by grief. He has read her letter three times, and each time it has made him feel helpless. He has knocked at her bedroom door, voice tender and contrite, humble with the effort of begging for forgiveness. She wouldn't answer. He pounded, voice enraged and outraged, manic with the desire to make her understand, until he heard the light switch by the door go clack. He kicked, he screamed, he threatened to break down the door with one of the metal chairs from the kitchen; she said that she didn't want to have to call the police, but that she wouldn't hesitate. "Do whatever you want, then," he'd screamed. "I don't give a goddamn what you do."

In the past three hours he has run the gamut of emotions, from guilt and panic to self-pity and hatred, and back again. He has flip-flopped from wanting to crawl into her on his belly and lick her toes, to wanting to stride in with giant steps and punch her in the mouth, hard. He has also run through the better part of a fifth of scotch. Paul is exhausted, sitting hunched in his chair like a buffalo skin with no buffalo inside of it any more. Paul is crying, salty, tepid tears – the sprinkler system of the soul – leaving damp snail trails down his handsome face. Paul has cried before – on the assassination of Martin Luther King, the time the cat fell out the window and the two times that he saw *The Sound of Music* – but he has never cried like this before. He neither sobs nor whines; chokes nor moans. He simply weeps: silently, numbly, devoid of all effort, and when he is done a part of him will be for ever dehydrated, ready to be blown away like a dry husk in the wind. But which part? he wonders, and then thinks the line "done, done the undreamed dreams and dead that dream my life", hoping he will still remember it when he's sober.

His empty eyes turn to his father's photograph, and with that movement, so normal, so casual, the smallest shift from left to right, the sound starts, the sorrow of decades colliding with the catastrophe that the present has just become. As surely as Walter's death changed the world has Linda's denial of him changed it yet again. The halo-like hoop hangs loosely on a corner of yesterday's *New York Times*, jammed into the wastebasket. His parents' love had been inevitable and eternal: neither poverty nor failure destroyed it; disappointment didn't dent it; death didn't end it. He cannot see or hear or feel or think, but his father's face burns through, and every memory collected of him, and every image of the four of them as a family – Lillian in her patent leather shoes, Walter in his old jacket and his hat with the ear flaps, Rita with her sticky red lips and *Evening in Paris* perfume, Paul on his bike grinning – all glow in his brain. He finally passes out, thinking that all he ever wanted from his marriage was to spend the evening sitting by the fire, reading in companionable silence, his wife sitting nearby, in her hands a book of poems.

★   ★   ★

He is dead but wanders through the rooms, flicking ash into coffee cups, kicking socks beneath the bed, shouting where is, where is, why . . . and then, at his burial, she had no weeping in her, all feeling burnt to cinders in the oven of her soul. She sits in the hollow of her life without him, crying, thinking of choirs and candles and chocolates and her head against his chest, his breath across her brow. He will come in right now, bearing gifts, singing some honkytonk song. He will come in right now, sit beside her, put his hand on her

174

shoulder, awkwardly, tenderly, like a boy, say, "You know, I really missed you", really, really missed you, really missed you, missed you. Movements heavy, she walks around the room, hearing whisperings deep in the night. Hadn't they stood together, arms entwined, and kissed such kisses, oh darling. She steps back from the doorway where once they had stood in love. He comes up behind her, puts an arm around her waist, says, sweetheart, how I longed for you, for you, always the only one, remember, only you you you my love. To the music playing somewhere else they begin to dance, dream lovers, moonlight filtering in through the starched thin curtains, bathing them in its magic light, marking them with the mystery, now known and realized, love love love and the kiss, slightly swaying, a kiss lingering and long, teeth touching.

★　　★　　★

Up in the Bronx, Rita, half sleeping and half hallucinating, has a revelation. It takes not quite three-and-a-half seconds, and though it will never be really forgotten, it will never be really remembered either, zip splash. The revelation is that her entire life was founded on one irrevocable mistake, a cataclysmic error in judgment that had her struggling, striving all her life and always in the wrong direction: like looking for strawberries in a cornfield. The revelation is that she married the wrong man, and that because of this she was always in the wrong place, fighting the wrong things, doomed to unhappiness and defeat. The revelation is that she had hated Walter, had hated his demands and his dreams, his childishness and his great wailing need, his maleness screaming for her to fuck him feed him and feel his pain. In those sizzling, sparkling seconds Rita is released by the knowledge that her dying is not a punishment but an end.

And out on Long Island, Lillian and Jimmy have come through a week in which there was as much ice inside as outside, blazing silences and slamming doors, bickerings over the right way to fill the oil bottle and the wrong way to slice a quiche. But tonight he brought home wine and a box of

175

chocolates the kids at school were selling to raise money for some new gym equipment, and she made him his favorite dinner, pork chop casserole and green Jell-O with pear halves in it. They have had a markedly peaceful and contented family evening, even Angela managing to behave as though she had some human qualities; they have watched television together, drinking the wine and laughing at the same jokes; they have made love, not exotically but fondly, each saying "sorry"; they have fallen into peaceful sleeps, asses touching. Things are all right somewhere.

He has been locked in his study all morning, phoning. It seems to him as though Patricia or David bangs on the door every four minutes and thirty-seven seconds to remind him that Mommy is waiting for him to leave, but that isn't true: they have each knocked once, an hour and a half apart, and David only wanted to know whether or not his baseball hat was in there. Linda herself has only disturbed him once, calling through the scruffy, finger-printed semigloss white door in her new voice – the voice of a woman who is prepared to be polite to you, maybe even friendly now and then, but never intimate – "Have you almost got it together, Paul?" pronouncing "Paul" as though she were saying his entire name, have you almost got it together now, Paul Theodore Sutcliffe. "I'm doing the best I can, Linda. I'm having problems." "Just remember that I want you out of here today. For real."

He has heard her moving through the house – walking down halls, shutting doors, turning on taps, calling to his children, yelling at the cat – as though all things have remained the same. While he sits in his room, dialling first the time and then the weather and, bored with that, the day's joke. He cannot call Janet and ask if he can stay there till he finds an apartment, because he knows she will say yes, making this new world official. He has called Liz and asked if he could stay with her, just for a day or two, and she responded in her informal, modern woman way with, "Are you nuts? I don't have enough room", meaning how would I explain you to my other lovers, the ageing Jewish poet whom Paul has met and despises and the young Colombian Marxist whom Paul hasn't met but whom he despises equally. Paul has no friends. He has read through every page of his neat, brown leathered address book, starting at the top of each and winding up at the bottom, silently chanting the names and numbers from Aboff and Bordavich to Wasserbach and Zelli, and nowhere among them has he found one person he could simply call and say to, my wife has thrown me out can I stay with you till I find a place? Not one: not one who wouldn't smirk or smile; not one who wouldn't pry or prod; not one who wouldn't think or even say, oh, God, isn't there somewhere else you could go? There are people in Chicago, Tampa, Los Angeles, Oregon and Oxford, England, who would gladly put him up for a time, but no one in New York. Paul has associates, acquaintances and admirers; he knows people who are jealous of him and others who think he and everyone else would be a lot better off if he were to be sucked into the void by a justice-seeking God; he knows women who would like to screw him and men who would like to screw him, a few of both sexes who genuinely wish him well and many more who are indifferent. But no friends. Typists, movers, money-lenders, legal advisers, friends of friends who know a guy in Flatbush, pushers and pussies – but no pals. No side-kicks. No blood-brothers. No one to whom he could say by the haunted orange light of the dying campfire, "Let's head out to Utah and see if our luck changes". No one who would pick out a piece of jerky from between his teeth with a twig, spit into the smoke and say, "Sounds okay by me".

Where is he going to go?

If he opens the door, will he discover husky, sweating men in T-shirts, their beer bellies brimming over their belts, moving his things from the house? painting the rooms? building shelves in the living room where he always said he would some day build them? shouting, "Hey, lady, whered ya wanustapudis?"? Men like his father's friends who always

177

called him "son" and "chip off the old block"; men who stank of sweat and cigarettes and who all owned one suit that had never fit them right; who thought that wrestling and musical comedies represented culture; men who stuck their napkins in the necks of their shirts. If he opens the door, will he find them wrapping his things in old copies of the *Daily News*, sitting on his luggage while they chew their bologna sandwiches on white bread, washing them down with beer from the can? "Hey, Mac," they'll say when he tries to slip past them, "Hey, Mac, yagotta truck comin' for disstuff?". "Ah, ya know those professor types," they'll shrug to one another, wiping their noses on the sleeves of their bleached-out shirts, "they're all queer anyway". Clumsy socially, inarticulate personally, they will be sitting on the boxes holding his books, his papers, his poems and back issues of his journal, with holes in their T-shirts and taunts licking at their lips, thinking what a poor bastard he is because his wife doesn't love him any more. Men who think that Lichtenstein is a country, smugly judging him as a loser, feeling sorry for him because they think he's a schmuck.

He'll never come out. He'll hold his classes in his study and have his students bring him food and water. He'll only use the bathroom when she isn't home; he'll come in and out via the fire escape, his briefcase gripped between his teeth as he drops like a cat to the ground. He'll make himself a legend: the man who wouldn't let go of love. He'll be a twentieth-century hero, dragon-slayer of the metropolis, an inspiration to his peers. They will write poems about him, compose songs and jingles, interview him on the evening news, air brush his image on shirts and bags with the slogan: Would You Want Your Children To Come From A Broken Home? And all the thousands of disowned husbands and fathers throughout the city – Uptown and Downtown, East Side and West Side, even into Queens and Brooklyn – as they sit in their silent one-bedroom apartments, furnished with the garage rubble of their undivorced friends and the things their mothers didn't want any more, as lonely and alien as a cheap hotel room in Wichita, will think of him and take hope, will

178

leave him messages in the personal columns of the *Voice*: at least there is one man who won't let them deball him . . . good luck, Sutcliffe, the West Seventies salute you. When they interview him on the Tonight Show, he will explain, with all the mighty force of logic and reason at his command, in as good-humored and straightforward a manner as he can muster, that the changing economic and social structure of post-war times has disowned, primarily, women from their place in the universe, from the spiritual and biological purpose which runs like blood through the veins and arteries of their souls and pulses like a warning light on the treacherous shoals of their confused minds. Women have forsaken love for rubbish (though, probably, he wouldn't phrase it quite that way; would, instead, cross his legs and tap his pipe and say "for temporal and superficial priorities") like sex, financial security and independence and a vapoury and vacuous equality ("whatever that is meant to mean, ha ha") – and, when he finished, all of the vanquished and banished ex-husbands and nominal fathers in the audience would stand up as one and applaud, and all over the regius city men who had been subdued and intimidated into marriages of compromise and deluded obsequiousness would sigh gently and whisper among themselves, "You know, I think that guy might have something". He might bend to Linda's delusions and whims, he might stagger and sway under the weight of her fickleness and lack of commitment, but his love, at least, would not be so easily disposed of as hers; his half of the marriage would remain unaltered, beyond time and place, beginningless and endless. Love, he would tell America on network television, is not a subway train, it does not stop and start, it does not open its doors to have its passengers flung out on cold and barren stations in the depths of treacherous nights. In a world with the profundity and meaning of an amusement park, only love was immutable, only love could offer salvation. What else is there for us? he would ask, looking straight into camera 3, what else?

Indeed.

There are four raps on his door. "Paul," says Linda, "if

179

you aren't out of this house within the hour I'll burn you out."

She is in the middle of the hall, sitting on David's tricycle with the multicolored fringes dripping from the handlebars, looking bored and, inexplicably, beautiful, when he opens his door. "I think we should talk about this," he whispers.

"We've been talking to each other for years and years and years. There isn't anything left to say."

"Things aren't settled."

"Talk to my lawyer." brringbrring goes the little silver bike bell.

"Lawyer? I don't want to talk to any fucking lawyer. What does the law have to do with us?"

She fiddles with the fringe, rocks the tricycle back and forth. "The law married us, the law will unmarry us." Honkhonk goes the little silver horn.

"The law? The law? For Chrissake, Linda, don't be such a fool. Marriages aren't made by signing a piece of paper – and they're not dissolved by signing a piece of paper."

Honkhonkbrringbrringhonkbrring.

"Just stop a minute, Linda, and look at what you're doing to us. Look at what you're becoming. Just another cog in the great societal wheel, just another soulless twentieth-century robot . . ."

"Wind-up person."

"What?"

"You used to call them wind-up people. In your youth, that is."

Has her mouth always been this hard? her eyes bricked-up? her voice so blocking?

"I don't give a damn what I used to call it. You used to believe in us. You used to understand. You used to be one of the few people in the world who knew . . . and now look at you, now look at what you've become . . . just another faddish flunky. You're just another kind of junky, Linda, just shooting all this crap into your head. You don't know where you are. You don't know what you're doing. You have no idea of what's going on . . ."

180

"Out."

"I'm not leaving, Linda. Not like this."

"Three strikes, Paul, and you're out. Get out."

"You can't throw me out like this, Linda."

With one foot she propels the brightly painted three-wheeled vehicle back and forth before him. "I mean it this time."

"You've said that before. You've said that before, Linda."

"But this time I mean it."

And he wonders to himself, as men have wondered through the centuries, by what secret word it was, by what divine sign let loose into the commonplace, by what wizard's look he was meant to be able to distinguish the real from the not-so-real. "Just like that."

"What do you mean 'Just like that'?"

His fingers snap. "Just like that. All our plans, all we've had, over" snap snap "just like that."

Is she looking at him from up close or from very far away? Is she seeing him with new eyes, or is she only at this moment seeing him at all, this man who has threaded her life through his, who has been the one image she sought to see from the first moment she set eyes on him sitting in the student cafeteria like Christ with the little children? "How much shit do you think I can put up with?" she asks with a certain amount of awe.

"How much shit can you put up with? How much shit can you put up with?"

She can see him still, one leg up on a near-by chair, his head thrown back, dribbling cigar ash onto the floor, surrounded by his hangers-on, surrounded by a room filled with childish hurly burly, he the hub and they the bub, he aloof and in control and everyone else confusion's pawns, indecision's dupes, children of chaos. She was carrying a brown plastic tray which held one cup of coffee and a perfect one-eighth slice of cherry pie and Richard Esposito was talking to her about the Nazi lying dormant in all of us, about how no one could say for sure that they wouldn't bayonet babies if that was the thing to do, and she saw him sitting there, the one who knew, the one who was different, and she

181

thought, completely missing what Richard was saying about doubt and assumptions, "oh".

She stands up and away from the bike. "Paul, you've walked all over me for years. Ever since the first time we met you've done nothing but use and manipulate me." She places her hands not quite on her hips. "And humiliate me. When you want me to be a wife everything else about me becomes expendable or rearrangeable." She moves her hands up and down, lets them drop. "When you want me to be a career woman, then the house and the kids are expendable. Send the kids to camp, send the kids to Rita, send the kids to bed . . . but when you want me to be a mother, then it's Linda don't you think you should spend more time with the kids, Linda don't you think Patricia's feeling a little left out, Linda don't you ever do anything with the kids any more, they just sit around like cabbages. Everything is always you you you. Who the fuck do you think you are?" In the indirect light of the corridor, on the makeshift stage of floor and wall, Linda's shoulders hunch inwards, her chin goes out and her hands punch air. It's the first time he's ever seen her impersonate him. "I am sick and tired of the whole damn universe having to accommodate itself to you. I am sick and tired of your judgments and your decrees. Let Paul Sutcliffe tell you who to vote for, what to eat for lunch and which deodorant to use . . ." she kicks the bike and sends it clickclacking down the hall, its pedals going round and round until it runs into the wall. "I am sick and tired of you, you pompous ass. Always telling everybody what to do, hiding behind your stinking little typewriter whenever you don't want to have to do something." She has moved so close to him that he is tempted to reach out and grab her, clamp her wrists and shake the sense back into her, slap her flushed face until the bad blood is dispelled and she is her old, sweet self again, but she's too fast for him, she's past him now, tanked up and speeding. "You and your fucking art and your fucking contribution to society and your patriarchal bullshit about the democracy of education. You and your we are all brothers and sisters bullshit, skulking around, leering at everyone, pretending to

182

be such a nice guy, begging people to publish your crappy articles and your trite, pretentious poems. All you ever do, Paul Sutcliffe, is masturbate. That's all you ever do, whether you're writing or you're fucking it all comes down to the same sick, revolting thing, just you pumping yourself like a madman. And you know what? You know what?" her skin damp with color, red and blue and green and brown, her skin seeming to dissolve and blend, some undreamt of process of interior war painting, sweat patching at her temples, herself transformed into Rita, Rita swinging at Walter with a broom, Rita yelling and yelling, her tears etched into her cheeks, ihateyouyoubastardiwishyou'ddropdeaddeaddeaddead, Rita moaning in the kitchen, her lips painted red, her nails dipped in banshee blood, my life my life why was I ever born, the peasant priestesses of all the boroughs huddled together, their gold-looking jewelry clicking and jingling, their chanting swelling through the house oh men oh men oh men, rattling their coffee cups and cake plates, their dreams all dreamed, their futures all behind them, their unused breasts sighing with futility. "You always make a mess." She looks at him but doesn't see him; she sees him but doesn't recognize him, this woman who used to call him honey bear. "Always. God you disgust me. Just who do you think you're kidding? Huh? Who?"

"Whom." He gives a warm little chuckle, the last sound of the last living thing after the apocalypse.

She moves nearer. He sees her coming, drawn by old forces, compelled by the old need, and makes a move to reach for her, to pull her to him in screeching tears and cognizable comfort. She spits.

"You bitch," he whispers, "you filthy bitch," and he slaps her so hard she dances across the corridor, one hand up to her face.

And bitch she is, she who was always so neat and poised, so quiet and so controlled, her face mutilated by fury, her voice howling, "You. You. You. Everything is you and how you feel and what you want and what you think. You've never done anything, not one thing that you didn't want to do when you didn't want to do it. You play daddy when you want, you play teacher when you feel like it, you play son or brother or supercock depending on your mood. And you still think everybody should feel sorry for you. You and your fuckin' artistic soul." She rushes at him with her loafer in her hand, pounding on his shoulders, banging at his head. He grabs her by the shoulders and pulls her against him, pinning her arms between them, she butting and he holding, she crazy and he crazed. And then his lips are on her hair, across her forehead, on her mouth, "Don't do this to me, Linda," pulling off her clothes and pulling at her breasts, she soft and succumbing, melting to the floor, a nipple hard between his teeth, his hand fierce inside her, "You bitch you bitch I love you so", pulling at the snakes of her hair. The universe crackles and rages and glows. The energies of the cosmos crash and collide.

Over, he lifts himself from her body, bruised and moist, jewels of semen dropped across her belly, and stares into her face. They are unconnected.

Sitting on the floor with his head in his hands. "Who is he?"

He watches her sit up and put her blouse back on, seeing how, when he leaves, she will lift the phone or grab a cab, rush to be kissed and consoled, race to be held and caressed; seeing how, when he is gone, her body will reshape itself around this other man, some Philistine fiction editor without morals or principles who would sell his daughter for a sixty thousand print run; seeing all he has trusted and loved, cherished and nurtured, breathing wetly and warmly into some strange ear, love me love me fuck me now.

He is one of her children in pain. She reaches out to touch him; he pulls away. He asks how long it's been going on; she doesn't say. He asks how many men there've been; she simply breathes. He wants to know if she is in love with this other man; she says, "No". And they go on watching each other for minutes from opposite sides of different dreams.

At last he turns his body away from her and murmurs, "I love you, I've always loved you."

184

Linda sits on the old floral rug, her hand half across a rose. She can see the walls and ceiling of the room, the pictures and books, the broken curtain ring and his father's beer stein with pens and pencils holding it down. She is feeling love for no one. She hears him speak the word and spells it in her mind, in curved neon letters of lilac, chartreuse and blue, l-o-v-e. On that morning that Richard Esposito had been saying "It's all right, here and now, getting our coffee and worrying about the psych exam, to say that we would have stood up to the Fascists . . . but how can you know – how can you ever be sure", she had looked across the room and in the left-hand corner, where the light squeezed in through low basement windows, she had seen Paul Sutcliffe with his feet up on a chair and his head thrown back, his smile cracking wide the world, and she had fallen in love. Had she? And since the moment he had stretched his hand to touch her hair she had behaved as though she loved him, had given what she believed should be given – and when she had hated, hated him, she had acted like she loved him even more. Had she ever loved him? And Mark? did she love him? would she ever? Is she too old now to let herself believe? Or has she always been that old?

There is a block beneath the desk, and a burn mark in the arm of his chair. If what Paul has given her is love, then what does he give to Janet and to the kissing girl in the car? If what Paul and she have had is love – then what is non-love? If Mark loves her, if he is offering her the love that will last – then what did he offer Marilyn in those summers long ago before he became interested in boating and she got into body massage?

She picks a paper clip from on top of a faded, curling leaf. Mark is right. She gave Paul everything, she humbled and denied herself for him, she surrendered all she had to him, she opened herself to pain and doubt – and pain and doubt was what she got.

He rubs his eyes and stares at the molecular movement of the air. What a fool he's been, how used and engulfed, how betrayed. All his sacrifices and chances lost, all nothing more

185

than bloodied beloved sons offered to a phoney god. And this woman he has clung to for so long, this woman he thought he knew as well as himself, this other half of his soul . . . "Is he the first?"

It is easy to tell the truth: you open your mouth and – without having to consider whys and wherefores, reasons and connections, without having to locate the correct pitch of voice and timbre of word to imitate sincerity – out it comes. If she tells the truth Paul will feel better. If she lies she will hold control. His fingers tear fluff from the carpet. She catches the look in his eyes.

"No."

He should have known. If he had looked, if he hadn't loved her so, he would have seen it going on for years: affairs with her colleagues, affairs with his; flings with friends, meaningless fucks with passers-by; perverse and passionate scenes with his students, mid-morning orgies with her lesbian friends. She has betrayed him in the kitchen, on the lawn, in the backs of cars and in the basements of rented houses near the Sound. She has barely had the time to wash the cum from between her legs as she has sped from bed to bed; and even while he was buying bonds and a teddy bear and dreaming out the life of his son, she was rolling her pregnant body on its front so they could fuck her from behind, like a large white goose, ass high, oh faster faster faster more . . .

"They're my children, aren't they? He's my son?"

She stands up, taking her underwear from the floor. "I don't know anything any more. I just don't know anything any more," she says, pausing as though to touch him. "Not anything."

There are no more presents to be bought; no more prayers to be said.

Alone in his room, Paul dials Janet's number.

He spent most of the night driving uptown and downtown, crosstown, then crosstown again, forming in tracks on the slick city streets a vanishing crucifix, stopping when he came to likely and unlikely bars. He doesn't remember deciding to come to Rita's, he simply arrived.

"What's wrong?" she called over the banister as he marched heavily up the stairs.

"Nothing."

"What's happened?" and she took his coat.

"Nothing."

"Where's Linda? Do you want some coffee?"

"I want a drink."

"Where's Linda?"

He opened the cupboard looking for liquor.

"Where are the children?" and she followed him from corner to corner, from square to square. He opened the refrigerator, hoping for beer.

"What children?"

He jerked the can out so hard that a jar of apple sauce and a bowl of rice came with it, smashing across the floor.

"Your children. Patsy and David."

He threw the can against the wall. "What children? What children? I don't have any fuckin' children," leaning against the sink waiting to be sick.

"Paul, what's happened? Tell me what's happened." She touched his rigid arm. "I'm your mother. Tell me what happened."

What could he say that she could understand, this old and ignorant woman, this pathetic creature who has played out her life like an old maid's melodrama performed by the amateur drama society of a small town in Georgia during a dry season? How could he transform into words the pain and sense of betrayal, the disillusionment and horrible nothingness that are torching through his heart and soul?

"Get away from me, you stupid bitch. Get away from me. Shut the fuck up and leave me alone!"

And she did.

He sat on the couch and watched her bring him sheets and blankets and an embroidered pillowcase; as the little Paul watched when he was ill, his mother change the bed and trim the corners, plump the pillow and turn the top edge of sheet

187

and blanket down, there, now it's nice and clean for you. But she didn't smile or offer to bathe his head; she didn't kiss his cheek or ask if he'd like toast and tea. She moved like a woman making up beds for enemy soldiers who had beaten her husband and ravaged her daughter, who had brushed their bayonets against her breasts. In a voice she'd never used before, she said, "There's a clean towel and washcloth in the bathroom", and looked at him directly. He stared into her oh–so–blue eyes – not as Walter once had done, with lust and longing, with loss and loathing – finding no end, their reflections shooting between them, bouncing off from the mirrors of hell.

He hasn't slept all night. Rita is still in bed, waiting, he supposes, for his call. He lies on the couch, trying to guess the time from the light struggling through the venetian blinds; a brave face and inside tears. As though he has slept and dreamed, he sees an image of himself, content and smiling, and behind it the double image, himself dressed in pompoms, ruffles and glossy paint. Himself the clown. He lies unmoving on his mother's couch and hears the universe laugh.

He is alone on a frozen planet, isolated on a barren rock in the middle of a glittering galaxy. Wifeless and childless, trying to see his son's face; trying to see if it is his face or someone else's. Where are they now, the lovely young women to hold his hand and sigh for him; where the colleagues to clap his shoulder and buy a drink; where the students to write down his wisdom on single ruled pads? His son, his son, who would grow to do the things he hadn't done, to have his eyes and his gift for words, to take his knowledge and hold his truths, his son. Whose son?

Paul lies with his head on a cheap foam–filled pillow, the case smelling of bleach and fabric softener, the old plaid blanket pulled up to his waist. He is lying on a beach with his son stretched out on top of him, body to body, heartbeat to heartbeat, but slowly the little boy's face melts away, fainter and fainter still, till there is only his little body and his little legs and his little arms and there is no tiny heart ticking in time with his. And finally sleeps.

188

It's not a dream he will remember. Women chase him, women with long hair tangled like baskets of live bait; women golden and gleaming in the rose-tinted moonlight; women dark as eternity breathing gently into the silvered web of his fears. He is a bat, he is an aged mage flying against the demon forces of the dark; he is a garnet-eyed stallion; he is energy made touchable and seeable, running against the static forces of doom. They shoot at him with rhinestoned spears, they lassoo him with beaded ropes; they offer him honeyed songs to which to fly; they offer him Elysian fields through which to roam. He is boy man god boy-man man-god. They hold him softly with careful caresses; they drag him back with their mourning mother wails, bejewelled with tears.

Rita lies on her bed, on top of the inexpensive pink spread which almost, in a certain light, looks like satin. She stares at the neat white squares of ceiling tile, but sees a salmon-pink ceiling, bordered in heavy, leaf-like molding, an intricate fixture in the middle of the room holding frosted glass goblets with glowing hearts. What room is this? Voices call, lips kiss, arms hug, laughter surrounds. What voices? What lips? What arms? Whose laughter? None. Outside the traffic sloshes by, the dog next door barks at passing children and they scream.

He wakes to hear the sounds of morning, Rita in the kitchen, water boiling in the kettle on the stove, and holds the blanket tightly. He will get up now and have breakfast with his mother, and he'll talk to her, he'll ask her, a woman, about women – about his wife. He is home and safe at last.

And Rita in the kitchen thinks that now she will beg him to take her home with him, take her home where she can die in peace, not in a hospital with tubes up her nose, urinating all over the pure white sheets and her own white thighs, but home with the TV going and the telephone ringing and the children squabbling down the hall.

Paul comes into the kitchen and stands back from where she is bent over the counter, leaning on her arms. "Mom."

She raises her head from where it rested between a bottle of some white liquid and a dirty spoon.

He is going to her, to put his arms around her, to lean against her, head to head and tear to tear.

Rita turns. "I'm dying," she says. "I'm dying, Paul."

He stares at his mother for one second, for two seconds, for three. "What?"

8

Paul calls it Death Row. In the bed nearest the door lies old Mrs Triolo, the curtain always pulled around her, crying steadily, almost stealthily, from morning to night to morning, a fine trickle of tears like fairy's jewels wending its way down her wrinkled, bloodless cheeks. Across from her, Eloisa Ortiz, connected to bottles and boxes, sleeps and doesn't sleep, lies conscious and not quite conscious, mumbling in Spanish to people who aren't there and who, perhaps, never were. And in the bed by the window rests Rita, strung with tubes like a giant marionette. Thinner and colorless, she seems to shrivel as she is watched, the visible shrinking woman of room 310, Wing C. Along the windowsill and over the tops of the bedside tables, cards and plants and boxes of candies sit, waiting. Rita watches the window, the light changing and the planes and clouds passing, waiting as well.

Paul hates the hospital. He bullies the nurses, he fights with Lillian, he never lets the doctors forget that he knows all about iatrogenics and the dehumanization and moral irresponsibility of technocratic medicine. Only to Linda is he civil and good-tempered, pretending that they are still together and that Janet isn't waiting for him somewhere – at home, or in the car. Only to Rita is he patient and kind, pretending that she is getting better and that they aren't all waiting for her to die.

His visits are short and frantic. He jokes, he meddles, he tells her stories about his children – some of them true and

191

some of them not – he comes in one evening wearing an old fedora, telling her she'd better be better by Easter. Rita says, smiling back at ghosts, "Remember when you were little and I took you to the Easter Parade? Remember?"

His visits are short and, as the old lady outlives the doctors' predictions, less frequent. He makes paper flowers explode from his empty hand, he smuggles in miniature bottles of whiskey for Rita who never liked whiskey and drinks them himself, he blows shimmering soap bubbles over the inmates of Death Row. He has so much to do, projects and plans: he must find a bigger apartment for Janet and himself, he must push the lawyers to get the divorce through as quickly as possible, he must hustle for promotion, he must finish his book. And through it all he must navigate the shark-infested familial waters, Linda's hostility, Lillian's hysterics and Rita's unnerving habit of hanging on to his hand when he's trying to leave, whispering "What's going on Paul? What's going on?"

Lillian weeps her way into spring. Soon curling green leaves and tiny pastel petals, each one perfect, will blossom across her face and down her neck, and bees and butterflies will hover around her head. Jimmy hugs her in the hallway, going in and coming out, patting her hand, saying, "Take it easy, honey. Don't get yourself so worked up." Paul screams at her in the hospital snackbar, "For God's sake, Lillian. You're not the one who's dying. Why don't you dry up?" Jimmy says, "Now, Paul. We're all a little upset right now . . ." "Go fuck yourself," Lillian screams back, spilling her coffee all over her new slacks. "Now look what you've made me do!" she sobs. "Just look what you've done now." "Don't let Mom see you like this," Paul says, carefully pushing his chair back into place. "Don't you do anything to upset her. Do you understand?" "I wish you'd been adopted," Lillian spits back, her smearing mascara making her look like a matronly raccoon, but he walks from the room as though he doesn't know her.

Linda comes every evening after work. She has agreed, for Rita's sake, not to let on that the case of Sutcliffe *vs* Sutcliffe is

192

stumbling along towards the courts. She has agreed, for Rita's sake, to say "We" and "Ours" and "Us" and to let Paul hold her hand when they stand next to the bed saying good night. For Rita's sake, she puts her wedding ring back on outside of the hospital entrance and says things to Rita like, "When they let you come home we'll fix up Paul's study for you". "When will that be?" Rita whispers, and Linda says, "When they finish the tests. We have to see how you do on the tests," and Rita leans back into her pillow and sheets, white on white, waiting to be graded by God.

Inside of room 310 all of the pieces of their puzzles fit as before. Outside of room 310 they are scattered and rearranged, they are bent and broken and reassembled.

What does Rita see? The ceiling with its cracks and staining. The Lilliputian landscape of the blankets, the hills and valleys and rounded slopes of a land now home, her hands on the covers, sculpted from time, the empty bed before her, the emptying beds around her, the four of them pinned and positioned around her, propping and plumping pillows, are you comfortable, Mom, how are you feeling, all right? better? is there anything you want? Comfortable? Hungry? Thirsty? Bored? What does she want that they could possibly give her? Magazines papers snapshots and anecdotes ten more years or two or one or one half?

What does Rita know? Remember, remember, remember – that blue coat, that meal at your aunt's, Lillian's Holy Communion, the trip to Bear Mountain, the time Paul smashed the glass top of the coffee table, when Lillian peroxided her hair, the weddings, the Thanksgivings, the bungalow on the Jersey shore, the cabin in the Catskills, Walter pushing Paul's pram down the street, Lillian on his shoulders, golden curls and a sunsuit with tiny blue bears dancing down the front – remember remember remember, pushing them all into the safety of the past, where she had some control and there was time, always time . . . too much.

Lillian sits in a metal-framed chair on one side of Rita's bed, Linda sits in a duplicate chair on the other. Jimmy, still grinning, leans against the wall by the window, jiggling the change in his pockets and laughing at jokes no one has made. Paul stands at the foot of the bed, pushing Rita's wheeled table back and forth, looking at his watch while pretending to adjust the height. They all look tired, the controls pushed to automatic pilot, as though they'd been keeping continuous vigil, nine dark nights and nine dark days, lighting candles and burning incense, the movements of the ritual self-perpetuating and sufficient, there being nothing to do but continue.

Rita has been crying, holding Lillian's hand, then Linda's. "If I'm dying," she says, "then I wish they'd just let me die. I wish they'd just let me die."

Lillian squeezes the shrunken hand. "Don't talk like that, Mom. They're doing all they can do. They're doing what they have to do." And looks at Paul as though it is all his fault; and looks at Jimmy as though there is something he should do.

Linda holds Rita's hand more tightly, afraid to let go; afraid that Rita will go poof! in a puff of blue Day-Glo smoke, leaving them behind calling come back, Mom, come back.

"Don't be a fool," drawls Paul, putting on his tough-guy voice. "We'll have you out of here by Easter, sweetheart. Who's going to glaze the ham if you're still locked up? Who's going to color the eggs?"

"Oh, I don't think so," whispers Rita. "I don't think they'll send me home for Easter."

"Of course they will," in his normal voice. Six eyes shoot paralyzing rays at him, two wash him down with love. "I'll have a little talk with the doctors, okay?" He comes to stand beside Linda, an arm around the back of her chair. "We'll watch the Easter Parade. And we'll have sweet potatoes. Sweet potatoes and ham and baking powder biscuits." He goes to pat her hand but misses and pats the edge of the bed. "No one ever thinks of hiding places for the eggs like you do." He smiles but only Rita smiles back. Linda flicks his fingers from her shoulder.

"I could die happy then," says Rita. "If I could have just one last Easter with the kids."

194

"Now, Mom," Lillian tucks the blankets in, smooths out a wrinkle in the collar of her mother's nightgown. "Don't go getting your hopes up. You'll have to see what the doctors say."

"We don't want to do anything to set you back," warns Jimmy.

"I want to go home," she moans. "I don't want to die here like this. I want to go home."

Paul almost pats her head but merely brushes a lock of hair away. "You just schtick widme, kiddo," kissing a dry and unfamiliar cheek. "You just wait and see."

"You'd better get some rest now," says Linda, standing up and signalling retreat.

One by one they bend and kiss and squeeze.

"What the hell is wrong with you?" Lillian hisses when they hit the hall. "Are you demented or something? Why did you go and lie to her like that?"

"I wasn't lying. I'll talk to the doctors." He pushes the button for the elevator.

Linda stands a few paces aside, her arms folded across her, staring at the crack in the doors. "And they'll say no. They'll say no and she'll be worse off than she was before."

There are a young couple and a middle-aged couple already in the elevator.

"Maybe they'll say yes."

"And what if they do?" She stands to make it look as though she isn't with him. "Where is this mythical home you're bringing her to? You don't think she might notice that Janet isn't me?"

"I'll take care of it," staring at the descent of numbers. The young man coughs, the older woman smiles at Lillian, who has begun to cry. "You three just go on acting like every little thing you do is a big deal. That's right, Lillian. You cry. You cry so everyone in the whole fuckin' hospital will know how much you're suffering."

"There's no need to shout," says Jimmy.

"Don't give me orders," shouts Paul. "Nobody wants your opinion."

"And no one wants yours," shrieks Linda. Janet is sitting almost directly in front of the doors when they open, looking patient and hopeful until she recognizes them, or Paul, then looking simply happy. "Oh, Christ," sighs Linda, all heads turning towards her, "there's little Mary Sunshine."

"Sarcasm doesn't become you," says Paul striding past her, and into the waiting arms of his new true love.

Lillian and Jimmy give Linda a ride home. "Are you all right?" Linda keeps asking Lillian. "Are *you* all right," Lillian keeps asking Linda. "I can never remember," says Jimmy, accidentally leaning on the horn, "whether or not your street is one way."

Linda can't sleep. She lies in bed not reading a book that Mark said she had to read, staring uncomprehendingly at the words of the blurb: vivid re-creation, penetrating insight, definitive statement on our times.

Mark can't leave his wife. She will have a nervous breakdown. He won't be able to live with his guilt. Linda isn't ready for commitment. He can't live in another man's home with another man's children. He isn't good enough for her. The children resent him. What about the vacation he and Marilyn had been planning in Puerto Rico?

"I thought you were in love with me," said Linda. "Maybe we can get away for a week in the summer," he sighed, tracing her profile with kisses. "Just the two of us."

Linda thinks of herself as an empty soda bottle lying on a beach visited only by screaming gulls in the white-ice heart of winter.

He told her about the friend of a friend who was madly in love with one woman but married to another. He told her how six years after the affair had ended, tragically and painfully, the wife had left the friend's friend and he had called his old but never forgotten love, she answering the ring just as she was leaving for two weeks in Bermuda; how he had begged her to meet him in Madrid instead; how now they were the happiest couple the world has ever seen.

Linda thinks of herself as an empty Cel-Ray bottle left lying on a beach in the white-heart ice of winter slowly being buried in sand and the shells of tiny dead creatures. "If you really loved me, you would understand," he pleaded. "I don't want the same thing to happen again." "I don't know what you want from me," she said. "I don't know what I'm doing any more." "Oh, love, love," licking the threat of tears from her eyes. "Just love. What more is there? What else counts?"

Is this where the world begins, or is it the precise point at which the universe ends? Linda throws the book onto the floor. She doesn't really care much one way or the other any more. All these years she has been waiting for her life to begin, only now noticing that it has started and carried on more or less without her. Linda lies with her hands across her stomach and her feet pointing towards Philadelphia.

Still, she really can't complain. Paul takes the kids every other weekend and Mark doesn't love his wife; Mark takes her out, buys her lunches and calls every night and Patricia and David don't care much for Janet. It isn't as though she was born retarded or deformed. It isn't as though she's a junky or a whore. It isn't as though she is poor or ignorant or disadvantaged, diseased by poverty or crippled by being born the wrong person in the wrong place at the wrong time. It isn't as though she'd been doomed at birth to a life of futile suffering, victimized by the world's malign indifference. She isn't some brown-skinned woman with babies with bowed bones and death-head eyes. She doesn't have to scrub floors or grovel for garbage. She doesn't have bleached hair and say "Ain't that cute". She's well read, she's cultured, she knows what's what and who is who; she gets more out of life than most.

Linda lies on her three-hundred-dollar mattress in her fifty-thousand-dollar apartment, her Bonwit's nightgown half-covered by her Jungle Dreams sheets. Oh, lucky lucky Linda, to have landed smack dab in the lap of the land of the affluent and free, to have everything a girl could want. And love.

Linda switches off the bedside light, watching shadows

tease each other on the wall. And love. The impression of his body on hers still lingers, the sweetness of his lips against her skin remains. If only she could curve against him every night; if only she could wake each morning to find his hand against her hair. She had doubted it before; guilt had confounded her, old habits had confused her, misconceptions had dogged and pursued her. But now she knows: the essence of life is love. And love is Mark Schwerner. Imperfect of face and thinning of hair; insensitive at times, at times even selfish and childishly cruel, self-centered, even. But love. Her love. If only she could turn now and see him sleeping, arms tucked against him, that silly little silver chain still against his neck.

Dribbling into sleep, the image that Linda sees is Rita, her eyes like laser beams zapping through the night, all alone in her room of empty dying. At least it won't be like that for her, Linda thinks, and so slides into sleep.

Janet is planning to be a June bride. It will be a small, unceremonious wedding – no church, no fragile, fantastical gown, no matchbooks embossed Janet and Paul with silver birds and silver bells – but it will be a wedding just the same: her parents neatly prosperous and respectably proud, a few chosen friends to wish them well, smoked salmon and champagne.

"We can't fix a date yet," says Paul.

"June?" she screeches. "June? Everything will be settled by June," over there, on the far side of tomorrow.

"Something could go wrong."

"Like what?" a change of mind, a change of plans, a flip flop of the heart?

"Like anything, for God's sake." He bangs the ashes from his pipe. "There are always delays."

"All we've had is delays. What's wrong with June?" A good month, warm but not too warm, lush and thriving, the bursting of life all around.

"Oh, Janet," his voice swinging out on the last syllable with a sigh. Oh, Janet, her mother would say, hands on hips, mouth puckered into anything but a kiss; Oh, Janet, her teachers would hum, eyebrows raised, fingers pointed at the incorrect answer, blazing on the blackboard like blood. Oh, Janet, oh, Janet, can't you ever do anything right?

"Oh, Janet, what?" she screams, throwing her party plans onto the floor. "Oh, Janet, what?"

He retrieves her pad, laying it carefully on the coffee table in the neutral zone between their cups. "Oh, for Chrissake, stop acting like a child. All I meant was that you're going to feel pretty foolish if you make all of these arrangements now and then find out that the divorce is held up for months over something. That's all. I don't think we should plan anything until we've got a court date."

"But the lawyer said . . ."

"Janet. Honey. Do you know how many men there are raising pigeons and studying ancient Greek behind bars whose lawyers said they could get them off?"

"Your lawyer said June by the latest."

"Probably, Janet, probably. This is a world of chance and illusion, not a Hollywood film."

"But your lawyer said that with all possible delays accounted for, the latest it would be was June."

"Probably. Janet. Probably. There is no guarantee. You know what bureaucracies are like as well as anyone."

"Better," staring straight at him with one of those peculiar looks in her eyes.

"All right, better." He pours himself a little more coffee from Janet's ornate, gold Turkish pot. "I'm only thinking of you, honey. What if your parents book a flight and everything, get someone to mind the angel fish and the finches for a week, and then Linda throws one of her girlish fits? Your parents will spend the week riding the ferry and trotting up and down the Statue of Liberty and the Empire State Building while my lawyer talks to Linda's lawyer and you lock yourself in the bathroom and we all spend the week eating old fish and stale bread. That's what will happen."

She carefully puts the cap on her pen. "I'll talk to Linda," she says. "I'll talk to her as one woman to another. I'm sure she'll understand."

He makes a face and a sound that mean he knows the light at the end of the tunnel is merely another train. "You don't know Linda."

"Paul," Janet says patiently. "Linda used to be one of my very best friends, you know. I think I have a good idea of what she's like."

"That was a long time ago."

"It wasn't that long ago," maintains Janet, sitting cross-legged on the floor surrounded by the spirits of female solidarity and instinctive communion, her blood the blood of sorceresses and mothers, in her cells those two X chromosomes that hold the crucial code. "I understand Linda a lot better than you think. A lot better than you do."

"Janet, can't you understand that Linda hates you? You're the last person she would behave decently to."

"We'll see." She places her pen on top of her pad, just below the heading "Food".

He sees raging winds of whipping hair and torrential rains of tears; he hears the howling of women with dripping hearts in their teeth, nails clawing at the walls of infinity. "Leave it alone, Janet. We're just going to have to wait and see."

"I've waited and seen enough."

"It's only a question of weeks."

"I told my mother June."

"Well call her again and tell her July. Or August."

"She has her heart set on it."

"Well call her back and tell her to move her heart over a month." He pauses; she pouts. "Janet, you do remember that my mother is dying, don't you? Can't you at least let me get through that before you make other problems for me?" and he lays, in her soft white palm, his own bruised and beaten heart, please.

Janet had forgotten: forgotten his grief, forgotten his empty eyes every evening that he returns from his mother's side, another teaspoonful of hope depleted. "If you're sure you don't want me to talk to her."

200

"I'm sure."

She takes his large, hard hand in hers. "I'm sorry I'm being so selfish, Paul. I wasn't thinking about you at all."

He kisses her tenderly, almost reverently on the top of her left ear. "I know how you feel, darling. I'm doing all I can."

Beyond them, the sun, a burnished bronze wafer, sets over Manhattan, trailing strands of red and gold and rose across the darkling sky. In another time, the warrior and the lover, the mage and the priest, the poet and the idiot, might have seen in it the workings of the gods, a portent or a promise. Paul sees the gleaming against the glass and says to Janet, "I think that it's time for a drink."

★   ★   ★

The old lady has come home to die. The barren earth and barren trees outline infinity against the grey, gone sky. One bird sings, a familiar sound in a world now faraway and strange. She sits by the window, knitting on her lap, a jacket for a child she will never see, born of a love still undiscovered, and, knowing now, waits for him to come for her, not with wine and roses in his arms but peace, preternatural peace and the immutable consummation of their love. What scenes she sees, what friends whose faces flash and fade against the night, what dreams she has dreamed in her greater dream, all come and go at once and leave her whole and warm at last, the cells of her body spreading out like stars against a perfect sky. All is complete, all balanced, all known – the smiling of an infant's mouth, the tapping of a finger, the meeting in a flowered park, the empty cup and tarnished silver spoon, the torn and twisted rag, the shredded leaf held forgotten in a book: all linked all shown as one fragile, fore-ordained form. She sighs and so sings the empyrean...

★   ★   ★

Linda has just come home from seeing Rita. Lillian and Jimmy are having car trouble and couldn't make it this weekend, Paul was battled down with work. She brought the children with her and left them in the waiting room with comic books and chocolate bars, calling after her "Is Grandma dead yet?". Now she slams the door behind them, locks all the locks, and shouts at them to get ready for bed as she picks up the phone. When Paul answers she doesn't even say hello, or hi, or this is your first wife speaking. "You damn shithead," she shouts back at the sound of his reassuring voice. "All she talks about is Easter. That's all she talks about."

"Is that you, Linda?"

"What to get for the kids, how to dye the eggs, what sort of cake she should make for dessert, whether or not she should go to church to see the lillies, will I let her buy Patsy a new hat like the one Lillian had when she was ten . . ."

"That is you, isn't it, Linda? You can't fool me," signalling to Janet that his children's mother has at long last lost her mind.

"It's going to break her heart, Paul."

He moves the receiver from one ear to the other. "What's going to break her heart?"

"Not coming home for Easter. They won't let her out of there. Why did you ever promise her she could come home?" Linda who has shed no tears and made no mourning sounds shrieks into the plastic phone. "Why did you lie to her like that?"

"To make her happy."

"But it's not going to make her happy. Even if they let her out it's not going to make her happy. It's just going to upset her even more."

Behind him, Janet whispers that if he wants she could have just the smallest and most friendly of words with Linda now. He shakes her away like a spiralling screen of smoke. Before him, as it were, Linda sucks back her sobs. But he can shake her away with just a simple motion, too. "You don't understand, Linda," he says into the uniform holes of the mouthpiece. "Rita isn't going to live till Easter. Can't you understand that? She'll be dead before the month is out."

"You can't know that," and he can see her face blotched with anger, her eyes boiling in her skull, her hand tugging on the coil of cord, "you can't be sure."

202

"You've talked to the doctors, you've heard what they have to say." He leans his back against his lover's white wall. "You don't think I'd promise her something like that if I thought she'd be alive, do you?"

In an old brown cardboard carton that once held Del Monte Canned Peaches and that now resides in Lillian's attic lies, at the bottom under an assortment of accumulation, a photograph of Rita when she was four. She is dressed in a white dress and black or, perhaps, brown boots, and her hair is in long curls, fastened with an enormous colored ribbon, maybe blue or yellow. In her right hand she holds a small American flag. Was it taken on the Fourth of July? Was it a morning filled with busy promises and small delights? After the photograph, was there a picnic, lemonade and chicken wings, sparklers and ice cream in the sculpted park, its green green trees heavy with the heat? And in the morning with so much to do, before the last traces of coolness were licked from the streets, did Rita sit at the table in the tiny kitchen, eating her breakfast from a cornflower-blue bowl, fingers of sunshine crawling across the table top and china, across her hands and wrists? Rita's beautiful, beautiful mother, rustling as she ices a cake, creating order as she pins in place her shimmering hair, looks over her shoulder at the small girl, squinting through the window to outside where the air is heady with the smell of flowers, water and horse shit. The ice truck rumbles and clop clops by, a young man takes a kiss and laughs, fire crackers explode, a tiny boy cries. A cat walks across the roof. Rita's mother gives her, as a treat, a peach saying, "Be careful you don't get it on your dress". It is the time before: before the Rita with breasts just swelling; before the girl who bleached her hair and the mother who dragged her crying through the Brooklyn streets to the iniquitous shop where the potion was purchased; before the nights of the mother waiting up in the kitchen demanding to sniff at her underpants; before before. Peach juice lies like dew across her mouth, a pigeon sitting on the fire escape blinks and

203

ruffles and shines in the sun. "Mama," says the little girl, studying the cat scratch on the index finger of her right hand, "Mama, is it true that some people don't believe in God?" Her mother wipes her dry and reddened hands on a corner of her apron, wipes a wanton wisp of hair away from her face, her beautiful beautiful mother who could have married well and wisely, who could have had a gentleman, a man of means and culture, but instead had chosen Rita's dashing, no-good father, sighs and says in tones of sorrow, "Yes. Yes there are people like that. And you should always stay away from them," the godless and depraved who will drag you into hell. Rita touches the Sunday school pin on the shoulder of her dress. "But who do they talk to if they don't talk to God?"

Rita talks to Lillian and to Linda, to the nurses and the volunteers, to the nightly visitors to other beds who know her now and stop in the door to say hello. Rita tells the nurses about her children – her attractive daughter with her lovely home on Long Island, her good husband who worships the ground she walks on; her brilliant, distinguished son who writes books and has three degrees – and her grandchildren – the adorable Angela like a little doll, the precocious Patricia who's really going to be something when she's older, the darling David, a chip off the old block. Rita tells them all that she is going home for Easter, that she always loved the Easter flowers in the Brooklyn Botanical Gardens, that she will buy her babies furry stuffed rabbits and chocolate eggs. The nurses check the tubes and pat the pillows, say, "Now don't get your hopes up, Mrs Sutcliffe, you have to see what the doctors say".

Rita hears phones ring, footsteps fall and doors opening and closing, sits again on the double decker going down Fifth Avenue, holding Walter's hand. Half-drugged, half-sleeping, half-dead, does Rita wait for Jesus, immaculate and kind, to walk through the entrance of room 310, his wounded hands outstretched, smiling the smile of the ultimate lover, his voice as gentle and as perfect as the curve of the petal of an amaranth, offering her the reward she was once taught she deserves? And is it just the night nurse that she hears, coming to check that none of them have died?

Paul strokes celestial circles on the belly of his beloved. "I want us to have a child," he whispers, his voice like another shadow in the night. "I want us to have a baby of our own."

"A baby?"

"A baby of our own," of his own, a seed he can be sure he's sown, a child who could never call some other man Daddy.

"But I thought you said . . ." she murmurs, afraid to trip over some subtle trap, recalling how she once lay boneless on the floor, pounding on the cushion by her head, I want a family, I want your child, I want some children of my own before it's too late, while he carefully buttoned his tweed overcoat and told her that he had all the children he wanted, that he was too old now to start all over again.

"Just yours and mine," and mine, patting the place where the miniature feet would some day kick and prod, some day soon.

"Do you mean that?" A perfect child with his father's eyes and his mother's smile, tiny hands to touch her cheek and little lips to suckle at her breasts, her own child, herself a mother, given permanence and credence, her child not Linda's, her husband, her family, her future firm.

Paul doesn't love his children any less because they may not be his, are probably not his, have been, since conception, conspirators in the female plot to disown and discredit him. He will still take them out on Sundays and fix a room for them to visit on weekends and during school vacations; he will still pay for their braces and their broken bones, their college educations and the psychoanalysis they will have to undergo after having been raised by the witch-woman, their mother. And they might even, of course, be his, or one of them might be his, but how will he ever be sure, how will he ever know. "I want you to have my child," he sighs and

205

pleads, begs and commands, offering her the gift no one else can give, to make tangible the promise of their love.

Janet cradles him in her arms, this man who is her love and life, this life that is her substance and her sense. "I never knew what happiness was before," she says. "I never knew."

And Paul, who had thought he did but now knows better, says, "Neither did I."

And they fall asleep beneath the crack in the plaster of the ceiling, like the crack in a cartoon heart.

He was on his way home from a reading in, could you believe it, Brooklyn, he'd had a few glasses of wine and was feeling rather mellow, he'd been in the neighborhood and thought it would be nice to have a cup of coffee with her and a few moments of tranquility, and so he had phoned from the box on the corner and she had said, sure come up.

She has given him coffee, bourbon and a few light kisses, has listened to his complaints against his ever-growing family, or families, has sympathized with his grief and mourning over Rita's dying and his marriage's death, has made him try one of the wholewheat brownies she was making when he called, and has summed up his and perhaps the entire planet's predicament by leaning her head back against the jumble of colors of the bedspread covering the couch, looking at him as though she hasn't quite thought about him before and saying, "Christ, you are such a jerk sometimes."

"Thanks."

"Oh, Paul," huffing an exaggerated sigh, topping up her drink and his, "why can't you ever do anything clean or constructive?"

"You mean like housecleaning?"

"In a manner of speaking, yes."

"I don't understand what you're talking about."

Liz is looking like an oasis tonight with her old plaid shirt and dungarees, her small, dark apartment cluttered and calm, the record player playing softly, a plate of brownies on the coffee table. "You always make such a mess," she says, smoothing out a wrinkle in the spread.

"I'm not the one who makes the messes," holding his drink on his knee, his voice emotionless with sadness, his free hand inching across the 100% cotton to touch her. "I'm the one who's trying to straighten everything out."

"Do you think you've straightened things out?"

He considers for some seconds, scanning all the separate compartments of his life, searching out the pulsebeat in her hand. "Yes. As much as I can. I can't be responsible for other people's behavior."

"But Paul," says Liz, "you're exactly where you always were, just different," removing her hand to reach her drink.

"You're mad because I haven't been around much." Or at all.

She could tell him to look around and see if he can see any traces of her missing him – an old wine bottle with a single rose, a postcard pinned onto the wall, his picture so unthinkingly propped up on a shelf. She could ask him where he thinks her dependence lies, she whose life he touches only at the edges, she who has always seen him only when neither of them had anything else to do, so casual, so controllable, so cool. Liz swallows a baby blade of ice. It sometimes surprises her that she actually likes him. "I don't care if you come around or you don't come around," is what she says. "We're friends, Paul. You don't have to pay for it all the time." She tilts her head, stretching her long and lovely neck. "But a little honesty wouldn't hurt."

"And how am I not honest?"

"What are you doing here?"

"I came to see you," claiming a round round knee. "I miss you."

"And what about Janet?"

"She's got a class tonight."

"And what about Janet? What happens when you get married? Are you still going to miss me?"

"My marrying Janet has nothing to do with us," says Paul.

"Does it have anything to do with you?" asks Liz, voice high with wonder. "Does anyone ever have anything to do with you?" and stares at him as though he is the magic molded man whom you can touch but never mark, the marvel man with the specially treated surface that wipes clean in minutes, who is heat and scratch resistant, impervious to wind and weather, the miraculous mannikin with the burglar-proof heart.

"I didn't come here for your women's group crap," snaps Paul, making as if to leave. "I came here for some understanding."

Liz is up and heading for the door. "You came here to get laid. That's why you came here." He is still standing at the couch, she is opening the door. "But it's not going to happen any more."

"Oh, for Chrissake, Liz," plopping into the lap of the couch, his arms spread to shape a cross, "we've been through this scene a hundred times. I should have thought that with all your men you'd have learned something by now."

Liz takes his jacket from the row of wooden hooks by the door and flings it into the hall. "Oh, I have," she says. "The hundred-and-first time is the charm."

Linda is wearing a new T-shirt dress in a becoming shade of sea-green, has permed her hair and lost ten pounds. She looks terrific, better than she has since she was twenty-two. Everyone at work has been complimenting her for weeks. She suspects they are trying to cheer her up, but isn't totally sure of why. She is in line for a promotion, she has been asked to give a lecture on children's literature at NYU and she has begun a night course in potting, for which she shows, the instructor assures her, an above-average aptitude. Linda's pearl is in her oyster.

Tonight as she sets the table, lights the candles, tosses the salad and chills the wine she is her own ideal image of a happy, independent and successful woman. She puts a single rose in an old cognac bottle and steps back to check the effect. Perfection, simple and pure.

She hasn't seen Mark for eight days – Rita is worsening, Lillian and Paul have intensified their hostilities, she has been pressured with work and David had the flu – but tonight he is coming for dinner and staying the night. Linda is about as high as the Himalayas. Every evening she and Mark walk from the office to his car, where they sit and kiss and fondle for up to twenty-five minutes, whispering sweet everythings before she has to go, still damp from his embraces. But tonight they have all night.

She opens the wine, pours herself a glass, puts a record on and sits to wait. And wait. She has another glass of wine and calls the time. And waits. She switches to scotch, puts another record on and turns the oven off. And waits – for his step in the hall, his knock on the door, his fingers ravaging her flesh.

When he does call it is from a pay phone at the hospital and he can't really talk because there is a waiting room full of people hanging on his every word. Marilyn, he says, has been mugged. She's not really hurt, but she's badly shaken. Somehow her thumb has been broken. She needs him. He can't get away.

"Oh, how awful," cries Linda, and means it. "How awful."

He says that he knew she'd understand. He can't possibly get away now.

"Of course not," says Linda. "Of course not."

And it's shaken him up, too. She might have been killed, or even raped, he whispers into the phone, his head as deep beneath the plastic bubble as it is possible to go. A child cries, a woman moans, a junky staggers behind him, dripping liquid coins of blood. "She might have been killed," he repeats. "She might have been killed."

Linda leans over with the receiver to her ear and blows out the candle, blows petals from the rose. "Will you call me tomorrow?"

"If I can," he comes close to promising. "I don't want to leave her alone. You understand."

Oh, of course, of course, of course she understands. "If there's anything I can do," she says, anything, anything I can do.

"If you could have seen her," he says, twisting the cord through his fingers. "If you could have seen her . . ."

At the sound of the tone, please deposit . . .

"I have to hang up now, Linda. I don't have any more change."

"I could call you back."

"I'd better get back to Marilyn. If you could've seen her, Linda . . . I thought my heart would break." Better a heart than a thumb.

Linda sits at the table, looking beautiful but beaten, pouring patterns of salt onto her willow pattern plate, pouring wine into her glass, pouring tears all down her face. Thinking that she would do it – were there anything she could do.

Like a sacrificial maiden – painted and bejeweled, clothes just-so – Linda stands at the entrance to the student cafeteria, looking as though she is about to be pushed into hell. Facing her is a mob of noise and smoke and shifting color, the pageantry of a hostile nation which is waiting to carve out her heart and serve it to their hungry gods, grind her bones to a powder for their darkling rituals. Was she ever part of such a scene, so young, so certain, so self-assured, tipping back a plastic chair, her feet up on another, hair so clean and teeth so white, radiating health, prosperity and a simple belief in her own possibilities for happiness? And then there is a hand at her shoulder, a voice in her ear: the push.

"Hello, Linda," says Janet as Linda turns. "I've saved a table for us in the corner where we can be alone," and points into the shadows, alone among the multitudes.

"Oh, good," whispers Linda, brushing back her hair, not quite sure of what else she can say.

"It's good of you to come," smiles Janet as they sit down with their coffees, wishing she'd suggested a bar instead.

Linda nods, only able to think of the things she can't say: so good to see you, gee it's been a long time, I don't know why we don't do this more often.

"This place certainly is a madhouse," grins Janet fondly.

Linda blinks, looking around her at this place, described by Janet over the telephone as "neutral territory", and says, "It certainly is."

"Well."

"Well."

Janet sips her drink, Linda dutifully sips at hers.

"I thought it was about time we had a talk together," Janet begins.

"So you said on the phone."

"After all, there's no reason we can't still be friends."

Linda can think of one or two.

"Friendly," Janet amends. "There's no reason we can't be friendly."

Linda stares into the liquid steaming in her Styrofoam cup, wondering once again just why she has come, why, before the onslaught of Janet's reasonableness, adultness and practicality, she crumbled so completely. "There's no need to get carried away," she says at last.

"It's not an unusual situation these days," Janet assures her with authority.

"It is for me."

Janet titters. "You always had a good sense of humor," proving they can be friends.

But not any more. Linda breaks her pretend plastic spoon in half, and then looks at it as though it did it itself. Has she come just to gather the final humiliation in person? Should she have brought her credit cards, the Sutcliffe cards, to be handed over publicly but informally, brought her children, each carrying their brightly colored overnight bags and favorite toys, this is your new mother now? "What is it you want to talk about?"

"It's about the divorce," says Janet in her forthright, no-nonsense, no-beating-about-the-bush way that has won her so many friends and admirers.

Having finished her coffee, Linda now begins to demolish, jagged bit by jagged bit, her cup.

"Paul doesn't tell me everything that's going on, but he's suggested that there might be some delays."

Linda notices the dirt along the windows and the chips in the paint on the wall. "I suppose there might be."

"It just seems to me," says Janet, holding her cup with both her hands, "that if there were some problems, you know, with the settlement of things . . . I mean, I don't know much personally about these things, but a lot of my friends . . ." and stops looking for light in Linda's eyes. "I just thought that maybe if we could talk things through there wouldn't be any need for delays."

In part, Linda has come to this first conference of the wives of Paul Sutcliffe because she didn't want to appear unreasonable, because her parents raised her not to be a spoil sport, because she didn't want to seem to be an hysterical ex-wife, the wronged woman. But now she wonders why. "Just what delays are you talking about?"

Janet's hands cut air. "Well, you know, delays. Paul seems to think that there are some things the two of you can't agree on."

"Like what?" she asks, beginning to get interested.

"Oh, well," shrugs Janet, "I don't know exactly."

"Unexactly, then."

"Well, he hasn't actually said. He just seemed to think that . . . to think that you might be difficult." It's not for nothing that Janet was the girl in her high school graduating class to win the good citizen award from the Daughters of the American Revolution.

"Ah," breathes Linda, and starts to drop the broken pieces of plastic into the ruins of her cup. "Paul says that I am causing delays."

"That you might," corrects Janet.

"But why should I?"

"Why should you?"

"Yes, why should I?"

Janet is rarely speechless, but now – thinking of all the reasons why Linda should be a bitch, reasons like hurt and bitterness, resentment and vindictiveness, failure and defeat – she slows down noticeably. "I'm sure you have your reasons," she says sweetly, and not unkindly. "It can't be pleasant."

212

"No, it's not pleasant. But that doesn't mean I should go out of my way to make it more unpleasant."

"I didn't mean to suggest that . . ."

"If you didn't mean to suggest it, then why did you want to see me?"

"I just thought there might be something that I could do. To make things easier."

Drop dead. Move to Iowa. Fall in love with someone else's husband. Good suggestions, but all, alas, too late.

Janet looks as though she may cry, and Linda, the veteran of so many tears, relents. "All you have to do is make sure that Paul does what he's supposed to do." And then decides not to relent too much. "I certainly don't want to stand in the way of your happiness." A person could get hurt that way.

They sit opposite one another, each with folded hands in lap, Janet staring at her neat white cup of standard size and standard shape; Linda staring at the wreckage of hers.

"Thank you."

It is just as they are about to leave that a strikingly pretty young woman passes their table, nodding hello to Janet. "Who was that?" asks Linda, looking after the unforgettable head.

"Oh, do you know her?" asks Janet, picking up her purse. "That's Liz. Liz Carmichael. She's doing a seminar with Paul."

For the first time in several days, Linda smiles. "I thought she looked familiar."

Rita dies, more or less suddenly, sometime in the early morning, well before Easter. She has left no last words or notes, made no touching bequests. When they go through the apartment, there is little there worth salvaging or worth having: no treasured letters, no precious photographs, no trinkets of jewelry or favorite things to remember her by. It is as though she did go poof in a puff of smoke, and with her went her past and all her presents, poof poof.

Lillian weeps and Paul laments. Lillian takes the sheets and towels, Paul takes the TV for the kids and calls the Salvation

Army to collect the rest. No one suggests that Linda should take anything, now that she is no longer Paul's wife, not really.

No one flings himself, or herself, onto the coffin as the first spadeful of dirt thumps on the lid. No flowers fall from a sky heavy with angels' tears, no voice of man or beast breaks the sound of talk and jingling coins and clicking heels with a howl of tangible pain.

Janet calls her parents on the evening of the funeral to tell them that June is almost certain now.

Paul calls Liz, barely able to speak from within his surging sorrow, but her one response is, "Your poor mother". He drives Linda home, and they get drunk and make love like they used to, so many and many lives before.

Lillian wakes in the night, thinking that she heard her father come into her room and tell her that she shouldn't worry, everything was all right now.

The world rests and Rita rots, or will soon.

9

Janet is not as good at being pregnant as Linda was, or so he tells Linda when he comes by to pick up the kids.

"It's different for everyone," says Linda, always fair.

"Christ, you'd think she'd invented it," he says, and looks at her with longing.

"The first few months can be the worst," says Linda.

"I can't get any work done with her carrying on," says Paul, and he makes a face she used to love.

She makes coffee and jokes, he tells her stories about his students that have her in stitches.

As he's leaving, the kids screaming through the hall, he gives her a kiss on the cheek. "Maybe we could have dinner one night, you know, and just talk over things. The kids and all."

"Oh," says Linda.

"Just dinner," and he kisses the other cheek before she can say no.

If no was what she meant to say.